Scandal ^{IN} ^{HIS} Arms

Scandal IN HIS Arms

DEBORAH HALE

Cover by The Killion Group Inc.

ISBN 978-1-9894080-4-9

Dedication

This book is dedicated with my deepest thanks to Andrea, Janice, Farris, Karen, Linda, Suzanne and Christine. Knowing you were waiting for Gabriel and Moira's story inspired me to keep working on this book when the going got tough.

And to Nikki McIntosh, Anne MacFarlane and the Writing Power Hours Group who challenged and motivated me to get to the finish line.

Chapter One

London, June 1811

"**M**ISS BRENNAN?" LORD Gabriel Stanford strove to keep his voice calm as he addressed the elusive lady he had been pursuing for weeks. "What a pleasant surprise to find you here this evening."

He bowed low but did not take his eyes off the Irish heiress with whom he'd once shared a brief but passionate Yuletide tryst. If she tried to flee, he would be ready to follow her. Gabriel assured himself that must be why she so powerfully captured his gaze.

Moira Brennan's blue-green eyes widened at the sight of him. Their meeting in the midst of the Prince Regent's Grand Banquet clearly came as a surprise to her as well. And not a pleasant one.

"Lord Gabriel." She made a stiff curtsey. "No doubt the only untitled Irish women you expected to find here tonight were servants. I assure you Father and I received a proper invitation. My dear godfather saw to that. You may have met him in the receiving line."

Gabriel nodded, though he had quite forgotten Miss Brennan was a goddaughter of the Regent's particular friend, the Earl of Moira. It explained how she had managed to gain admission to such an exclusive event.

Silently, he blessed the earl for bringing about this meeting. He had begun to fear it might never happen. "I did not expect to see *you* in London at all. I was told you had gone to

Bath from Brighton. Before that, I believe you spent several months on the Isle of Jersey."

"You seem very well informed about our movements, sir." Miss Brennan did not sound flattered by his interest. "We did visit the places you mentioned. But Father could not refuse an invitation that does us such honor. We do not intend to remain long in London."

Around them in the vast banqueting tent, hundreds of the Prince Regent's aristocratic guests took their places at the richly arrayed tables. Almost as many liveried servants circulated among the company dispensing choice wines. Mouthwatering aromas from the buffet competed with the sweet fragrance of the floral arrangements. Dulcet music flowed beneath the loud buzz of conversation.

Yet for all Gabriel noticed their surroundings, he and Moira Brennan might have been alone in the gardens of Carlton House on that warm June night.

"I am delighted you chose to attend," he replied, astonished to recognize a ring of truth in his voice. Until that moment, he had anticipated their meeting with a number of emotions. Delight had not been among them.

Irritation, certainly, on account of the frustrating chase the lady had led him. Indignation, that she might have abandoned their child like a stray cat. Perhaps a mild qualm of guilt for having taken her into his bed on that distant winter night.

Yet from the instant he laid eyes on her again, for the first time in over a year, Gabriel's pulse began to beat a rapid-fire tempo in his veins. He recalled the taste of her kisses, a delectable mixture of festive punch flavors — nutmeg, wine and lemon zest.

"I only came tonight for my father's sake." Moira Brennan spoke with a beguiling Irish lilt that years of English schooling had not managed to erase. "If you will excuse me, I must find him before it is time to dine."

She started to turn away, but Gabriel reached out and caught the tip of her fan. "Please stay a moment longer. There is an urgent matter I must discuss with you."

"I think not, sir." She glared up at him and jerked her fan from his grasp. "You can have nothing to say that I am the least inclined to hear. I thought I made that clear when we parted."

"You did indeed." Gabriel tried not to flinch at the memory. Moira Brennan had refused his marriage proposal with the bitter scorn usually reserved for a mortal insult. At the time he had been vastly relieved to escape the parson's mousetrap. He'd hoped he would never see her again, yet here they were and he could not deny the intense awareness humming through his flesh. "But a great deal has happened since we last met. It is vital that we speak."

Her fresh features which had once sparkled with blithe eagerness were now frozen into a cool, conventional mask. "I have no idea what you mean, nor do I wish to. I must go. I bid you good evening, sir."

Gabriel sensed she was desperately anxious to avoid his inquiries, which made him all the more determined to confront her with his suspicions.

Though he did not try to restrain her physically, he could not let her go without making an effort to get the answers he sought. The future of a child was at stake — one who had come to mean the world to him.

He pursued the Irish beauty with his voice alone. "Perhaps you did not hear about the infant my friends and I found abandoned in front of our lodgings a few months ago."

Miss Brennan jolted to a halt, like a spirited filly that had been reined-in hard. She spun back toward Gabriel. "A b-baby ... left on your doorstep? This is the first I have heard of it."

She sounded genuinely surprised. Or was she only shocked that he dared to mention the scandal in such a public place? The throng of guests in the banquet marquee seemed oblivious to their exchange. Considering the delicate subject of their conversation, Gabriel was happy to be ignored.

Beneath the lady's astonishment, he thought he glimpsed a

flicker of panic in her eyes. What possible reason could Moira Brennan have for alarm unless she knew far more about the situation than she claimed?

"*If* you are unaware of the gossip," he stressed the first word to convey his doubt, "you must be one of the few here this evening who can make that claim. The incident caused considerable gossip among the *ton* for many weeks."

Moira Brennan tilted her chin at a defiant angle. The spectre of anxiety had disappeared from her blue-green gaze, as if ruthlessly quenched. "I do not belong to your precious *ton,* Lord Gabriel, remember? And you know very well I have been away from London for several months. There must be a great deal of society gossip of which I am unaware."

She was hiding something. Gabriel had never felt so certain of anything. "Then allow me to acquaint you with the details."

Being near her again roused many feelings he had not experienced since their last meeting. All his senses seemed sharpened to an intensity that was almost disagreeable ... but not quite. "Jack Warwick, Rory Fitzwalter and I returned from the Regent's first levee to find a baby girl in a basket on our doorstep. A note left with the child gave her name and claimed that one of us is her father."

The intrepid thrust of Miss Brennan's chin faltered. If Gabriel had not been watching her so closely, he might have missed the subtle tremor.

"Indeed?" She composed her features into an expression of impersonal interest. "Given your reputations, it is a wonder that such an unfortunate incident did not occur long ago."

The fierce jab of her disapproval stung Gabriel. He recalled the way Moira Brennan had once looked up to him. Now her reproach stirred his defences. "Not all reputations are as well-deserved as they might seem," he snapped. "Have you no interest in what became of the child?"

He watched her face for any sign that might betray excessive concern.

"Of course I do! As would anyone with a heart." Miss Brennan glanced around, perhaps to check if anyone was listening to their conversation. "Finish your story and be quick about it. I must rejoin my father."

Gabriel was tempted to spin his tale out for as long as possible, to keep her near. "My friends and I did everything in our power to locate little Sarah's mother. Jack engaged his cousin's widow, Lady Southam, to assist us in caring for the child."

"Assist *you*?" Miss Brennan gave a derisive chuckle, so unlike the carefree laughter he had once coaxed from her. "Do you mean to tell me three notorious bachelors undertook to rear an infant?"

A blaze flared in Gabriel's cheeks. "Perhaps it is more accurate to say that my friends and I assisted Lady Southam. We took it in turn to help feed Sarah by hand, to change her linen and bathe her, to amuse and soothe her. We became greatly attached to the dear little creature."

His voice warmed with pride and affection for the tiny child who had captured his heart. As he spoke of little Sarah, a change came over Moira Brennan's expression. Her bristling coldness seemed to thaw into a wistful mist.

"For a time," Gabriel continued, "we were all certain Jack must be Sarah's father by Madame Reynard. He was prepared to marry the woman, in spite of her reputation, to provide Sarah with a proper family. But it turned out Madame was only claiming the baby in order to secure an advantageous marriage."

"How infamous, to use an innocent child for her own gain!" The words burst from Miss Brennan's lush lips like a cork exploding from a bottle of the Regent's finest champagne.

Was righteous indignation the only reason for her passionate rebuke? Gabriel wondered. Or might the Irish heiress resent another woman trying to claim *her* child?

"The discovery of Madame's deception left us in a quandary," he explained. "It meant that Jack could not be Sarah's father after all and Rory is adamant he cannot be. That leaves only me and my romantic history is not as extensive as rumor would have it."

Gabriel lowered the volume of his voice but not the intensity of his tone. "If Sarah *is* my child, only one woman could be her mother. Tell me, was it you who left her on our doorstep?"

After an instant of stunned silence, Moira Brennan's Irish temper exploded.

"How dare you ask me such a question?" Her gloved hand flew, striking Gabriel a smarting blow on the cheek.

Until that moment, no one else in the crowded banqueting tent had paid them any heed. But the lady's violent outburst caused many heads to turn and gazes to fix upon them. The buzz of conversation hushed then intensified again, like a swarm of wasps whose nest had been shaken.

Miss Brennan pivoted with furious grace and dashed away, leaving Gabriel to rub his cheek and ponder what her volatile reaction could mean. In the fleeting instant before she struck him, he had glimpsed shame and deep pain in her eyes. Why should she look that way unless what he'd suggested was true?

Though he knew it would only fuel the fever of gossip Miss Brennan's furious display had sparked, Gabriel ignored the staring crowd around him and raced off in pursuit of the woman who might be the mother of his child.

⸺•◆•⸺

Why had she let her father persuade her to attend to this ridiculous, extravagant spectacle? Moira berated herself as she fought her way through the throng of guests making their way toward the dining tents in the garden of Carlton House. Hopefully their departure would leave the upper rooms of the Prince Regent's residence less crowded. She had told Lord Gabriel Stanford that she must find her father and that was true. But first she needed a few moments to collect her composure, which had been badly shaken by her encounter with the Duke of Cheviot's youngest son.

Encounter? It had been more like an ambush!

The nerve of that man! After not exchanging a word with her in more than a year, to make such a scandalous accusation in the midst of the most public event of the Season!

It was not entirely Lord Gabriel's fault that they'd had no contact since Lady Killoran's Christmas house-party, her conscience protested. She had not made herself easy to locate.

Perhaps not in recent months. Moira tried to dismiss the inconvenient pang. But following the house party, she and her father had resided within riding distance of London. Lord Gabriel had been too busy drinking, gambling and wenching to pay a single visit.

The discovery of a misbegotten infant on his doorstep had compelled him to seek her out. Lord Gabriel claimed to care for this child he could not even be certain was his. The irony of it threatened to overwhelm Moira. How had a helpless babe managed to secure his devotion in a way she had not?

The further she fled from the Prince's gardens, the thinner the crowd grew. By the time Moira reached the Great Staircase, she was able to ascend to the upper floor without difficulty — a feat that would have been impossible an hour earlier.

She breathed a sigh of relief to find the grand rooms overlooking the gardens all but deserted. Pausing by one of the bow windows in the Rose Satin Drawing Room, she inhaled deep drafts of night air scented with food and flowers. The grounds below sparkled with lights, laughter and music.

It was a great honor to be invited to the Prince Regent's fête. But Moira would rather have languished in obscurity if it meant avoiding Lord Gabriel Stanford. Her past dealings with the Duke's son had shown her that newly-prosperous Irish folk had no place in his world.

"I do not believe you will find your father up here." Lord Gabriel's voice startled Moira.

She gasped and raised one gloved hand to her throat.

"What business is that of yours? And why did you follow me when I made it clear I do not wish to speak with you?"

Fluttering her fan rapidly to cool her flushed face, Moira noticed a faint red mark on Lord Gabriel's chiselled cheek where she had struck him. She found herself torn between the urge to reach out and soothe it with a caress and the impulse to inflict a matching blow on the other side. Then perhaps he would leave her in peace — curse him!

"It *is* my business since you excused yourself from our conversation on the pretext of locating your father." He planted himself squarely in front of her so she could not easily escape, short of jumping out the window. "It appears that was a falsehood. I suspect it is not the only one you have told me this evening."

His voice had a ragged, breathless edge that did not detract in the least from its appeal. It reminded Moira of the endearments he had murmured to her in the intimate darkness of a winter night. That night seemed a lifetime ago in some ways, yet strangely immediate in the feelings its memory aroused.

She lowered her fan to glare at Lord Gabriel. Perhaps that was a mistake, for it exposed her to the peril of his melting dark gaze.

"Do you reproach me for trying to exercise a measure of civility?" she demanded. "Would you rather I had declared the impolite truth that I cannot abide the *sight* of you, much less your conversation?"

Something in his gaze made her wonder if he would have preferred a physical blow to her hostile words. But Moira refused to feel the least twinge of sympathy for the man who had thrown her life into such turmoil. "What makes you think I owe you the truth or anything else after what you did? Were you not satisfied with ruining me? Must you make certain everyone in Society knows of your conquest?"

A look of deep chagrin twisted Lord Gabriel's handsome features. Moira sensed that he had only begun to realize how badly he'd behaved toward her this evening.

Before he had the chance to offer a properly abject apology, his expression hardened again. "I did not intend any such thing. Our fellow guests were far too occupied with their own amusement to take any notice of us. If they did, it is only because you responded to my question with such a violent outburst rather than a simple, truthful answer."

He had the gall to blame her? Moira longed to throttle him! If only she could be certain that placing her hands around his neck would not tempt her to do something weak and foolish.

"After the quantity of wine they are likely to drink tonight, I doubt the Regent's guests will recall much of anything they see or hear." Lord Gabriel cast a glance through the bow window to scan the glittering garden below. "Yet I cannot deny it was badly done. I should have made a greater effort to question you in private about such a delicate matter. I beg your pardon for allowing my frustration to get the better of discretion."

The gentleman's unexpected apology affected Moira more than she dared let him see. "How can you expect me to excuse such an insult after a few words of doubtful sincerity? They are your speciality as I recall. If I were a man, I would be justified in challenging you to a duel."

"Perhaps so." One corner of Lord Gabriel's well-shaped mouth arched briefly as if amused at the thought of them locked in mortal combat. "And you might win, for I have never been a skilled marksman . . . much to the Duke's displeasure."

Moira recalled how Lord Gabriel had made light of the fact that he was such a disappointment to his father. It had stirred her indignation and sympathy . . . until he'd disappointed *her* with his irresponsible behavior.

"My apology was quite sincere," he insisted. "If it were in my power to alter the past, I would act differently. Since that is impossible, can you suggest any other way I might make amends?"

His offer left Moira breathless. Would Lord Gabriel truly grant *any* favor she might ask?

Of course not. That was ridiculous! Besides, as he'd said, it was impossible to correct the past. Some mistakes could never be mended.

"There is one favor you might do me that would ease my offense …"

Lord Gabriel did not hesitate. "Name it and I shall make every effort to oblige you."

He seemed so eager and sincere, Moira almost regretted what she was about to say. Then she reminded herself what was at stake. "Kindly stop pestering me with your ridiculous questions and leave me in peace."

Lord Gabriel's countenance hardened into a forbidding look. "I shall be happy to do as you ask if you will give an honest answer to my inquiry, regardless of how ridiculous you consider it. For little Sarah's sake I must know if you are her mother."

"I am not," Moira insisted with firm conviction. She could not afford to let Lord Gabriel sense the slightest doubt.

"Are you *quite* certain?" An ache of disappointment suffused his voice. "It seemed the most likely possibility."

Moira refused to feel sorry for him. "It is not a matter about which a woman is liable to be mistaken."

"I suppose not." It was clear Gabriel Stanford wanted to believe the child belonged to him. "But if Sarah is not our daughter, whose can she be?"

What made him so anxious to claim that tiny foundling? The thought provoked a tight ache in Moira's chest and made her eyes sting. She must escape Lord Gabriel's company before he noticed her distress and drew the wrong conclusion.

Or, worse yet, the right one …

———◆◆◆———

Several hours later, the midsummer sun was beginning its early rise as Gabriel sat drinking with Rory Fitzwalter in one of the banqueting tents. The place was a good deal quieter than it had been. But there were still a few hardy revellers prepared to carouse at the Regent's expense until someone showed them the door.

"There you have it, old friend." Rory spoke with a more pronounced Irish accent when he was in his cups. "The answer you have been seeking all this time. The beauteous Miss Brennan is not Sarah's mother after all. By your own insistence that means you cannot be her father."

He beckoned a yawning servant to refill their glasses then raised his to Gabriel. "Shall we toast your fortunate escape from the bondage of parenthood and other disagreeable responsibilities?"

"I will do no such thing!" Gabriel made a determined effort not to slur his words. "I think the world of that dear little creature. I would have been proud to claim her as my daughter."

He heaved a sigh that seemed to rise all the way from the toes of his silver-buckled shoes. "If I drink, it will not be a celebratory toast, but rather to drown my sorrows."

Having made his motives clear, Gabriel took a deep draft of his wine. Though he knew it must be a costly vintage, the stuff had a bitter aftertaste. "I suppose this means I must congratulate *you* on having sired such a fine young daughter."

Until that moment, he'd never had envied his friend.

"Do not be so hasty." Rory wagged his forefinger. "I am fond of the child too, but I still maintain it is impossible that she could be mine."

They had discussed the matter at length after the baby first appeared on Jack Warwick's doorstep. Rory Fitzwalter was seldom without a very willing woman in his bed. But his paramours tended to be past the age of breeding and able to support a child if they found it necessary. He insisted none of them would have the bad manners to abandon an infant at his door with an anonymous note.

Now Rory regarded his friend with narrowed eyes. "What makes you so certain Miss Brennan was telling you the truth?"

Part of Gabriel resented the question, while another part

latched onto it with desperate hope. "Why would she deny her own child?"

Even as he spoke, Gabriel recalled the scrupulously maintained web of deceit that had surrounded *his* true paternity. Instead of seeking to learn whether Sarah might be his daughter, perhaps he ought to investigate the identity of his natural father.

"Why?" Rory repeated, as if the answer must be obvious. "A great many reasons I can think of, even in my present state of inebriation."

He took a drink and cast a glance around the banqueting tent. Small knots of guests sat about eating and drinking. A few were slumped in their chairs snoring.

Perhaps satisfied that no one was within earshot, he lowered his voice just the same. "Unlike *my* dear ladies, yours is young enough to care about her reputation. She may want a husband one day. The presence of an illegitimate child would deter the sort of suitors Miss Brennan might prefer, don't you think?"

The notion of Moira Brennan being courted by other men sent a fierce possessive blaze through Gabriel's chest.

"That makes no sense!" he protested with such savage intensity that Rory startled, fumbling his wine glass. "If Miss Brennan admitted to being the mother of my child, I would marry her, of course. Then neither of us would need to be parted from our daughter."

Initially, he'd resisted the notion of marrying Moira Brennan ... or any woman. Growing up in the Cheviot household had convinced him that marriage and happiness were mutually exclusive. Yet, by degrees he had warmed to the idea, until he'd almost made peace with it. Jack and Annabelle Warwick's happy union had made him question some of his long-held beliefs about matrimony. Not that it mattered now.

"It is all well and good to tell *me* you are prepared to marry Miss Brennan." Rory drained his glass. "Does *she* know you would be willing to make an honest woman of her?"

Did she? His friend's question cut through Gabriel's haze of fatigue and tipsiness. Had he told her so plainly, or had he assumed she must understand? He plundered his memory to no avail. Instead it dwelt on images of Moira Brennan's blue-green eyes, the appealing cascade of her auburn hair and the tantalizing sweep of her shoulders.

Perhaps Rory was right. If the lady was not certain of his honorable intentions, she might be inclined to deny their love child. He must make sure she knew it was safe to tell him the truth.

Chapter Two

TWO EVENINGS AFTER the Regent's banquet, Moira strolled along one of the wooded paths of Vauxhall Pleasure Gardens with Mrs. Trimble, her trusted companion of many years. "I do not know why Father insists on prolonging our stay in London. If the weather grows any warmer, the city will be unbearable."

She chided herself for complaining. Ever since her encounter with Lord Gabriel Stanhope, she had been out of temper. Only one thing might lift her spirits and it was not to be found in London.

"Now, now my dear," the older woman replied with her usual motherly good sense. "Your poor father is feeling well again at last. Is it any wonder he wants to enjoy a bit of company before you settle down in Surrey for the summer?"

"I suppose not." Moira stifled a sigh. "Though I worry he will overtax his strength with all this gadding about."

Her father had fallen dangerously ill last autumn, forcing them to extend their stay on the Isle of Jersey so he could recover. In a way the situation had been providential, yet Moira could not bring herself to think of it like that.

Mrs. Trimble gave an indulgent chuckle. "You used to be quite fond of gadding about, don't forget. You're still a young woman, my dear. Enjoy these years. They go by far too quickly."

"I am well aware how quickly time passes," replied Moira as the melody of a popular ballad wafted from the music pavilion in the heart of the Pleasure Gardens.

Mrs. Trimble lowered her voice. "I know you must be anxious to return to Ardmore and see … how everything is getting on. But all will be well, I'm certain."

Moira was about to answer when a familiar female voice called out. "Miss Brennan, is that you? I heard you had come to town. How good it is to see you again!"

She turned to find the Countess of Killoran bearing down on them, followed by the earl and some other gentlemen. Moira had known her ladyship for some years and found her well-meaning, though inclined to *manage* everyone around her.

"Lady Killoran, the pleasure is mine. Your lordship." She curtsied to the earl and countess. "May I present my companion, Mrs. Trimble?"

"I believe we have met." Lady Killoran smiled warmly. "Though, as I recall, you were not able to accompany Miss Brennan to our Christmas gathering the year before last."

Mrs. Trimble beamed with felicity, no doubt flattered that the countess recalled her absence after so many months. "That is true, your ladyship. My sister was taken poorly and Miss Brennan insisted she could manage with one of the maids to do for her."

The countess nodded as she motioned the other two members of her party forward. "You must remember my brother-in-law Rory Fitzwalter and his friend Lord Gabriel Stanford. They were with us that Christmas as well. What an unexpected reunion this is!"

Unexpected? Certainly Moira had not anticipated meeting Lord Gabriel again so soon. As she and Mrs. Trimble curtsied to the gentlemen, she tried not to scowl. Was this meeting truly by chance or had he contrived it somehow?

Lady Killoran seized Moira's arm and began to stroll down a broad tree-lined path that led away from the Music Pavilion, while Mrs. Trimble and the gentlemen followed. "How is your dear father? I heard he'd been taken ill, poor man. What a worry that must have been for you."

"It was indeed." Behind them, Moira heard Rory Fitzwalter and his brother the earl exercising their Irish charm on her companion. Lord Gabriel remained silent, which would continue if he knew what was good for him. Moira feared what Mrs. Trimble might let slip if the gentleman tried to engage her in conversation.

Somehow Moira managed to walk without tripping over her feet and to converse more or less coherently with Lady Killoran. Most of her awareness remained concentrated on Lord Gabriel, who trailed quietly behind them.

After several minutes, the countess paused in mid-sentence and called to her husband. "Look, Frederick. Is that not Lady Cork? I know you are anxious to speak to her."

The Killorans begged Moira's pardon and excused themselves. She expected Lord Gabriel and his friend to follow, but they did not. When she glanced behind her, Moira spied Mrs. Trimble deep in conversation with Rory Fitzwalter. What a notorious man-about-town might say to interest a respectable middle-aged widow, Moira could not guess.

She had no time to ponder the question for Lord Gabriel stepped forward to take the countess's place by her side. "So we meet again, Miss Brennan. Fate seems bent on throwing us together this week."

"Fate?" Moira sniffed, though it was all she could do to keep her foolish lips from arching upward at the sound of his bantering voice. "Is that what you have taken to calling yourself? I do not believe for a minute that we met this evening by chance."

She expected Lord Gabriel to deny the charge. Instead, he replied with a disarming chuckle. "It would be a rather unlikely coincidence, would it not?"

Part of Moira wanted to demand how he'd known she would be here this evening, but she could guess a well-placed coin had found its way into some talkative footman's pocket.

"What do you want now?" She kept her eyes fixed firmly ahead when they practically itched to glance in Lord Gabriel's direction. "Are there a few people in London who might not have heard you accuse me of scandalous behavior at the Prince Regent's fête? Perhaps you ought to stand on the balcony of the Music Pavilion and shout it out for everyone else to hear."

"I did apologize for my thoughtless behavior," he reminded her in a tone that seemed to caress her ears. "I promise I will do nothing to embarrass you this evening."

Moira scarcely noticed as he steered her down a side path toward a more secluded area of the Pleasure Gardens.

"That is reassuring." She meant to infuse her voice with biting irony. Instead the words came out in a flirtatious tone. Before she could prevent it, a fleeting smile crossed her face and her glance strayed toward Lord Gabriel.

Their eyes met and he returned her unintended smile. That look seemed to ferment her blood into the finest champagne, sparkling and thoroughly intoxicating.

With great difficulty, she wrested her gaze away and struggled to regain her self-possession. "I have not forgotten your apology, but *you* seem to have forgotten your offer to make amends. I answered your question about the child, now I wish you would stop pestering me!"

"I do not blame you for being vexed with me," he replied, as if he had not heard a word she said, "nor for perhaps being … less than forthcoming."

What did he mean by that? Moira's heart plunged while all the air seemed to rush from her lungs. What did Lord Gabriel Stanford know?

He seemed oblivious to her inner turmoil. "In my urgency to discover Sarah's parentage I fear I bungled my approach. I ought to have made it clear that if the little one is ours I have every intention of doing what honor demands."

"A-are you proposing to me, sir?" There had been a time when she'd wanted nothing more. Later she'd desired nothing less. How did she feel about the prospect now? Moira could scarcely sort out her turbulent emotions.

Her indifferent response seemed to take Lord Gabriel

aback. "That depends. *Are* you Sarah's mother?"

At least he had the consideration to lower his voice to a barely audible murmur. That did little to soothe Moira's temper. Lord Gabriel would reluctantly submit to taking her as his wife, for reasons that had nothing to do with his feelings toward her, whatever they might be.

"You think I was lying when I denied it?" Moira wished she could feel as indignant about that as she tried to sound. "You assume an offer of marriage is sufficient incentive to make me tell the truth. You forget that I refused a proposal from you once before. Do you suppose the fact that I am a year older has made me desperate to secure a husband by any means?"

"Of course not!" Lord Gabriel bridled. "I only wanted you to understand my intentions and know you have nothing to fear from telling me the truth."

He sounded sincerely offended that she had misinterpreted his motives. "I recall only too well that you refused me once already. I hoped that if the welfare of our child were at stake, you might reconsider your disdain for me."

Disdain was all she *wanted* to feel for him. It was what he deserved, surely. Her stubborn heart had other ideas. It urged her to tell Lord Gabriel Stanford the whole truth — not simply the strict answer to his question. But he had shown her what his reaction would be and it confirmed her worst fears.

"In that case, it is fortunate for everyone concerned that my answer remains unchanged. The child left on your friend's doorstep is not mine. I resent your suspicion that I would be capable of abandoning a helpless infant. If I had found myself in such a predicament, you and your disreputable friends are the last people I would leave her with."

She was being too harsh, Moira's conscience warned her. What had happened between them at Lady Killoran's house party was as much her fault as his. And he had offered to do the honorable thing, no matter how distasteful he might find it.

But he had made her believe he was in love with her, Moira's wounded heart protested. And he had not disabused her of that false notion until after he'd bedded her. The last thing she wanted was to let him back into her life to cause more havoc.

"Regardless of what you think of me and my friends," Lord Gabriel replied, "we have done our best to provide Sarah with proper care and a loving home. I had hoped to give her a family with her natural parents — an idea you seem to find offensive. I beg your pardon for doubting your earlier denial, but I could not escape the sense that you were concealing something from me."

If a gang of ruffians had burst through the high hedges that lined this path to menace her, Moira could not have felt more threatened than by Lord Gabriel's simple declaration. She wanted to rage at him and insist that he was wrong. But her conscience was already too overburdened to support an outright falsehood. Besides, too strenuous a protest might only increase his suspicions. She could not afford that.

Instead she forced a mirthless chuckle. "I fear you have allowed your affection for that little foundling to run away with you ... which is commendable in its way, I suppose."

She must get rid of Gabriel Stanford before he caused her any more heartache. "There is one matter which I have *concealed* from you, but only because I did not believe it should be of any concern of yours."

Even as she considered what she was about to say, Moira hesitated. She had struggled with her decision for some time now, torn one way then the other. Her encounters with Lord Gabriel Stanford had left her more confused than ever, until this moment.

"Perhaps you should let *me* be the judge of its significance." His tone betrayed an intrusive degree of interest.

She needed protection from Lord Gabriel's curiosity and from his equally dangerous appeal. "Very well, then. One of the reasons your offer of marriage does not tempt me is because I am already betrothed."

"B-betrothed?"

Moira stole another brief glance at Lord Gabriel Stanford. This time she had the grim satisfaction of seeing his mouth hang slack.

She should have taken vengeful delight in his obvious bewilderment, but that was not possible. Clearly Lord Gabriel could not imagine why any man would want to wed her unless circumstances forced him to.

———◆———

When Gabriel arrived at the Warwicks' townhouse on Bruton Street the next day, Annabelle flew to take his arm and lead him to the nearest chair. "Poor fellow, you look perfectly dreadful! Did you and Rory stay on at the Prince Regent's fête until the bitter end? I thought you intended to reform your habits, for Sarah's sake."

Gabriel tried to protest that he had not been carousing ever since the night of the banquet.

Before he could get a word out, Annabelle turned to her husband. "Jack, will you ask Mr. Godfrey to make up one of his tonics for Lord Gabriel? And please ring for Polly to fetch Sarah down the moment she wakes from her nap."

"With pleasure, my love." Jack Warwick beamed at his pretty wife. Once the most incorrigible rake in London, he was now the very picture of domestic felicity. "Though I expect a visit with his favorite young lady may be the only tonic our friend requires."

Gabriel tried not to envy them. He was warmly attached to both Jack and Annabelle and wished them nothing but joy. Yet he recalled the misery they had endured when circumstances conspired to keep them apart. It confirmed his long-held belief that when it came to marriage, love and happiness seldom went hand in hand.

Annabelle nodded in response to her husband's remark as she sank onto the settee opposite Gabriel. "Sarah will be delighted to see him too, I'm certain."

She fixed Gabriel with a penetrating blue gaze, which he endeavored to avoid until Jack rejoined them a few moments later.

"Tell us then," Jack took a seat beside his wife. "Have your vile looks anything to do with Miss Brennan? She fetched you quite a clout the other night. I am surprised it did not leave a bruise."

"Saw that, did you?" Gabriel rubbed his cheek where Moira Brennan had struck him. Though the blow had not left a mark, his flesh still tingled when he recalled it. "I cannot blame her for being provoked by the impertinent remarks I made to her in such a public place. I was so eager to ask her about Sarah that I did not consider who might overhear us."

"Were you able to find her again after she ran off?" asked Jack. "Among such a crowd of guests at a vast establishment like Carlton House, it would be easy to slip out of sight."

"I tracked her to the drawing room overlooking the garden." A vivid image of Moira Brennan rose in Gabriel's mind. The dapple of tawny freckles and her billow of auburn curls made her look even younger than her years. Together with her white gown, those features had given her an air of virginal innocence. He had good reason to know such an impression was false.

Whose fault was that? Gabriel's conscience demanded.

Not entirely his, he silently protested. The impetuous heiress had stolen into *his* bedchamber on that cold winter night, not the other way around.

His conscience refused to relent. Miss Brennan had been young and naive. She'd fancied herself in love with him and assumed he returned her ardor. He should never have taken advantage of her mistaken ideas to satisfy his desire, no matter how intense.

"What happened then?" Jack's query interrupted Gabriel's rueful reflection. "What did you say to her? How did she reply?"

"I pressed her for an honest answer to my question about

the baby, of course. Miss Brennan insists she is not Sarah's mother. She claims that she and her father were on the Isle of Jersey from before Sarah's birth until long after she was left with us."

"I am sorry, Gabriel." Annabelle addressed him in a tone of gentle sympathy. "I know what high hopes you had of being Sarah's father. But never fear. She belongs to *all* of us now. As long as Jack and I have her in our care, you and Rory will be welcome to spend as much time with her as you wish."

"In fact …" She clasped her husband's hand. "We are planning to have Sarah christened. We would like you and Rory to be her godfathers."

Did the Warwicks expect him to be grateful for the honor? Gabriel bridled. "Was it not premature to make such plans when Sarah might have turned out to be *my* daughter?"

"Perhaps." Jack's hushed but ominous tone warned Gabriel that he would not tolerate any criticism of Annabelle. "But since that is not the case, surely it is in Sarah's best interest for us to have her christened."

Just then, Jack's indispensable valet appeared bearing the tonic Gabriel had often imbibed after a night of overindulgence. It was a vile concoction involving raw eggs, pepper, ginger and capers. But since he could not deny its curative powers, he drained the cup as quickly as possible. Somehow he doubted even Godfrey's celebrated tonic could relieve what ailed him today.

Returning the empty cup with a grimace, Gabriel thanked Jack's valet for his assistance. His grimace transformed into an eager smile a moment later, when Sarah's nursemaid bore the child into the sitting room. His heart, which had throbbed as if bruised, now swelled to contain a rush of fond warmth.

The baby's plump cheeks were still flushed from sleep but her eyes sparkled with delighted recognition of Gabriel. She clapped her tiny hands together and cried, "Ga!"

"Clever girl!" He peppered her face with kisses. "You are trying to say my name, aren't you? Ga-bree-ell."

"Ga-ga-ga!" Sarah chortled in reply.

"I vow you grow bigger and bonnier every time I see you." He rubbed his nose against hers, making her laugh harder. "Have you cut more teeth? Any new accomplishments for which I should praise you?"

"One more tooth on the bottom, sir." Polly spoke for her small charge. "I was afraid she would chew her teething coral clean through."

"She can sit up on her own and hardly ever topple," Annabelle announced with a ring of maternal pride. "And she can stand up for a good while holding onto a chair."

"Sarah," she called to the baby, "where is Papa?"

The child turned at the sound of her name. She looked toward Jack, who grinned and winked at her. She promptly burst into gleeful laughter. "Ga!"

Gabriel's heart sank. Sarah had not been trying to say his name after all. Did he only *imagine* she recognized him from one visit to the next?

He'd been thoroughly intimidated when the tiny screaming creature had appeared on their doorstep. In hindsight he was ashamed of himself for leaving so much of her early care to Jack and Annabelle. He had not believed for a moment that she might be his daughter. But as his attachment to the baby had deepened, Gabriel's thoughts turned increasingly toward the lovely Irish heiress with whom he had shared a passionate Yuletide tryst.

Such thoughts tumbled through Gabriel's mind as he played with the baby and quizzed the women about her health and growth. He would gladly have continued both longer, but after a while little Sarah grew restless.

"She is not tired of your company," Annabelle assured him as Polly approached and lifted the baby from Gabriel's reluctant arms. "It is time for her feeding. What an appetite she has these days!"

"Goodbye, little one." Gabriel gave the baby's fingers a parting squeeze then released them with a pang of regret.

"I shall see you again soon. Do not grow up too fast in the meantime."

Sarah stopped fussing and lavished him with an adoring smile that reminded Gabriel of the way Moira Brennan had once looked at him. Were there more points of resemblance between the two? He was certain there were.

After Polly swept her little charge off to the nursery Gabriel turned his attention back to the Warwicks. "Do not be too hasty about this christening business. Regardless of what Miss Brennan claims, I am still not convinced she is telling the truth."

"I sympathize with your desire to claim Sarah as your daughter," said Jack. "I was prepared to believe any outrageous tale and forfeit my future happiness to protect her. But in the end, I could not rearrange the facts to suit my wishes."

"Remember, Gabriel," Annabelle's tone begged him to see reason, "the note that came with Sarah said her mother could not care for her. Surely an heiress like Miss Brennan would have no such difficulty."

Her words had a ring of good sense, yet Gabriel found himself desperate to doubt them. "You assume her mother's motive for abandoning Sarah was financial, but the note made no mention of money."

"What other reason —?" Jack began, his tone growing heated.

"Moira Brennan has gotten engaged!" Gabriel blurted out the news. It left a bitter taste in his mouth. "To a clergyman, no less. Do you suppose she would want to take the chance of her suitor discovering she had a child out of wedlock?"

The thought of her with another man made his heart pulse with violent heat. He told the Warwicks about his conversation with Moira Brennan at Vauxhall.

Jack's brow creased. "An heiress like Miss Brennan could secure a much better match than to a mere curate."

Annabelle gave a furtive glance around the sitting room, as if to make certain no one would overhear. "Do you suppose

Miss Brennan assumes a man of the cloth will be too inexperienced to realize her virtue was compromised before their marriage?"

Her question made Gabriel's stomach sink. Even if he had not gotten Moira with child, his lapse in judgment might have done her harm in other ways. In his eagerness to claim little Sarah, he'd neglected to tell her how deeply he regretted that.

When Gabriel did not answer Annabelle's question, Jack offered a comment. "If that is her reason for accepting the fellow, I hope Miss Brennan will not be taken advantage of. Her fortune would be a great temptation to the wrong sort of man."

A fierce rush of heat suffused Gabriel's face. One of the reasons he had been reluctant to propose to Moira Brennan was the certainty that he would be condemned as a fortune hunter.

"Now, Jack," Annabelle protested. "I believe your experience with Madame Reynard has made you too suspicious. Surely a clergyman would not have designs on Miss Brennan's fortune!"

Jack gave a rueful shrug. "I wish I could be certain his vocation would preclude the fellow from being a fortune hunter ... or worse."

"Worse?" Gabriel's head snapped up. "What could be worse?"

"I do not mean to alarm you," said Jack. "Nor to accuse anyone. But these are dangerous times with Bonaparte rampaging all over Europe."

A shadow of grief fell over both the Warwick's faces. Gabriel knew they must be thinking of Annabelle's first husband, who had been Jack's beloved cousin. Young Lord Southam had perished in battle against Napoleon's forces.

"What does that have to do with Miss Brennan?" he demanded.

"You said the lady met her fiancé on the Isle of Jersey," Jack replied as understanding began to dawn on Gabriel. "The Channel Islands lie perilously close to the coast of

Normandy. What better disguise for a French spy than as a humble clergyman?"

His friend's suggestion made unsettling sense. With access to the Brennan fortune and connections, what sensitive information might a French spy be able to pass along to his masters? A surge of outrage swept through Gabriel, followed by a cold qualm of shame.

It was his fault that Moira Brennan had fallen prey to a man who might do her, and perhaps the whole country, a great deal of harm. That meant it was *his* responsibility to assess the threat and thwart it if necessary.

Chapter Three

"**Y**ou've been awfully quiet today." Mrs. Trimble glanced up from packing Moira's trunk to fix her with a look that mingled curiosity, concern and mild disapproval. "Come to think of it, you haven't seemed yourself since last evening at the Pleasure Gardens. Did *that young man* say something to upset you?"

For this brief visit to London, the Brennans had chosen to stay at the exclusive Pulteney Hotel. After her unsettling encounter with Lord Gabriel Stanford, Moira had persuaded her father they should make an early start for home the next morning.

Once he agreed, she had done her best to put Lord Gabriel out of her mind, but her companion's question roused unwelcome memories of their conversation at Vauxhall. It was not so much what Lord Gabriel had *said* that troubled her, though his unexpected marriage proposal had set off a fierce tug-of-war within her. What truly dismayed her was the powerful response to his presence that she could not control.

It was perfectly ridiculous! She'd been acquainted him for less than a month before they'd parted over a year ago. By rights, she should scarcely recall his name. Yet, in a sense, she had carried him with her ever since.

Mrs. Trimble heaved a sharp sigh as she tucked the last of Moira's dresses into the trunk. "I should never have let him speak to you on your own, but that Mr. Fitzwalter diverted me so. He has a way about him, that one. It took me the longest time to notice that Lord and Lady Killoran were no longer with you."

Clearly that had been Lord Gabriel's plan from the outset. Moira bristled. She might have been flattered that he'd gone to so much trouble to speak with her in private. But she knew he was only doing it for the sake of the little foundling he clearly doted upon. Though part of her resented Lord Gabriel's preoccupation with a child who was not even his, an unwelcome flicker of sympathy stirred within her also. How could she blame him for wanting to take responsibility for his actions and reunite an abandoned infant with its family?

Once again she told herself to put the attractive but troublesome nobleman out of her mind. She would soon be back in the country and with luck he might never cross her path again. To her dismay, the prospect left her feeling oddly deflated.

"I have not been quiet on account of my conversation with Lord Gabriel Stanford," she insisted. "The gentleman means nothing to me anymore."

Perhaps if she said those words often enough she could make herself believe them. "If you must know, I have been giving Mr. Clarkson's proposal a great deal of thought and I have made up my mind to accept."

Had she left herself any choice after telling Lord Gabriel that she and the curate were betrothed? Moira could not decide whether she was more annoyed with herself for making such an impulsive announcement, or with him for goading her into it.

Fortunately her words had the desired effect of diverting Mrs. Trimble from quizzing her further about Lord Gabriel Stanford.

"Thank heaven!" The good lady clasped her hands to her motherly bosom while her plain features blossomed into a rapturous smile. "My prayers have been answered."

Mrs. Trimble belonged to one of Ulster's most respected clerical families. Her father and both grandfathers had been vicars, while a distant cousin was Bishop of Tyrone. In her eyes, a ministerial beau was preferable even to the son of a duke.

"I'm certain you will have a contented, respectable life with Mr. Clarkson, my dear. *He* will never give you cause to repent your feelings for him."

"That is precisely the conclusion I came to," Moira replied. Privately, she acknowledged that it would be impossible to repent what she did not feel.

Why could she not summon up any deeper feelings for the reverend gentleman than respect and tepid fondness? He was the most obliging man she had ever met, ready to agree with her every opinion and comply with any request. He was an attentive listener and in spite of his spiritual vocation he never preached at her or quoted Scripture. There were times she could almost forget he was a man of the cloth.

Mrs. Trimble closed Moira's trunk and dusted off her hands. "Now that you've made up your mind about Mr. Clarkson, you have no reason to look anxious, do you? No sense letting that pretty face get wrinkled before its time."

Moira tried to appear serene, which was not easy while thoughts of Lord Gabriel Stanford continued to lurk in the back of her mind.

An abrupt knock on the door provoked a guilty start from her.

"That must be Father's man," she squeaked, "come to tell us what time we are to dine."

Rather than waiting for Mrs. Trimble to answer the summons, Moira hurried to the door and prepared to greet her father's valet.

The words froze in her throat when she found her Papa standing in the parlor of their suite, his ruddy visage glowing with satisfaction. Behind him hovered Lord Gabriel Stanford, looking equally pleased with himself.

Apparently she had not seen the last of him after all. A fierce urge to slam the door in his face warred with a bewildering flutter of exhilaration.

Mr. Brennan chortled. "Surprised to see this young gentleman again are you, my love? So was I when we chanced to meet today. You remember Lord Gabriel Stanford, I hope?"

"How could I forget him?" Moira made a polite curt-sey quite at odds with the glare she aimed at Lord Gabriel. "You have an uncanny knack for being all over London, sir. Especially wherever we happen to be."

His meeting with her father was no more a coincidence than his appearance at Vauxhall the previous evening. She did not want to leave him in any doubt that she saw through his machinations.

Lord Gabriel responded to her bitter quip with a warm chuckle, as if it amused him. "I assure you, Miss Brennan, I have been nowhere near Cheapside nor the Smithfield Market. I suspect you would find many of our acquaintances gath-ered in a small number of exclusive locations around town this week."

Next he addressed himself to her father, who looked rather bemused by their exchange. "I should have mentioned, sir, that it was my good fortune to encounter your lovely daughter at the Prince Regent's fête and again last evening at Vauxhall. Now I see the old saying is true, that good things come in threes."

"Well, think of that." Mr. Brennan looked from Lord Gabriel to Moira. "Why did you not tell me you had seen our young friend?"

"I have seen a great many people since we arrived in London, Papa." Moira recalled how Gabriel Stanford had once endeared himself to her father with his attentiveness. At the time it had endeared him to *her* as well. "Surely you cannot expect me to report them all to you."

"Hardly." Mr. Brennan shook his head. "But you should have known I would wish to hear of *this* gentleman. He is not some chance-met acquaintance, is he? We celebrated Christmas in his company. I reckon that creates a special bond."

"I quite agree, Mr. Brennan." Lord Gabriel nodded eagerly.

Moira barely stifled a derisive sniff. Could Papa name *any* of the other guests who had celebrated Christmas with them at Lady Killoran's house party?

If he noticed her baleful look, her father gave no sign. "I came to tell you that Lord Gabriel has invited us to dine with him this evening at Cheviot House. Quite an honor, wouldn't you say?"

What was Gabriel Stanford conniving at now? Moira's glare intensified. How many times must she deny being the mother of his little foundling before he would believe her? And what might he do if he discovered the secret she was so desperate to keep from him?

———◆◆◆———

Moira Brennan looked anything *but* honored by his invitation to dine. Gabriel had not expected her to. Then why did her pointed lack of enthusiasm cause him a foolish pang of dismay?

He could not deny she had good reason to be vexed over his past behavior. She'd made it clear she resented his continued efforts to question her about a matter that might easily destroy her reputation. But he could not wash his hands of her until he made certain her fiancé was worthy of her devotion.

"Thank you for the invitation, Lord Gabriel." Miss Brennan swept into the parlor of their hotel suite as if marching to do battle. "But we intend to make an early start for Surrey in the morning. We have already ordered a light supper to dine here and all my evening attire is packed away."

"By all means come dressed as you are," Gabriel insisted. "You look quite charming and this will not be a formal occasion. The duke and duchess have retired to the country and left only a small staff behind."

Fortunately, he had always been a favorite with the servants. Gabriel had no doubt they would provide him and his guests with a very good dinner.

A rosy flush suffused Miss Brennan's cheeks when he complimented her appearance. If he assumed that signalled a more receptive attitude toward his invitation, he was mistaken.

"We would not want to put your servants to extra work when the house is shut," she protested.

Gabriel dismissed her objection with a chuckle. "Our servants often lament the lack of opportunities to entertain. I wish you could have been here in April when Mama hosted a ball for the first time in years. Since you and your father were not available to accept my invitation then, I should be delighted to entertain you now in this small way."

He could imagine how the duke would have reacted to a suggestion that they invite a newly wealthy Irishman and his daughter to their grand ball. Might suspicion regarding the theft of Lady Halston's magnificent sapphire bracelet have fallen on the Brennans rather than the infamous Mayfair Shadow?

Before the lady could raise any further objections, her father spoke. "You heard the gentleman, Moira. It will be no trouble. Why should we dine in a hotel parlor when we could be welcome at one of the finest houses in Mayfair? If it means we set out a little later tomorrow, what will it matter? It is not as if we have anything particular awaiting us back at Ardmore."

Gabriel sensed that Miss Brennan had a reply on the tip of her tongue but she bit it back. *Was* there some compelling reason why she wished to return to Surrey as soon as possible? Her mysterious fiancé perhaps?

"If your daughter would rather not accept my invitation," he suggested, "I hope that will not prevent *you* from joining me, Mr. Brennan. I'm sure we can find a great many interesting topics for conversation."

Though he addressed his words to her father in a casual tone, Gabriel fixed Moira Brennan with a level stare that warned her she would stay away at her peril.

The lady clearly recognized his threat. "I did not refuse your invitation, Lord Gabriel. I only mentioned our plans and expressed my concern about inconveniencing your servants. If Father is so anxious to dine at Cheviot House and you are certain it will not put anyone out, of course I shall accompany him."

She did not claim she would be *delighted* or even *pleased* to accept his invitation. He was an unwelcome reminder of a regrettable incident from her past. It was clear she would prefer never to set eyes on him again. Gabriel could scarcely blame her.

Yet that was all the more reason he owed it to her to make inquiries about this fiancé of hers.

"Excellent!" he responded with enthusiasm that was not entirely feigned. Though Moira Brennan might feel nothing but contempt for him, he still found her more stimulating company than any woman he had ever met. "Then I shall go and make the arrangements for our dinner."

Mr. Brennan shook his hand. "I look forward to it most keenly, Lord Gabriel!"

"Until then." Gabriel cast Moira Brennan a conciliatory smile and made a respectful bow.

She replied with a correct but rigid curtsey and a glance that glittered with passionate antagonism. Somehow it had the opposite effect on Gabriel than she might have hoped.

He departed the hotel with a spring in his step and an undeniable hum of anticipation coursing through his veins. Matching wits with Moira Brennan promised to be more exciting than an evening of gambling. Gabriel sensed the stakes could be even higher and the potential reward more elusive.

What was Lord Gabriel Stanford playing at? Moira wondered as their carriage drew up in front of the imposing edifice of his family's Berkeley Square mansion. Did he still not believe her denial that she was little Sarah's mother? Perhaps he sensed she was keeping something from him, which was true, even if the particulars were not what he suspected.

Perhaps he hoped to worm some incriminating information out of her father. If so, he would be sorely disappointed.

Papa suspected nothing of her secret, which was how she intended to keep it. Still, she did not trust him in the company of Lord Gabriel Stanford on his own. It would be better if she was there to deflect dangerous questions and coach her father's answers.

Patrick Brennan leaned forward to peer out the carriage window. Any closer and his nose would have been pressed against the glass. "When I was a young lad in County Carlow, who'd have reckoned I would one day be invited to dine at such a place?"

Many of his countrymen had turned rebel and rejected the English nobility who kept them down, but Moira's father was entirely the opposite. Though proud of his Irish roots, he aspired to be accepted by the highest-born in England.

"How can you be so impressed by Cheviot House," she demanded, "when we were guests at the Prince Regent's magnificent mansion only a few days ago?"

"That was quite a sight," her father agreed, "but more than a trifle gaudy wouldn't you say? The Stanfords were a powerful family in this land long before the Regent's great-grandfather ever thought of coming from Hanover to claim the throne. The Dukes of Cheviot have no need to make a great fuss to proclaim their position."

Perhaps not, but that was precisely why Moira doubted she and her father would have been welcome at their grand ball. She wondered what the duke and duchess thought of their son's interest in a foundling of questionable parentage.

As the Brennans ascended the broad, shallow steps to the elegant portico of Cheviot House, Moira wondered if she ought to have worn a more fashionable gown. She feared they might be curtly bidden to use the tradesmen's entrance.

But when the door was answered by an ancient man-servant in handsome livery, she and her father received as respectful a welcome as any royal visitor.

They had scarcely crossed the threshold when Lord Gabriel appeared to greet them.

"Mr. Brennan, Miss Brennan, thank you for doing me the honor of dining with me on such short notice. It is my pleasure to welcome you both to Cheviot House!"

Whatever his motives for inviting them this evening, Moira found it impossible to doubt the sincerity of their welcome.

"The honor is ours, sir." Mr. Brennan gazed around with an air of deep satisfaction. "I must say, I admire this place a great deal more than that confection of the Prince Regent's."

Inwardly, Moira cringed. Did it sound presumptuous for newly-rich people to comment on the arrangements of a ducal family?

Gabriel Stanford responded with a tolerant chuckle that fell on Moira's ears like a caress. "His Grace, the Duke would be the first to agree with you, Mr. Brennan. The Prince does prize extravagance over restraint, though Carlton House is nothing compared to his pavilion at Brighton. Would you care to see more of Cheviot House before we dine?"

"Very much indeed!" Moira's father beamed at their host while she gave a grudging nod of agreement.

Lord Gabriel ignored her lack of enthusiasm.

"Right this way," he gestured toward a wide, dimly-lit gallery then instructed the servant who had admitted his guests. "Jepson, kindly send someone to fetch us when dinner is ready."

"Very well, sir." The old man regarded his young master with a doting expression. Then he bowed and withdrew.

Lord Gabriel turned his full attention back to his guests. "I am most grateful for your company this evening. Cheviot House is a splendid old place, but ridiculously large unless the entire family is in residence, which rarely happens. My brothers were already in school by the time I was born, so I used to dread coming to town and rattling around here on my own. Foolish the ideas children get."

Behind his hospitable banter, Moira thought she detected a note of wistful longing at odds with his usual rakish charm.

Perhaps Lord Gabriel realized he had betrayed more than

he intended, for he gave a laugh that sounded forced. "Now that I am older, I have the sense to appreciate the advantages this house has to offer. You must see the Italian Room. It houses a collection of paintings and sculptures from the Continent."

As they passed a number of large rooms with drawn curtains, Moira glimpsed clusters of furniture swathed in dust sheets, like parties of ghosts. The thick carpeting in the gallery muffled their footsteps, but when Lord Gabriel or her father spoke, their voices echoed. Walking past portraits of august Stanford ancestors, Moira's neck prickled as she fancied their disapproving gazes following her.

No wonder Lord Gabriel had disliked coming here as a child. For all its splendor, the great house was positively oppressive! Had she been wrong to assume he must have an ulterior motive for inviting them to dine here this evening? Perhaps the poor man simply wanted a bit of cheerful company.

Scarcely aware of what she was doing, Moira drew closer to their handsome host.

He led them into a vast chamber hung with many pictures that were clearly not family portraits. Instead, the ornately framed canvases contained scenes from Classical mythology. The latter made Moira blush and look away, flustered by the quantity of naked flesh on display. But when her gaze fell, it settled upon the sculpture of a sleeping youth, every sinew of his bare body faithfully replicated in pristine marble.

Was that how Lord Gabriel looked without his clothes? The wicked thought crept into Moira's mind and resisted her strenuous efforts to dismiss it.

There had been no light by which to admire his naked form on the midwinter night when she'd stolen into his bedchamber, reckless with a mixture of intoxication and infatuation. Now, as she strove to wrench her gaze away from the statue, the sight of its lithe arms, firm-muscled torso and supple thighs set unbidden desire smoldering within her.

"My word!" Her father's voice, hushed with wonder, jolted

Moira from her carnal musings. "What a remarkable collection you have here, Lord Gabriel."

"I can take no credit for any part of it." Their host sounded more chagrined than flattered by Mr. Brennan's praise. "Past members of the family acquired various pieces during their Grand Tours. I never had that opportunity. With the situation in Europe so unsettled, my mother would not hear of my going abroad."

It had long been the custom, Moira knew, for aristocratic families to send their sons to the Continent to acquire a bit of polish and perhaps sow their wild oats prior to marriage. Denied a Grand Tour, Lord Gabriel indulged his youthful excesses nearer to home, under the disapproving eyes of his parents.

An ember of sympathy for him ignited in Moira's heart, only to be stamped out by his next words to her father. "You and your daughter have been nearer to the Continent than I have ever been. Do tell me about your visit to the Channel Islands. Were you not nervous to be so near the coast of France in time of war?"

Before her father could reply, Moira spun away from the provocative sculpture of the sleeping youth. "We were in no danger on the Isle of Jersey. General Bonaparte learned his lesson at Trafalgar."

Just then, the servant who had answered the door reappeared and addressed their host. "Lord Gabriel, Mrs. Valentine wishes me to inform you that the meal is ready whenever you wish to dine."

"Thank you, Jepson," his master replied in a tone that sounded almost affectionate, "and thank Mrs. Valentine until I am able to express my gratitude in person. We shall come at once to savor her excellent cooking at its freshest."

He headed toward the far end of the gallery, beckoning his guests to follow.

Moira hoped the servant's timely interruption would get them off the subject of Jersey. But as Lord Gabriel ushered them into the immense dining room, her father remarked, "Our visit to the island was perfectly peaceful, at least what I can recall of it. I was quite ill then, you see. I would scarcely have known if the French *had* overrun the place."

Could they not find a less risky topic of conversation? Moira wondered as they approached the dining table, which looked capable of accommodating at least a score of guests. For tonight, only three places had been set at one end.

Lord Gabriel held a chair for Moira, as he addressed her father. "Miss Brennan mentioned that you had been ill, but I did not realize your condition was so serious. You seem well-recovered now. How anxious your daughter must have been for you."

Mr. Brennan nodded as he took his seat opposite Moira. "The poor lass fretted herself quite ill for a while, but she came around soon enough and tended me devotedly until I began to improve. Once we returned to England, nothing would do but I must take a course of sea-bathing at Brighton, then those vile waters at Bath."

Jepson served them fragrant, steaming bowls of oyster soup, but Moira's stomach clenched when her father mentioned her spell of illness during the worst of his. *Anxious* did not begin to describe her state of mind at the time. Knowing those she loved were depending on her, she had somehow found the strength to do what needed to be done.

As her father spoke of his recovery, Lord Gabriel nodded, his handsome features composed in a sympathetic look.

But when he replied, his words struck Moira like a threat. "How comforting it must have been to have had a clergyman to call upon during such trying times. Pray tell me about the Reverend Mr. Clarkson. He must be a worthy fellow to have won the hand of our fair Miss Brennan."

Her father fumbled his spoon. His brow furrowed in a puzzled scowl. "Won the hand? You must be mistaken, sir. Is he not, Moira?"

Dash Lord Gabriel Stanford! In the few days since he

had barged back into her life, the man had made nothing but trouble. How could she have felt pity for him, let alone guilt for keeping her secret?

"Lord Gabriel is correct, Papa." Willing her hand not to tremble, she paused to consume a spoonful of the hot, salty soup. "Mr. Clarkson has proposed to me and I intend to accept, if you will give us your blessing. He means to ask you once we are settled back at Ardmore. I hope you will not stand in the way of my happiness."

"But . . . but . . .," her father sputtered. "I had no idea there was any feeling of that kind between you and Clarkson."

Moira shot Lord Gabriel an icy glare. "Do you suppose because I was not simpering and blushing, it meant I was indifferent to the gentleman? Those are not signs of love, only fatuous folly!"

She recalled with mortification how she had responded to Lord Gabriel Stanford in her first fever of girlish infatuation. How could that delirious madness ever be the foundation for a lasting union? Her feelings for Mr. Clarkson were more sober and mature. They would stand her in better stead and keep her from committing any more disastrous errors.

Mr. Brennan retrieved his spoon and took a slow, deliberate sip of his soup. "I shall have to think on it and see what Clarkson has to say for himself."

Her father's reaction to the news eased Moira's irritation with Lord Gabriel. Papa did not sound determined to withhold his consent altogether. That was encouraging.

An awkward silence settled over the table as they ate the rest of their soup.

After the footman had removed their bowls and served a dish of poached sole, Lord Gabriel spoke again. "So Mr. Clarkson was not obliged to remain behind on the Isle of Jersey? How fortunate for you."

Though he tossed off the comment in a casual tone, Moira sensed a spark of dangerous curiosity behind it. She must stamp out that spark before it ignited any tinder.

"Mr. Clarkson was only visiting the Channel Isles for his health," she replied in a tone that suggested Lord Gabriel should mind his own business. "Now that summer is here, he has found employment near Ardmore."

Their host's dark brows shot up, warning Moira her effort to quench his curiosity had failed. "How convenient for the gentleman to find employment so near you. I should very much like to make his acquaintance."

Though the fish was cooked to moist, flaky perfection, Moira nearly choked her first bite. The last thing in the world she wanted was for Mr. Clarkson and Lord Gabriel Stanford to meet!

Much as their host's suggestion dismayed Moira, it seemed to cheer her father. "That can be easily arranged, sir. If you have nothing pressing to keep you in London, why not come to Surrey for a visit? You can give me your opinion of my daughter's suitor and advise me whether I ought to consent to their engagement."

The bottom of Moira's stomach seemed to give way. Surely her father could not place control of her future in the hands of a man who had shown so little regard for her.

She could scarcely summon breath to cry. "No, Papa! I am certain Lord Gabriel must have too many other social obligations to accept an eleventh hour invitation from us."

"Not at all," their host replied with vexing good humor. "The city is growing too hot and malodorous for my taste. I enjoyed spending Christmas at Beckwith Abbey, but this is the time of year when the Surrey countryside is at its most idyllic. I should be delighted to accept your kind invitation, Mr. Brennan. When do we depart?"

Lord Gabriel took a sip of his wine. His smile shone with a glimmer of triumph that sent a midwinter chill through Moira.

He was like a stubborn hound that had caught a whiff of her secret and would not rest until he ran it to ground. Would he ever believe her denials that she was the mother of his precious little founding? And what might Lord Gabriel do if he discovered that she'd secretly borne a child who *did* belong to him?

Chapter Four

A S THE BRENNAN'S travelling coach drove through the verdant Surrey countryside the next day, Gabriel reflected with satisfaction on how easily he'd procured an invitation to Ardmore. He hadn't been forced to take such extreme measures as Aaron Turner had to secure a place at Lady Killoran's house party. The enterprising privateer had won his invitation in a high-stakes card game with Rory Fitzwalter. Captain Turner's audacious scheme paid off in the end — though not as he had planned.

Recalling the events of that fateful gathering, Gabriel gazed across the carriage box at Moira Brennan. She and her companion were chatting quietly together as if he were not even present.

During the early part of their journey, Gabriel had conversed happily with Moira's father. The Duke of Cheviot might have sneered at Mr. Brennan's lack of *breeding* but Gabriel admired the resourcefulness and industry with which he had made his fortune. Unlike some men who'd struggled to rise in the world, the genial Irishman had retained his generosity and good humor. During their brief acquaintance, Gabriel had exchanged more pleasant words with him than he had in years with the duke.

Gradually the motion of the carriage had lulled Mr. Brennan into a peaceful doze. His chin fell to rest upon his chest and his breathing became a soft, rhythmic snore. His daughter and Mrs. Trimble seemed too engrossed in their conversation to notice. Was that a deliberate ploy to avoid addressing Gabriel?

He thought so, judging by the effort they made to keep their exchange from lagging. He sensed their unspoken agreement to prevent him from getting a word in, which would force them to acknowledge his presence.

Tempted as he was to provoke the women by interrupting, Gabriel restrained himself. He had managed to secure an invitation to Ardmore against Moira's wishes. He did not want to antagonize her further. The barely concealed antagonism he sensed from her was a painful reminder of his younger years.

Her recent behavior was a sharp contrast to the admiration she'd shown him at Lady Killoran's house party. Then, she'd hung on his every word, ready to laugh at his feeblest jest, approve all his opinions and discover everything about him that he was willing to confide.

Her adulation had gone to his head, like a lad's first taste of strong spirits. The more time he spent in her company, the more he wanted to spend. In spite of Lady Killoran's obvious intention to match Miss Brennan with Rory and Gabriel with Lily Crawford, he'd been drawn to the enchanting Irish heiress, instead. She made him feel as if any attachment between them would be an honor for her, rather than an act of mercenary opportunism on his part.

His churlish behavior had shattered her innocent illusions about him. Though he knew there could be no hope of regaining her good opinion, Gabriel could not bear for her to despise him more than she did already.

Since the women seemed determined to ignore him, Gabriel decided to return the favor. He leaned back in the comfortably upholstered seat and closed his eyes. The conversation between Miss Brennan and her companion immediately lost its urgency and gradually subsided altogether. Before long, Mrs. Trimble's snoring rose to compete with Mr. Brennan's.

Gabriel opened his eyes to discover Moira Brennan gazing at him with what he might have mistaken for affection.

The instant she realized she'd been caught, a fierce blush

suffused her fair cheeks. Her delectable lips twisted into a scowl that almost spoiled their pretty shape.

"I should have known you were only feigning sleep," she muttered. "You are very good at that."

Gabriel could not follow her meaning. "Good at sleeping?"

Her blue-green eyes flashed. "Good at *feigning* — at pretending you are one way when you are quite the opposite. Pretending to sleep when you are awake. Pretending to care for a woman when you only wanted to amuse yourself with her. Pretending to be open and straightforward when you are clearly up to something."

She pitched her voice low so as not to wake her father and Mrs. Trimble, yet her tone crackled with hostility.

Her accusations struck a raw nerve with Gabriel, perhaps because he could not entirely deny them. He often did speak and act in a manner that was contrary to his true feelings, though not in all the ways Moira Brennan had suggested. It was a skill he must have learned from his family, his mother in particular. It had been a necessary defense, to conceal his vulnerability and pretend that the duke's constant fault-finding did not distress him.

For years he had pretended to care for nothing beyond his own superficial amusement. That performance was so convincing, he had almost persuaded himself it was true. His Christmas tryst with Moira Brennan had made him glimpse the truth. The discovery of a helpless infant on Jack Warwick's doorstep had shattered his illusions once and for all.

Gabriel might have confounded Miss Brennan by telling her what he was truly feeling at that moment, but his accustomed defences were strong. Besides, he sensed she might have more power to wound him than anyone he had known in a great while.

"You are a fine one to talk about pretending innocence." Gabriel parried her glare with a look of sardonic amusement. "If you suspect *I* am guilty of something underhand, perhaps it is because *you* are."

"How dare you?" she sputtered, but her protest could not disguise a flush of guilt.

Whatever perverse sense of satisfaction he gained from baiting her was not enough to compensate him if her outrage grew loud enough to wake the other passengers. That would rob him of the opportunity for a private word with her.

"If I am mistaken, I apologize." Gabriel offered a flag of truce, knowing full well he was not sorry because he was not wrong.

"I … I …" Moira put him in mind of a duelist who had just discovered her pistol was not loaded.

Gabriel took advantage of her confusion to pose a question he had been itching to ask since last night. "I hope you have recovered from the illness you suffered while nursing your father last autumn. What manner of ailment was it?"

The guilty start she gave told him far more than her vague, evasive reply. "Of course I recovered. That was months ago — so long that I scarcely recall what ailed me at the time. The ague, perhaps, or more likely just the strain of tending Papa and fretting that I might lose him."

Gabriel nodded as if he believed her, when every nerve he possessed seemed to jangle, warning him that she was hiding something.

He recalled that disquieting intuition all too well from his childhood. He had been puzzled and hurt by the way his mother petted and spoiled him in private, only to treat him coolly in the duke's presence. His father's constant fault-finding had troubled him less than the fact that his doting mother never once objected or took his part.

When he once asked her why that was, she'd turned pale and tongue-tied. Gabriel forgot what sort of explanation she'd offered, but he vividly recalled his conviction that whatever she said was far less important than what she had *not* said. His mother's distress troubled him enough that Gabriel had never again questioned her behavior. He'd taught himself to ignore the bothersome instinct that warned him something was not what it seemed.

Only recently he'd discovered the secret his mother had kept from him all those years. It turned out the Duke of Cheviot was *not* his father at all. He was the by-blow of an illicit liaison between the duchess and an unknown lover. Ever since making that discovery, Gabriel had regretted ignoring his suspicions and allowing himself to be deceived all those years. He was not about to let it happen again.

"I can imagine what a strain your father's illness must have placed upon you," he replied with sincere sympathy. Whatever had transpired, he had no doubt it would have been enough to make a person ill. He would never wish that upon her on any account. "How much worse it must have been for you, finding yourself in a strange place, far from home and the assistance of friends."

Moira Brennan gave a derisive sniff that seemed to spurn his sympathy. "I doubt being on the Isle of Jersey made our situation any worse. Our distance from the services of fashionable London physicians, with their potions and purges, may have done Papa more good than harm."

"Perhaps so." Gabriel chuckled at her tart observation. "I cannot claim such fellows ever did any good for my ailing relations. Their *cures* can truly be worse than the disease. But I was referring to you lacking the assistance of friends and neighbors at such a trying time."

The lady shook her head. "We scarcely know our neighbors in Surrey. They have all lived in the area for generations and do not welcome outsiders. As for friends, we have a number of congenial acquaintances who are willing to share the pleasures of life with us, but few we could turn to in time of need."

Her challenging gaze informed Gabriel that she did not number him among those staunch few.

Though her judgment stung, he was forced to admit she might be right. The young gadfly who'd courted her at Lady Killoran's house party had little experience standing by his friends when the seas of life turned rough. Pitching in to help raise little Sarah had given him a taste of responsibility, both its challenges and rewards. When Jack and Annabelle needed their friends to rally around, he had done everything in his power to assist them.

"You might be surprised," he replied. "Sometimes people can rise to the occasion if you give them the opportunity."

He was trying to help her now, Gabriel assured himself with a touch of self-righteous satisfaction — even if she had not requested his aid or realized she might need it.

"Indeed?" Moira Brennan declared her scepticism by raising one delicate brow. "Are you referring to yourself by any chance? Tell me how you propose to demonstrate that sort of friendship."

Her frank challenge caught Gabriel by surprise, though not nearly as much as the ill-considered reply that fell from his lips. "Perhaps I could use my influence with your father to persuade him to give his blessing to your engagement."

Could Gabriel Stanford be sincere about helping to secure her father's consent to her engagement? Moira mulled over that question as the carriage drew within sight of Ardmore.

Never in her life had she been so relieved to conclude a journey. She practically leaped out of the carriage the moment it stopped.

Being confined for several hours in such a small space with Lord Gabriel Stanford had been almost more than she could bear. Even when she pretended to be engrossed in conversation with Mrs. Trimble, she'd been disturbingly aware of his presence. His nearness gave her an unnerving sense that he could overhear her most private thoughts.

For most of the journey, she and her companion had prevented him from getting a word in, but it had taken more effort than Moira expected. Her grim triumph, when it seemed their conversation had lulled Lord Gabriel to sleep, was short-lived. No sooner had Mrs. Trimble drifted off than the gentleman opened his eyes and launched the very inquisition she'd been trying to avoid.

Had he believed her when she insisted the *illness* she'd suffered on the Isle of Jersey was nothing of consequence? She doubted it, but could hardly be surprised. How could she expect him to swallow such a blatant falsehood when she could not bring herself to pass it off with conviction?

Now that they were home Moira welcomed the diversion of her duties as lady of the house. She directed the servants to prepare guest quarters for Lord Gabriel, and listened to the butler's exhaustive account of everything that had happened while she and her father were away.

All the while, part of her mind remained preoccupied with picking apart every detail of the journey from London.

How had their conversation gotten around to the subject of people one could rely on in times of crisis? It had seemed a safe enough topic after his suspicious questions about her visit to the Channel Islands. Yet somehow it had led Moira to betray private sensitivities she'd never shared with anyone else. It troubled her that she'd been so quick to lower her guard around Gabriel Stanford. That was a weakness she could not afford.

She'd expected him to take advantage of her blunder, but instead he offered to help her persuade Papa to accept her engagement. Moira could not decide how she felt about that. On one hand, she welcomed any assistance in winning her father's consent. Surely if Lord Gabriel urged him to let her wed another man, Papa would see it was hopeless trying to make a match between her and the duke's son. And yet, Moira sensed their guest might have an ulterior motive.

In addition to those conflicting reactions, Moira could not suppress a foolish pang of disappointment that Gabriel seemed so eager to promote her marriage to another man. Only a few days ago, he had claimed to want her as *his* wife.

Had that been a trick to persuade her to acknowledge the Bruton Street foundling as their child?

If so, how could she risk telling him the truth about their baby?

The butler seemed to be winding down his account of all the recent doings at Ardmore when one of the footmen appeared. "Begging your pardon, Miss Brennan, but there is a clergyman asking to speak with you."

"Mr. Clarkson?" That was quick work, Moira marvelled. She had not been home for an hour yet her suitor was already come calling. Had news of their arrival spread through the neighborhood at lightning speed? Though she knew she ought to be flattered by Mr. Clarkson's eagerness to see her, she found it difficult to summon up equal enthusiasm.

That was reserved for her tiny daughter.

All the way from London, part of her mind had been preoccupied with planning how she might contrive to see her daughter and all the questions she wanted to ask the child's faithful attendant.

Now she struggled to concentrate on the present situation. The sooner she wed the amiable curate the sooner she might be able to do more than watch her daughter grow up from a distance.

"That's right, Miss," replied the young footman. "The gentleman is waiting on you in the library."

"Thank you, Samuel." Moira practiced a welcoming smile with which to greet her suitor. "Pray excuse me, Mr. Norris. As always, I appreciate the care you have taken of the household while we were away."

The butler nodded in acknowledgement of her praise. "Shall I instruct Cook to expect another guest for dinner?"

"Oh." The notion of inviting the curate to dine had not crossed her mind. Something within her resisted the idea. She was not certain she could bear to have both Gabriel Stanford and Mr. Clarkson at the same table.

She shook her head. "I think not. One unexpected guest is

quite enough for Mrs. Rollins to accommodate. I feel certain Mr. Clarkson had no idea of it being so late in the day to pay a call. Nor would he wish to impose."

"Very good, Miss," the butler replied. "Though if the gentleman would care to stay, Mrs. Rollins always prepares plenty."

Acknowledging his suggestion with a vague nod, Moira headed off to the library.

When she saw her admirer after an absence of several days, she offered him a smile that she hoped would improve with practice. "Mr. Clarkson, what a fortunate surprise. Did word of our arrival spread so quickly, to bring you calling?"

"Should I have awaited your summons, Miss Brennan?" The poor man looked so dismayed, Moira instantly regretted her uncordial greeting. "The truth is, I have strolled past your gate on each of the past three days, hoping I might find you returned from London. On this occasion, my hopes were rewarded. I could not resist the opportunity to welcome you home."

"How thoughtful of you." Moira gestured toward a nearby armchair and settled onto a matching one opposite. "And how resourceful."

She should be flattered by the trouble he had taken to pay her a call as soon as she arrived. Any sensible woman would be delighted to have such an attractive, attentive suitor, even if he was a clergyman of no fortune. If an heiress chose to marry a man without property, better it should be one with a respectable profession and regular habits who would not drink or gamble away all her money.

"Of course you do not need to await a summons," she added, not wanting to leave him in any doubt. "I am very happy to see you so soon."

Of course she was. Moira took in Mr. Clarkson's familiar appearance with an appreciative gaze. She found nothing in his looks to remind her of Gabriel Stanford in any way. He was not quite as tall and lean as the duke's son. His thick golden-brown hair might have given him a leonine appearance if his features had been broader. Instead they were sharply chiselled with a slight cleft to his jutting chin. His eyes were the blue of a cloudless summer sky.

If only the sight of him made her heart flutter, just a little …

"Happy is hardly adequate to describe my feelings." Mr. Clarkson lavished Moira with a smile of pearly perfection. "I hope your recent travels agreed with you and did not overtax your father's strength."

His tone and gaze radiated such sincere concern that Moira chided herself for her earlier wish. A foolish fluttering heart would not help secure a stable future for her and her daughter. A calm, cool head would serve them much better.

"I found nothing disagreeable about our travels," Moira replied, though she wondered whether Lord Gabriel Stanford might belong in that category.

No matter. She was not yet ready to inform Mr. Clarkson about her father's inconvenient houseguest.

Instead, she told him everything else she could recall about the Prince Regent's fête and her excursion to Vauxhall.

When she finished speaking, the curate heaved a poignant sigh. "With so many pleasant diversions, I wonder if you had any opportunity to consider the question I asked before your departure. I have hardly been able to think of anything else in your absence, dear Miss Brennan!"

"Your question … of course." His reminder caught Moira off-guard. She'd considered the decision so settled in her own mind that she had failed to realize Mr. Clarkson was still in doubt of her answer. "You are greatly mistaken if you suppose I did not think of it."

That must be why he had come every day to see if she'd returned. She must not keep him in further suspense, Moira chided herself. And yet, some invisible barrier prevented her from forming the necessary words. Giving him her answer would make the matter so … irrevocable.

"I am pleased to hear it," said Mr. Clarkson when her

hesitation continued too long. "May I inquire if you have reached a decision?"

"I have."

Another exasperating pause.

"And?" The gentleman prompted her with only the slightest suggestion of impatience, which he had every right to feel.

Moira drew a deep breath, determined to conquer her foolish reluctance.

At that moment the library door flew open and Lord Gabriel strode in. Moira's wayward heart immediately began to flutter.

The duke's son gave a violent start at finding Moira and her caller together, but he swiftly recovered his composure. "I beg your pardon, Miss Brennan. I did not realize you were entertaining company. Indeed, I had no notion of finding anyone here at all. Your father kindly suggested I might amuse myself with a good book until dinner."

A good book? Moira barely contained an unladylike snort of disbelief. Her father seldom entered the library. He had bought this collection of books, like most of the furniture and pictures, with the house. As for Gabriel Stanford, Moira did not recall him making any use of Lord Killoran's fine library during their stay at Beckwith Abbey.

While those thoughts raced through her mind, Lord Gabriel continued with suspicious fluency for someone who had interrupted by accident. "I apologize for the intrusion. I shall come back later to look for a book."

Instead of doing what he proposed, he marched toward Moira's visitor with his hand extended. His lips were fixed in a smile that looked too cordial to be genuine under the circumstances. "Forgive me, sir. We have not been introduced. I am Gabriel Stanford and I presume you must be Mr. Clarkson, of whom Miss Brennan has spoken so highly. I am delighted to meet you so soon after arriving at Ardmore!"

Why was he offering to shake hands like old friends rather than the more formal bows usually exchanged upon first introductions? Moira scowled.

Mr. Clarkson rose from his chair and fumbled with his hat as he freed his right hand to be shaken with jovial vigor. "Lord Gabriel, I am honored to make your acquaintance."

Gabriel's smile widened further, until it looked oddly menacing. "I take it Miss Brennan must have mentioned me to you as well."

The curate shook his head. "I do not believe so. Or perhaps I have forgotten. Why would you suppose she had?"

Gabriel chuckled as if the other man had made a deliberate jest. "Only because you called me *Lord Gabriel*, just now, rather than Mr. Stanford."

Had he not used his title when introducing himself? Moira tried to recall, but she had been too vexed by his sudden appearance to notice his precise words. Now, vexation did not begin to describe her feelings.

The sooner she could get the duke's troublesome son away from Ardmore and out of her life, the happier she would be!

———————

Lord Gabriel, indeed! There was definitely something suspicious about this suitor of Moira's.

As Gabriel awaited the curate's explanation, he congratulated himself for having put the other man on the spot so quickly in front of Moira Brennan. Not that he could take credit for laying a deliberate ambush. Ever since the humiliating discovery about his parentage, Gabriel could not bear to refer to himself in a style to which he was not entitled.

How fortunate his reticence had proven. It would have been more better yet if Miss Brennan's suitor had hesitated and stammered a reply that would betray his deception. But the curate did neither, confound him!

Instead, he countered Gabriel's chuckle with one of his own. "I fear you underestimate how widely the Stanfords of Cheviot are known. Perhaps if your Christian name had been

John or George, I might have been in some doubt of your identity. *Gabriel* is far more memorable."

Clarkson's response was so smooth and plausible, he must be either perfectly sincere or a practiced liar. Of course, a spy would need to be the latter, Gabriel reasoned, turning the man's appearance of innocence against him.

Moira Brennan did not seem to interpret her suitor's reply in the same light. Her fine eyes looked far more green than blue, as she directly a blistering glare at Gabriel. Did she guess that his excuse for interrupting her conversation with Clarkson was a ruse?

He'd overheard one of the footmen telling Mrs. Trimble the curate had come calling. The good manners that had been drummed into him in the Cheviot nursery balked at the rudeness of intruding upon a private interview. But he could not take the chance that Moira Brennan might say something imprudent and commit herself to a man who might not mean her well.

"Now that you have introduced yourself ..." The lady sounded as if her jaw was stuck tight. "Perhaps you will excuse us, Lord Gabriel?"

In spite of her rising inflexion, her words were clearly not meant as a question or suggestion. How could he keep her from being left alone in Clarkson's company without making her even angrier him?

"Of course." Gabriel backed toward the library door slowly, giving him time to consider his next move. "I have no taste for playing gooseberry. I hope Mr. Clarkson will be joining us for dinner, so we may have the opportunity to become better acquainted."

It surprised Gabriel to hear those words come out of his mouth. He would have preferred to have Moira Brennan's company more to himself during their first meal at Ardmore. But since Clarkson had surely been invited to dine, he intended to ask all manner of innocent, interested questions that might expose inconsistencies in the curate's story.

"Dinner?" Clarkson sounded genuinely taken aback by Gabriel's suggestion, though an air of ill-concealed eagerness hinted that he'd been hoping for just such an invitation. "I had no idea the hour had grown so late. I would not think of imposing on the Brennan's hospitality."

So Moira had not asked to her suitor to dine with them? Gabriel was not certain what to make of that. Had his thoughtless remark played into Clarkson's plans?

"Of course you do not mean to impose." Moira's fixed smile looked thoroughly at odds with her flashing eyes. "You must not suppose your company is anything but welcome at Ardmore. I would have asked you at once, only I thought you might have other plans I would not wish to spoil."

"Plans?" The curate gave a derisive chuckle, as if to suggest there could be no social obligation worth planning for in the country. "Quite the contrary, Miss Brennan. My good landlady has gone to visit her sister in Guildford for the day, so I should be obliged to get my dinner at the village inn."

"In that case, I insist you stay to dinner," replied Moira, though the prospect did not seem to please her as much as Gabriel expected.

Why on earth would the lady be reluctant to dine in the company of a man she was so determined to wed?

Chapter Five

DINNER THAT EVENING was one of the most uncomfortable meals Moira had ever endured! The only worse one she could recall was breakfast at Lady Killoran's house party on the morning after her passionate tryst with Gabriel Stanford.

Instead of taking a tray in bed like some of the other ladies, she had ventured down to the Killoran's breakfast room, hoping to exchange furtive smiles and fond glances with her lover. Perhaps he would help her to a muffin or kedgeree from the buffet and his hand might accidentally brush against hers.

Instead, Lord Gabriel had deliberately avoided sitting beside her and kept his eyes resolutely downcast. He'd scarcely taken his seat when he abruptly excused himself and rushed away. Dismayed by his behavior, Moira wondered whether he might have stayed long enough to eat if she had not been there. She got her answer when Rory Fitzwalter quipped that Lord Gabriel must be regretting his conduct from the previous night, *as he so often did.*

At that moment Moira realized their night of passion had not meant to Gabriel what it had to her. To him, she was merely the latest in a long string of amusing conquests, perhaps even less valued because she'd presented so little challenge. A year and a half had passed since that awful morning, yet the humiliation she'd suffered remained as fresh and raw as if it were only yesterday.

By contrast, Gabriel Stanford seemed nothing like the morose, regretful young man who had fled the Killoran's breakfast room that winter morning. His dark eyes sparkled in the beguiling manner Moira recalled from the Twelfth Night ball at which he had made the final conquest of her heart. This evening his charm seemed focussed upon her father and Mr. Clarkson rather than her. That irritated Moira, hard as she tried to deny it.

"The Channel Islands must have a very wholesome climate." Lord Gabriel beamed at Mr. Brennan and the curate. "If both you gentlemen went there for your health, it has been perfectly restored. Neither of you look as if you have been ill a day in your lives."

Moira's father regarded Gabriel with jovial fondness. Clearly he was taken in by the young gentleman's show of attentiveness, just as Moira had been when they first met. "You must persuade my daughter of that, sir. I feel perfectly recovered, yet she still insists on treating me like an invalid. If we were dining alone tonight, I fear the menu might consist of beef tea, calves-foot jelly and milk pudding!"

When he made a face at the mention of such fare, the younger men both laughed, much to Moira's consternation.

Lord Gabriel lifted a forkful of their cook's specialty, scallop of veal. "Is that why you were so eager to invite me to visit, sir? So you would not be obliged to suffer an invalid's diet?"

Was he mocking her concern for her father's health? Moira's cheeks grew hot.

"There is nothing wrong with good, plain, nourishing food!" she snapped. "It is one of the things that helped you get well, Papa, along with rest and quiet. I believe they did you as much good as the mild weather and fresh air of the Channel Islands."

"Do not forget your devoted care." Her father seemed bemused by Moira's bristling irritation. Did he suppose she was vexed with his teasing, and wished to make amends? "That was the best medicine of all. Do not think me ungrateful because I crave richer food and livelier amusement. Now that I feel better, neither will harm me, I promise you."

"Of course not, Papa!" Moira could not bear to have her

father imagine she was cross at him. "Only, I was so very anxious about your health for such a long time, I find it difficult to stop."

His illness had made her realize that her father would not always be there to protect her. She must learn to look out for herself and her child. Depending on anyone else was too great a risk.

An uneasy hush fell over the table. Moira found herself almost grateful when Lord Gabriel broke the silence with his accustomed genial grace. "And you, Mr. Clarkson, I presume you found the climate of Jersey equally restorative. Were you fortunate enough to have as devoted an attendant as Mr. Brennan? Your mother or sister, perhaps?"

He observed the curate closely, as if there could be no detail about Mr. Clarkson too insignificant to engage his interest. That was how he'd regarded Moira when they first met. She had made the mistake of believing it meant he cared for her. Now she knew it was only a sign that he wanted something. What could he possibly want from Mr. Clarkson?

The curate did not appear to suspect any ulterior motive behind Lord Gabriel's question. He shook his head with an air of wistful resignation. "I have no sisters or brothers, and both my parents are long deceased. Fortunately, I was not so very unwell as Mr. Brennan. And my landlady proved most kind."

Poor man! He knew what it was to have no one in the world to care for him. Was it any wonder he had become attached to her so quickly? Moira wished she could summon up deeper feelings than sympathy for him.

"How unfortunate." Gabriel Stanford feigned an expression of concern that Moira did not trust for an instant. "I wondered if you might be some relation to Rev. Clarkson, the abolitionist who did so much to assist Mr. Wilberforce in his campaign to end the slave trade."

The remark caught Moira by surprise. She had never suspected Lord Gabriel knew or cared about the Abolition movement.

Again the curate shook his head. "I wish I could claim such an esteemed connection. Perhaps there is a distant one, but if it exists I am not aware of it."

"I was not sorry to see that infernal slave trade abolished, "Moira's father piped up. "I knew plenty of men who made their fortunes from it, but I would sooner have starved than profit from such wickedness!"

Lord Gabriel regarded Moira's father with respect that seemed entirely sincere, while Mr. Clarkson appeared relieved that his fellow guest's questions had been interrupted.

As the meal progressed, Moira sensed a growing undercurrent in the gentlemen's conversation that did not please her. Beneath their show of cordiality they seemed to be sparring with one another. Why and over what, she could not be certain.

Her, perhaps? Surely that was absurd. Gabriel Stanford only cared about whether she was the mother of his little foundling. He had even offered to urge her father to accept her engagement to the curate. As for Mr. Clarkson, did he view Lord Gabriel as a romantic rival?

All this conjecture and veiled tension was enough to give a lady a violent headache. Moira reached up to rub her left temple, which had begun to throb.

Lord Gabriel was too much occupied with quizzing her suitor about his schooling to notice anything else, but her father was more observant.

"Are you feeling quite well, my dear?" he asked during a brief lull in the conversation. "It has been a long day and quite a drive from London in this warm weather. I know you can never sleep in the carriage as I can. I felt fresh as a daisy when we got home, yet you insisted I rest while you saw to our baggage, ordered dinner and who knows what else."

Moira seized the opportunity. If Lord Gabriel and Mr. Clarkson would not leave her alone to do as she wished, she would leave *them*. "I do feel a trifle indisposed, Papa. If you gentlemen will excuse me, I believe I should retire early."

As she rose to leave, Lord Gabriel and the curate scrambled to their feet, as if in a race to demonstrate their courtesy.

"Of course, dear heart." Moira's father beckoned over for a fond embrace. "I shall do my best to entertain our guests in your absence. Though they seem to have hit it off so well that I doubt they will need any other entertainment."

Was he truly fooled by their guests' pretense? Moira kissed her father on the cheek. "I believe you are right, Papa. Lord Gabriel and Mr. Clarkson seem quite capable of amusing each other. Gentlemen, I hope I can rely on you not to keep my father up too late."

"Of course, Miss Brennan." Lord Gabriel's brow furrowed in a look of dismay. "I beg your pardon for being too preoccupied to notice you were unwell. Is there anything I can do to assist you?"

His concern seemed so sincere that it almost made Moira regret misleading him. She reminded herself that *he* had once misled *her* about a far more serious matter.

"If the lady requires any assistance," said Henry Clarkson, "surely it is *my* place to provide it."

Were all men so anxious to compete over everything? Moira found it tiresome. "Thank you both, but I am quite capable of finding my way to bed."

The instant the words left her mouth, her cheeks blazed. No doubt Lord Gabriel remembered the night when she had found her way into a bedchamber where she had no business being.

If he did, the duke's son gave no sign he exulted in his easy conquest. "I hope with all my heart that a good night's sleep will set you to rights, Miss Brennan."

"As do I," echoed Mr. Clarkson.

"Thank you, gentlemen." Moira forced her feet to a sedate pace as she left the dining room. "Good evening to you."

Once the door closed behind her, she began to move faster until she reached her bedchamber at a swift run.

She was pulling on a lightweight cloak when Mrs. Trimble

appeared, looking worried. Her companion cast a questioning glance at Moira's attire. "One of the footmen told me that you were taken ill at dinner."

"Only sick with longing to see my little one," Moira explained. "I could not wait another instant and I was afraid the gentlemen would keep me occupied until all hours."

"Let me come with you," Mrs. Trimble begged. "I shall fret about you making that long walk all alone."

"Long walk?" Moira scoffed. "It is less than two miles across country with nothing more dangerous between here and there than Farmer Brown's cows. Besides, two women out walking will draw more attention than one."

"Very well, then," her companion agreed grudgingly. "But try not to stay out too late. I'll make certain the side door is left unlocked for you."

"Thank you, dear friend." Moira gave Mrs. Trimble a reassuring peck on the cheek. "I do not know how I would have managed all this without you."

A few moments later, while her companion acted as lookout, Moira stole down the servants' stairs and slipped out the side door. Fortunately, her destination lay in the opposite direction from the dining room, so there was no danger of the gentlemen spotting her out a window.

So soon after midsummer, the friendly shadows of evening had not yet begun to gather. But Moira's green cloak blended in with the verdant countryside around her. She drew the hood up to cover her bonnet and further obscure her identity in case anyone happened to notice her.

The warm evening air smelled of clover and early hay as she made her way through pastures and past hedgerows. An impudent squirrel chattered at her from its perch in a young oak tree. It seemed to scold her for trespassing on its property. Moira hurried on, drawn by thoughts of what awaited her.

Her heart bounded when she caught sight of the snug cottage that had been home to her young daughter for the past several weeks. Plucking up her skirts, she ran the last few yards and knocked softly on the door in case the baby might be sleeping.

A plump, pretty girl with dark hair and friendly brown eyes answered her summons. This was Betsy Aubin, the young Jersey woman Moira had engaged as Nora's wet nurse and foster mother.

"Good day, Miss." Betsy welcomed Moira with a warm smile. "I heard you were back from London, so we've been expecting you." She nodded toward a blanket on the floor where little Nora sat, clutching a large wooden spoon and waving it about.

"My word!" Moira scooped the child into her arms. "I cannot believe how much she has grown since I saw her last."

Delight at seeing her daughter again warred with a sharp pang of alarm at how swiftly Nora was growing and how much she was missing of her baby's first year.

As she pressed the dear little creature to her heart, Nora stiffened and let out a piercing wail, followed by another and another.

"What is the matter, my sweeting?" Moira cried, rubbing the child's back and holding her close. "Are you hurt … or ill?"

She hardly knew which dismayed her more — the fact that her baby was in such distress or that she had no idea how to comfort her. Until now, Nora had been a calm, cheerful infant … at least during her mother's visits.

"I think you took her by surprise, Miss." Betsy approached and held out her arms to take the child. "Lately she has grown quite shy around strangers."

That word caught Moira like a hard, cold blow. "I am not a stranger! I am her mama."

She resisted surrendering her daughter to Betsy, but the child grew more and more distraught, tears streaming down her plump, flushed cheeks. Her tiny dimpled hands reached toward Betsy as she bleated like a lost lamb, "Maaa!"

Moira's knees threatened to buckle.

"Let me have her, Miss," Betsy pleaded. "I'll get her settled for you."

Nora's nurse sounded anxious to comfort and protect the baby . . . even from her own mother.

Moira's arms seemed to lose their strength, just like her legs. When Betsy pulled the wailing infant away, she could not resist. Staggering a few steps to the nearest chair, she sank onto it, her stomach churning.

Meanwhile, Betsy bounced little Nora in her arms, crooning to her in a dialect of French spoken on her native island. As soon as the child was back in her nurse's arms, she began to grow calmer. Her cries subsided into sniffles.

"That's better." Betsy pulled a handkerchief from her apron pocket and tenderly wiped the child's tear-streaked little face. Then she took a seat on the other chair at the small kitchen table.

"Of course I didn't mean *you* are a stranger, Miss," she murmured in a rueful tone. "But little ones cannot seem to recall folks they don't see all the time."

"I suppose not." Moira's chest ached with every beat of her heart. "The time I have been away is quite a large part of her young life."

Her gaze ranged over the baby, like the caresses she longed to bestow but did not dare. "Perhaps I *have* become a stranger to her."

Betsy seemed to sympathize, though she made no effort to return the child to her mother. "Now that you are back in the neighbourhood, it will be different. You can visit us as often as you like and she'll soon get used to you again."

"I shall *never* be able to come here as often as I'd like." Moira sighed. If she could spend every moment of every day with her child, would it be enough? Even then, she would regret all the moments of her daughter's life she had missed. "For the next little while, I may be hard pressed to steal away for many visits. My father invited a guest from London and I fear the gentleman may occupy my time. At the very least, he might question my comings and goings."

At that moment, she wished she had never set eyes on Lord Gabriel Stanford!

Then their daughter tilted her head and caught sight of the wooden spoon she had dropped in all the excitement. Her delicate features lit up as if she had never been fussy for a moment. Her delighted expression was one Moira had seen often on Gabriel Stanford's face. There were other reminders of him in the shape of the baby's eyebrows and the silky dark hair that peeped out from beneath her bonnet.

Conflicting emotions tugged at Moira's heart. Without Lord Gabriel, she would not have this child, who meant the world to her. Yet, if he lingered at Ardmore she would not be able to see little Nora as often as she wished — perhaps not often enough for her daughter to remember her from one visit to the next.

More than ever, Moira felt the spur of urgency to wed and make a home for Nora before her daughter became even more deeply attached to Betsy Aubin.

***

Miss Brennan need not have worried about them keeping her father up late, Gabriel reflected as he tossed and turned, trying to get to sleep much earlier than he was accustomed to.

After she'd fled the dining room, a pall seemed to descend on their small party, which was strange considering how little she'd contributed to the conversation. Perhaps he and Clarkson had needed her to witness their game of cat and mouse. Without her, their repartee lost its zest for Gabriel. It was obvious the curate could hardly wait to make his escape.

The final plate had scarcely been cleared when the curate suddenly remembered a call he had promised to make on an ailing parishioner. With barely courteous haste, he made his excuses, leaving Gabriel and Mr. Brennan to their own devices.

Moira's father did not appear sorry to lose Clarkson's company. He leaned back in his chair and released a slow breath, as if he had just unfastened the buttons of a constricting waistcoat. "Will you join me in a wee tot of brandy, Lord Gabriel, and oblige me by not mentioning it to my daughter? She would only fret about it when there is no need."

"I should readily agree to both," Gabriel replied in the jovial tone he would have used with one of his friends. Yet he could not stifle a qualm of guilt for agreeing to conceal information that Moira would surely wish to know.

Once the brandy had been poured, Mr. Brennan raised his glass to his young guest. "What do you make of our curate friend? Will he do for my daughter, do you suppose?"

Gabriel sipped his drink slowly to give him time to consider his answer. He had promised Moira he would urge her father to give the engagement his blessing. Though he had no evidence to support his suspicion, Clarkson made his nerves jangle with a silent but insistent warning he could not ignore.

"He *seems* a worthy enough fellow." As he had back in his gambling days, Gabriel sought to hedge his bets. "Though in my experience, people are seldom what they seem."

The *ton* was a hotbed of hypocrisy. The high and mighty pretended to be respectable, even virtuous, while behind closed doors they indulged in precisely the vices they condemned in public. His own mother had betrayed her husband with another man, while the duke had tolerated a young cuckoo in the Stanford nest, rather than risk public humiliation.

Mr. Brennan greeted Gabriel's cynical observation with an indulgent chuckle. "I reckon that's true of most of us."

Gabriel shook his head. "Not you, sir. I observed you at Lady Killoran's house party and again in recent days. I have never once seen you put on grand airs, like some I could name."

When Mr. Brennan rolled his eyes, Gabriel knew they were both thinking of Lady Killoran's haughty brother, Viscount Uvedale. "What has that young coxcomb been up to, I wonder?"

Gabriel scowled. "Running up his debts, from what I hear,

while trying to find an heiress desperate enough to exchange *her* fortune for *his* title."

He had long despised fortune-hunters like Uvedale and could not bear to be counted among their number. Yet once the words left his mouth, he realised how his remark must sound. "Forgive me, sir! I did not mean to imply that Miss Brennan ... or you ..."

As Gabriel stammered an apology, his host responded with better grace than he deserved. "Do not fret, young man. I take no offense. I cannot deny I have certain ambitions for my daughter and any grandchildren I might have. What were all the hard work and risks of my youth in aid of, if not to see my family rise in the world? I am not anxious for Moira to throw herself away on a poor curate, but I would welcome him with open arms over that toplofty Lord Uvedale. She deserves a better husband than that."

"Indeed she does." Gabriel raised his glass in a rueful salute to Moira Brennan.

The lady deserved better than a penniless reprobate of dubious reputation, who had no right to the courtesy title he bore. Even Mr. Clarkson, if he was who he claimed to be, deserved Moira more than Gabriel believed *he* did.

Yet he stood by his assertion that Mr. Brennan was a better man than Lord Uvedale or the Duke of Cheviot. His frank admission of what he wanted for his daughter proved that.

What might it have been like to grow up with a father like him? Gabriel would have gladly exchanged his unmerited title and all the material advantages of his childhood to find out.

The two men talked awhile longer. Gabriel coaxed Moira's father to share stories of his youthful adventures in the army and later in the shipping business. Despite his objections, Mr. Brennan refilled his glass twice with well-aged, potent brandy. By the time Gabriel insisted they must get to bed or risk Moira's displeasure, he was feeling drowsy and a trifle unsteady on his feet.

After bidding his host good night, he shuffled off in search of his bed chamber. Fortunately he had enough wit to hold tight to the railing as he climbed the stairs and to extinguish his candle not long after he entered the room.

As he untied his cravat, Gabriel paused by the window and gazed down at the moonlit garden. It looked a good deal more peaceful than the grounds of Carleton House on the night of the Prince Regent's fête. Had it truly been less than a week since he'd encountered Moira there? The time seemed much longer.

Gabriel was fumbling with one of his waistcoat buttons when some movement below caught his eye. Was it only a trick of the moonlight, or did he spy a cloaked figure hurrying through the Brennan's garden?

The suspicious shadow detached itself from the cover of a neatly clipped topiary bush, dispelling any doubt that it was indeed a person. Gripping the windowsill to steady himself, Gabriel pressed his nose to the glass and peered at the hooded figure, straining to make out further details. It moved in quick, furtive bursts, the head turning this way and that as if anxious to avoid detection.

Suddenly Jack Warwick's warning about French spies echoed in Gabriel's mind. His heavy eyelids flew wide open and his heart hammered against his ribs.

He briefly considered opening the window and shouting to frighten the intruder away. But before he could raise the sash, the figure froze and glanced toward the house, perhaps aware of being observed.

The bright moonlight fell upon the intruder's face. A jolt of recognition shook Gabriel. What was *Moira Brennan* doing stealing through the garden at this late hour?

Chapter Six

MOIRA'S HEAD ACHED with weariness the next morning after her late night and a restless sleep. In her dreams, little Nora had disappeared from Betsy's cottage, only to turn up in a basket on the doorstep of Cheviot House. Discovering her there, Lord Gabriel had seized the child and whisked her into his family's imposing mansion. When Moira tried to retrieve her baby, the door had been slammed shut in her face.

She'd hammered on it with her fists and tried to call out but the words stuck in her constricted throat, threatening to choke her. She jolted awake at last with an unuttered cry ringing in her mind. Her heart pounded as if she had run all the way from Betsy Aubin's cottage.

Though the first wrens and sparrows had barely begun their morning song, Moira dragged herself out of bed and dressed with fumbling haste. Last evening she had not been able to contain her impatience to see her baby, yet she knew the early hours would be a better time to visit. A lady out for a morning stroll would draw far less notice than one venturing abroad at night. No doubt the child would be in better spirits after a good sleep than she'd been at the end of the day.

Bleary-eyed, Moira stumbled off to Betsy's cottage, determined not to startle her small daughter with any sudden outbursts.

She returned to Ardmore two hours later, her heart aching with fierce maternal affection and the cruel deprivation of having to leave her baby in the care of another. If only she had been brave enough to confess the truth to her father in beginning, he might have been able to devise a better arrangement. But he'd been so dangerously ill Moira had feared the shock and disappointment might be the end of him. Every day that passed made it all the more difficult to admit her deception.

As she passed through the garden on her way into the house, Lord Gabriel's voice jolted Moira from her guilty musings. "You seem well recovered from your indisposition, Miss Brennan."

The note of censure beneath his polite remark made Moira wonder again if he could overhear her private thoughts. At that moment, she could imagine few things more alarming.

She gave a violent start. Her hand flew to her chest, as if to keep her heart from bursting out. She spun around to face Gabriel Stanhope.

"Blast you!" Moira cried as soon as she caught her breath. "Were you trying to frighten the life out of me?"

"Hardly." The gentleman did not sound repentant as he rose from a low bench beside the rose trellis. "I assumed you had seen me. But perhaps you were too preoccupied. With what, I wonder?"

Every nerve in Moira's body screamed that he was a danger, yet she sensed her racing pulse was not altogether fuelled by fear. Though part of her longed to get as far away from Lord Gabriel as possible, it warred with a contrary yearning to draw closer than discretion and propriety dared permit.

"Preoccupied?" She tried to sound calm, but feared she fell far short. "I suppose I might be, between supervising the household and making certain the excitement of our visit to London does not harm my father's health."

Before Lord Gabriel could throw her further off-balance with another probing observation, Moira lobbed one of her own. "I hope you and Mr. Clarkson did not keep Papa up too late last night."

For some reason her inquiry made the gentleman smile as he sauntered toward her. "Your suitor did not find our company to his taste, I'm afraid. Your father and I made an early night of it after Mr. Clarkson's departure."

As Lord Gabriel approached Moira resisted the prospect of letting him get too close. But neither did she wish to be intimidated into a cowardly retreat. The only option left was to turn and walk beside him.

"I beg your pardon for giving you a fright," he said as they skirted a small ornamental pond. "I had one myself last night, so I understand how unpleasant a sensation it can be."

"Indeed." Moira struggled to suppress a flash of curiosity, but it got the better of her. "What gave you such a fright?"

Gabriel affected an ominous shiver. "On my way to bed, I thought I saw a ghost."

Of all the answers he might have given, that was not one Moira had expected. She turned toward him. "What sort of ghost? Where did you see it?"

"In this very garden, from my bedchamber." Gabriel pointed toward a second-floor window. "It appeared in the form of a cloaked lady."

A gasp of alarm burst from Moira's lips before she could prevent it. The windows had all been dark when she'd returned to Ardmore last night. She never imagined anyone might be watching her.

Fortunately, Gabriel appeared to mistake the cause of her reaction. "Have you seen the phantom lady, too? In the moonlight, she appeared quite spectral. But when I caught a glimpse of her face, she looked like you."

This time Moira was prepared to betray nothing of her inner turmoil.

But before she would produce a plausible-sounding denial, Gabriel shook his head. "That is impossible, of course, since you had retired to bed several hours before."

"Indeed I had," Moira replied, grateful for a moment to devise a credible explanation. "But I am certain it was not a ghost you saw. Likely it was one of the housemaids who has a beau in the village. She and I look enough alike to be mistaken for one another at a distance. I shall ask Mr. Norris to speak with her about being out so late."

"You should." Gabriel seemed to accept Moira's story without question. "Even the countryside is not without its perils for a young woman out after dark."

Was the gentleman as credulous as he pretended to be? Moira thought she glimpsed a shadow of doubt, or perhaps warning, in his dark eyes.

One thing she knew for certain. She would have to be more careful to conceal her comings and goings from Ardmore as long as Gabriel Stanhope was a guest here.

———◆———

Did Moira Brennan take him for a fool? Gabriel silently fumed as he confronted her in the garden.

Morning sunshine sparkled off the drops of dew still clinging to the leaves and flower petals, intensifying their brilliant colors. Songbirds warbled from trees. The fragrance of roses and sweet peas perfumed the air, all conspiring to make the garden seem wholesome and innocent. Last night, bathed in silvery moonlight and shifting shadows, the place had appeared almost sinister.

Moira had seemed far less innocent then, too. In spite of her story about the lookalike housemaid, Gabriel was more certain than ever that he'd seen *her* stealing through the darkened garden. What had she been doing abroad at that late hour and why was she so intent on keeping it a secret from him?

Had she been meeting her suitor for a moonlight tryst? Might that be why Clarkson had left so early last night? The notion made Gabriel's cravat tighten around his neck. Yet somehow he could not picture the pair in an amorous embrace.

If not that, what other furtive doings might have kept Moira out so late? Could Jack Warwick's farfetched speculation about Clarkson be correct? Might he be spying for the French and somehow have involved the lady in his intrigue?

She seemed eager to divert their conversation from what Gabriel had seen last night, which only intensified his suspicion. "Now that you have met Mr. Clarkson, I hope you will keep your promise to persuade Papa to give our betrothal his blessing."

Gabriel strove to conceal his true feelings with a show of amiability. If Moira sensed his suspicion, she might take greater care to cover her tracks.

"As a matter of fact, I began my campaign last evening. After Mr. Clarkson went home, your father asked me what I thought of him. I said he seemed like a worthy fellow." Gabriel neglected to mention his suggestion that people were seldom as they appeared.

"Is that all?" Moira heaved an impatient sigh. "It is hardly an enthusiastic endorsement."

Gabriel shrugged. "Perhaps not, but it is a beginning. I have had little opportunity to become acquainted with the gentleman. I fear your father would have been sceptical if I'd waxed effusive in my praise of a man I just met."

"I suppose . . ." Moira sounded doubtful. "In that case, you must get better acquainted with Mr. Clarkson straightaway. Then you can truthfully tell Papa how well he will suit me. You owe me that much, surely."

Gabriel felt his eyebrows rise. "What places me in your debt?"

"Let me think . . ." Moira raised her forefinger to her chin and furrowed her brow in a comically exaggerated look of reflection. "Perhaps it was the way you hounded me all over London with your intrusive questions and infamous accusations. Not to mention your behavior when we first met, charming me into losing my head over you when you only wanted to amuse yourself."

Amuse himself? Gabriel recalled her saying something similar during their journey from London. Why had he not disabused her of the notion then?

Immediately he stopped walking and turned toward her.

"If you lost your head over me once upon a time, it is no more than I did over you."

Moira came to an abrupt halt. Her expression changed to one of genuine surprise overcast with mistrust.

Before she could question his claim, Gabriel hurried on. "My ardor so affected my judgment that I lost all sense of propriety. I was consumed with regret from the moment I awoke to realize what I had done. Ever since then, I have wanted to make amends for my behavior. I suppose *that* does place me in your debt, though not for the reason you claimed."

He lowered his voice. "What happened between us at Beckwith Abbey went far beyond callous *amusement* on my part. You may accuse me of a good many vices which I will readily own, but that is not one of them."

Gabriel met Moira Brennan's wide, blue-green gaze without looking away, determined to let her see the true feeling his would show. It was not easy to withstand her scrutiny, having confessed that he judged himself as harshly as she must … though perhaps not for the same transgressions.

Whatever she glimpsed in his eyes clearly affected the lady. Her dewy complexion paled and her full lower lip trembled. Her guarded wariness muted to an air of uncertainty that seemed far more vulnerable.

When she spoke, her lilting voice emerged in a barely audible murmur. "At breakfast the next morning, you would not sit beside me. You refused to look at me or exchange more than a word. After you bolted from the room, Mr. Fitzwalter said you must regret your behavior from the previous night, *as you often did.*"

His memory of that morning was far from clear, Gabriel realized as Moira shared hers. "Rory has been known to make all manner of foolish remarks, usually at the worst possible times. He may have been referring to my drinking. I recall feeling more than usually vile that morning, not least because I had behaved in such a contemptible manner toward you."

Moira's delicate eyebrows drew together in a look of

bewilderment. "I thought you regretted what took place between us, because it would force you to marry me. The reluctance of your proposal confirmed my suspicions. I believed you were disgusted that I had thrown myself at you like a perfect wanton. Or worse, tried to trap you into marriage because I was so desperate wed into a noble family."

Her bewilderment must be contagious, for Gabriel suddenly found himself overcome by it. How could two people share an experience yet interpret all they had seen, heard, and felt to mean something entirely different?

As he reflected on that morning, trying to put himself in Moira's place, it became distressingly clear how his actions could have given her the wrong impression.

With more than a little hesitation he reached for her hand, relieved when she allowed him to take it. Considering the warmth of the morning, her fingers were colder than on that winter night when he'd first held them.

Gabriel shook his head with slow certainty. "I vow neither of those thoughts crossed my mind for an instant. I had far too much contempt for myself to spare any for you, even if you'd deserved it … which you did not. You did me a great honor that night, offering your innocent virtue with no assurance but your trust in my honor. I am sorry I disappointed you so cruelly. That was never my intention."

Moira lowered her gaze, her cheeks suffused with color as a self-conscious smile played over her lips. "You did not disappoint me, I assure you."

Her softly murmured words acted like a provocative caress. Gabriel's face burned as if with a raging fever. "I am relieved to hear it. Flattered, too, I must admit. I fear I did disappoint you, though not in quite *that* way."

"No! Of course not …," she stammered, snatching her hand back. "I should never …"

Did she believe he would condemn her for admitting she'd taken pleasure from his attentions? The notion might have made Gabriel laugh, if not for the lady's obvious embarrassment.

"Please, Moira …." He hoped she would not resent his familiar use of her given name. "You drew an understandable conclusion about my meaning. I had no business making such a ridiculous jest. I only meant to make light of it, not distress you."

His words seemed to reassure her, for the furious blush faded from Moira's cheeks and her manner grew calmer. "If what you say is true, it seems I have a habit of misunderstanding you."

Her features took on a delicate cast of sorrow that Gabriel longed to relieve. "I cannot reproach you for mistaking my feelings, when I have the same weakness where you are concerned."

He sought to explain in clear enough terms that she could not possibly misunderstand. "When you spurned my proposal that day, I thought you must regard me with the same contempt I had for myself. I was certain you viewed me as a despicable fortune hunter, so desperate to secure a rich wife that I would sink to any depths to ensnare you."

He had spent the past year and a half wretchedly certain she'd judged him in that light. Why was it so difficult to tell her?

"What would make you think such a thing?" Moira demanded, as if she could not imagine anything more ridiculous.

Gabriel shrugged. "Perhaps because you said as much when you rejected my proposal."

"I never …" Moira launched an emphatic denial which lapsed into a self-conscious sputter. "Oh gracious, I did!"

The memory of her scornful refusal had haunted Gabriel, igniting bitter resentment. Now that he recognized her true feelings, which mirrored his, it felt as if he had finally extracted a barbed thorn from deep in his heart. The wound might bleed, but at last it could heal.

"Do not blame yourself," he begged her. "There was some truth in what you said, which may be why it offended me so much at the time."

His words seemed to startle her back into wariness. "Truth?"

Gabriel gave a rueful nod. But before he could explain, Mrs. Trimble's voice rang out, calling Moira's name. The two of them sprang apart as they turned toward the sound of rapidly approaching footsteps.

An instant later Moira's companion appeared, looking fretful. "There you are, my dear child. I was beginning to worry when I could not find you."

Gabriel strove to stifle his resentment at being interrupted during the first civil conversation he'd had with Moira in months. He moderated his tone to one of good-natured banter that had served him well over the years. "You had no reason to fear, Mrs. Trimble. Miss Brennan has been perfectly safe here with me."

Moira's companion addressed her as if Gabriel had not spoken. "Mr. Clarkson has come to call."

Moira did not greet the news with much enthusiasm, which pleased Gabriel. "This is an early hour for visiting."

Mrs. Trimble puffed up, like a mother hen defending her chick. "The gentleman wanted to inquire if you had recovered from your indisposition last night. I felt certain you would want to thank him for his concern and let him see that you are quite well."

A reproachful note in her voice irritated Gabriel. He had no doubt that if Mrs. Trimble accompanied Moira to the Christmas party, the young lady would never have ended up in his bed. Much as he regretted his actions that night, he could not bring himself to wish their impetuous tryst had never happened.

Mrs. Trimble had been a devoted companion whom Moira had come to regard as a mother figure. Their bond had been strengthened by the secret they shared and the desperate measures Mrs. Trimble had taken to prevent her ruin. There was no one in the world she trusted more.

Yet at that moment, Moira could barely contain her impatience with the older woman's unrelenting interference. How dare Mrs. Trimble presume to know what she would make of Mr. Clarkson's unexpected call at such an early hour? Just then, she wished to speak with no one but Lord Gabriel Stanford.

They had been in the midst of a most enlightening conversation — one she wanted very much to continue. In the past half hour, she had learned several pieces of information that challenged opinions she'd held for many months — opinions upon which she had based important decisions. Suddenly her whole world threatened to turn upside down, a situation Moira found alarming yet strangely exhilarating. The prospect of exchanging conventional pleasantries with Mr. Clarkson did not begin to compare.

"*Are* you quite well?" Mrs. Trimble fixed Moira with a gaze of fond concern. "Your color looks very high for such an early hour and you don't seem like yourself."

Perhaps because she'd been standing there mute, lost in her thoughts, Moira realized. It was true she did not feel like the same person who had woken in her bed that morning then stolen away to Betsy Aubin's cottage. Thoughts of little Nora restored something of that other Moira Brennan. For her baby's sake she could not afford to jeopardize her plans for the future.

"Not myself?" she responded with a mirthless chuckle. "Who else would I be? Of course I shall speak to Mr. Clarkson and let him see that I am well."

She cast a glance at Gabriel, whom Mrs. Trimble had pointedly ignored. "If you will excuse me, sir, I hope we may resume our conversation later."

What had he meant about there being some truth in the uncivil things she'd said when he proposed? Moira could scarcely stifle her curiosity, but for the moment she had no choice. She hoped it would be possible to recapture the singular openness of their recent exchange. After months of hiding her feelings, it felt refreshing to speak her mind and hear the truth in return.

"Of course," Gabriel replied with a slight bow. "I look forward to it most eagerly."

Mrs. Trimble scowled as if he had uttered an insult. She beckoned Moira. "Come along then. You mustn't keep the poor man waiting."

Repressing a flash of rebellious annoyance, Moira followed her companion into the house. But she could not keep from glancing back at Lord Gabriel. When she did, she caught him gazing after her with a brooding air that was far too attractive for her peace of mind.

The memory of their conversation lingered in her thoughts as she entered the drawing room to find Mr. Clarkson pacing back and forth in front of the bow window, which overlooked the garden. Had he been watching her while she spoke with Gabriel?

When he caught sight of Moira, the curate's anxious expression lightened. "Dear Miss Brennan, I hope you can forgive me for making a nuisance of myself by calling at this hour. I could not rest until I had learned whether you were recovered from your indisposition. Fortunately, one look is enough to reassure me that you are quite well, which is a great relief indeed."

Moira chided herself for being annoyed with him. The gentleman clearly cared about her well-being. How could she resent that? On the contrary, she had every reason to be grateful to him. Mr. Clarkson offered the best opportunity for her to be a real mother to her beloved daughter, while the child was still young enough to forget her infanthood in the care of Betsy Aubin.

At least, it had seemed that way before she discovered how badly she'd misjudged Nora's father. If only she'd confessed her true feelings eighteen months ago instead of jumping to the worst conclusions and acting upon them, how different her life might be now.

She could not change the past, another part of her countered. No good would come of continually looking back over her shoulder, pining for what might have been.

"I'm sorry to have made you anxious on my behalf." She smiled at Mr. Clarkson, but found the warmth of her expression difficult to sustain. "I was only fatigued from our travels. A good night's sleep in my own bed was the best medicine for what ailed me."

"Excellent!" The curate beamed, as if he had never heard such welcome news. "Then, perhaps, since I am here already, I might propose an additional tonic — a stroll in the fresh air."

It was all Moira could do to keep from greeting his thoughtful suggestion with a groan of dismay. She had already walked to Betsy's cottage and back this morning, as she had last night. At this rate, she might soon wear out her shoes!

But since she did not dare mention her secret comings and goings, she replied, "That sounds like a fine idea. Where shall we walk, around the garden?"

Though the curate gave no obvious sign of aversion, Moira sensed her suggestion did not meet with his approval. "The gardens of Ardmore are very fine, but I had thought we might venture farther afield. Perhaps to Hazel Hill, if Mrs. Trimble would accompany us as a chaperone?"

"I am certain she would be happy to come along," Moira replied. A bewildering impulse compelled her to add, "If we are going to make an excursion of it, I ought to ask Lord Gabriel as well. He is Papa's guest and I fear he must find the country quite dull after all the excitement in London of late."

Mr. Clarkson's countenance fell. "I'd hoped the two of us might have an opportunity to keep company *without* Lord Gabriel. I am anxious to discuss our future … if we are to share one, which is my dearest hope. Though, perhaps you have decided to refuse my offer. I am well aware that I have little to offer by way of material advantages …"

He looked so forlorn Moira could not bear to injure his

feelings. He had been an agreeable companion and steadfast friend to her at a time when she desperately needed both. Besides, she had told Gabriel Stanford they were engaged. She could not back out now, even if she wanted to.

Shaking her head emphatically, she seized his hand and clasped it tight. "You of all people should know there are more important things than material advantages to consider when making such a decision. You have a great deal to offer the fortunate lady who joins her future with yours."

She sounded as if she were referring to another woman, Moira realized. Did she wish she were? The contrary inclinations of her foolish heart and her unfeeling head tugged her back and forth.

Mr. Clarkson seemed unaware of the silent war being waged within her. His downcast expression transformed instantly to one of ardent felicity.

"Dearest Miss Brennan!" He raised her hands to his lips and showered them with kisses. "I declare you have made me the happiest man in the world!"

She had not accepted his proposal in so many words. A quiver of panic rose from Moira's stomach to lodge in her throat. Yet clearly Mr. Clarkson believed she had. How could she disappoint him when she had so many compelling reasons to go ahead with the match?

He seemed to care for her a great deal more than she did for him, but surely that was a point in his favor. During her brief infatuation with Lord Gabriel Stanford, she had never been certain his feelings equalled hers. That had left her in a permanent state of anxiety, which fuelled her desperate desire for him. It had been a heady sensation, but it was not one a reasonable person would care to sustain.

Far better to entrust her heart to a man whose devotion would prevent him from hurting her. She could not bear to be hurt in that way again.

"Shall we set the date for our nuptials?" Mr. Clarkson's blue eyes sparkled with excitement.

His innocent question seemed to steal all the air from the room, until one thought restored Moira's power to breathe. "There is still the matter of my father's consent. You must know he has rather lofty ambitions for me when it comes to marriage."

For an instant the curate's upper lip seemed curl in a sneer. But the sour expression disappeared so quickly, Moira was certain she must have imagined it.

"One can hardly blame him," Mr. Clarkson replied, "considering your great beauty and charm."

Not to mention the fortune she stood to inherit. Moira thrust that thought from her mind.

"However," her suitor continued, "I feel certain your father places an even greater premium on your happiness. Surely you can persuade him that you could only be happy with a husband who holds you in the surpassing esteem that I do."

Perhaps her father would give his consent, if she could assure him no other man had the power make her happy. But could she truthfully make such a claim?

The curate's grip on her hands began to feel uncomfortably tight.

"Papa sets great store by Lord Gabriel's opinion," she said. "If he were to intercede on our behalf, I believe my father might give us his blessing."

Mr. Clarkson released Moira's hands abruptly and turned away, though not before she glimpsed his handsome features clenched in a hard scowl. "Why should he do that when it is clear he wants you for himself!"

That could not be true, could it? The possibility made Moira's head spin.

Gabriel Stanford had twice offered to wed her. He'd admitted his feelings for her were once deeper than she'd permitted herself to believe. But so much had changed since then. The duke's son had many appealing qualities, but she doubted constancy was one of them.

"Nonsense!" she insisted. "When I told Lord Gabriel you had proposed and that I feared Papa might object, he *offered* to assist us. Why, only last night after you departed, he spoke in your favor."

Moira knew she was painting a more promising picture of Gabriel Stanford's motives than she fully believed. If it disposed Mr. Clarkson in his favor, where was the harm? Better her fiancé should view the duke's son as an ally than a rival. That might make him more amiable, which in turn might persuade Lord Gabriel that the curate would make her a good husband.

Which was precisely what she wanted, Moira insisted to herself so strenuously that she almost believed it.

Chapter Seven

So Moira Brennan had not despised him as a fortune-hunting seducer after their night of tipsy passion? As Gabriel watched her head into the house, shepherded by her vigilant companion, he could scarcely believe what she had told him.

Yet when she glanced back with an air of pensive longing, that brief look persuaded him that she'd spoken the truth. Moreover, it suggested she would rather remain in *his* company than go anywhere else, even to greet her betrothed.

When she disappeared from view, Gabriel exhaled the breath he hadn't realized he was holding. It gusted out in a slow sigh, the meaning of which he could not work out. Was it relief, yearning, chagrin, or something else altogether?

Lost in thought, he ambled out of the garden, further in the direction he and Moira had been going. He could almost fancy she was still beside him, reminiscing more about the Christmas house party where he'd lost his heart to her. Those events were etched in his memory, as deep as ancient writings carved into stone. He'd been so certain he could interpret their meaning, only to discover he had misunderstood the cypher completely.

Now that he possessed the proper key, he must re-examine everything he'd experienced to make sense of it. One realization he could not escape was that he'd been a blind, obstinate, self-justifying ass.

How could he blame Moira for drawing the wrong conclusions about his intentions toward her? Had he not gone out of his way to act the role of a shameless rake, like his friends? The arrival of a helpless infant on their doorstep had shown him what a ridiculous pose that was.

Why could he not have learned his lesson sooner? Gabriel kicked a tuft of grass in his path, wishing it was his own backside. Then perhaps he might have had the sense to confess his true feelings to Moira and insist on knowing hers, even if they were not in his favor. The two of them still might have parted, perhaps not on the best of terms, but at least it would have been for good reason. And he might not have been left with this aching sense of futile loss.

Suddenly, from some distance behind him, he heard Moira calling his name in a tone of breathless urgency. It jolted Gabriel from his abstraction, like someone shaking him awake in the midst of a dream. His heart bounded as he turned toward her, exhilarated by the fervour he heard in her voice.

The sight of her dashed his spirits again.

She raced toward him, tendrils of ruddy hair dancing around her flushed face, her full lips slightly parted, but not in a smile. Her brows were drawn together in an expression of alarm, the cause of which he could not fathom.

Nor was she alone. Mr. Clarkson trailed behind her like a dogged shadow, denying her and Gabriel the opportunity to resume their conversation any time soon.

"Lord Gabriel," she gasped, slowing her rapid pursuit of him as she approached. "What are you doing all the way out here? A few more yards and I would never have spotted you from the garden."

Her shapely bosom heaved as she struggled to catch her breath. Was she anxious that he might have gotten lost?

Gabriel endeavored to set her mind at ease. "I must confess, I was not paying much attention to where I headed. Though I have no doubt I could have found my way back."

"If you fancy a walk, there is nothing worth seeing over here," she insisted, though Gabriel felt certain it was the direction from which she'd returned earlier. "Mr. Clarkson has invited me for a stroll to Hazel Hill. Why not join us? The view is far superior to this."

He had not noticed the view as he wandered, but now Gabriel glanced around him and decided Moira was right. There was nothing to see but a high hedgerow on one side and an upward-sloping hayfield on the other. He wondered where the lightly-travelled footpath led.

"It is kind of you to invite me." Gabriel nodded toward the curate, who hovered behind Moira, closer than propriety might have allowed if they were not engaged. "But I doubt your fiancé is anxious to share your company with a gooseberry from London."

"Fiancé?" Clarkson's bland blue eyes flashed with unclerical fury. "How do you know about our betrothal? Miss Brennan only just gave me her answer. I hope you were not eavesdropping on our private conversation!"

Gabriel bridled. He'd been guilty of his share of transgressions over the years, but it rankled to be accused of one he had not committed. "Don't be a fool! How could I have gotten all the way out here if I'd loitered around the house, listening in on you?"

The curate's mouth opened and shut several times before any words emerged. "I ... suppose you could not. But how *did* you learn of my engagement to Miss Brennan?"

Gabriel gave an exaggerated shrug to indicate the answer should be obvious. "The lady herself told me, several days ago. She said you'd proposed and that she intended to accept if her father could be persuaded to give his consent."

"Oh."

The wind of righteous indignation had clearly been taken from Clarkson's sails, which amused Gabriel. If their positions had been reversed, he would have questioned why another man should be informed of Moira's answer to such a vital question before he did.

Why *had* she confided in him about such an important decision?

Moira did not attempt to explain, though she continued to look troubled. "Of course Lord Gabriel did not intrude on our privacy."

"Nor would you on a walk to Hazel Hill," she told Gabriel. "Mrs. Trimble will be coming with us; why shouldn't you?"

That would be quite a different matter, Gabriel reflected. Any sympathetic chaperone would stay close enough to the couple to satisfy propriety, while maintaining enough distance that they might talk quietly together without being overheard. He did not fancy trailing Moira and Clarkson at a discreet distance, in the disapproving company of her companion.

"Please." Moira's blue-green gaze implored Gabriel as clearly as her words. "I would very much like you to come."

His perceptions about her had been wrong more often than he cared to recall, yet this time he was certain of her sincerity. She wanted to spend time in his company even if she was newly betrothed to another man. It stung to realize that within minutes of their last conversation she'd accepted the curate's proposal. Gabriel had hoped their talk might give her second thoughts about wedding a man she'd as good as admitted she did not love.

"Very well, then." He met Moira's gaze and held it. "I cannot refuse you anything you have your heart set on."

"Splendid." A faint blush crept into her cheeks. "It will give you and Mr. Clarkson an opportunity to become better acquainted."

Was that the only reason she wanted him to accompany them? Gabriel tried to suppress a pang of disappointment.

"I look forward to it," declared the curate in hearty tone that sounded forced.

An instant before, Gabriel could have sworn he glimpsed a scowl on the other man's face that mirrored his own feelings precisely.

On their ramble to Hazel Hill, Moira's cheeks soon began to ache from holding her lips in a bright false smile. In the past she had found both Mr. Clarkson and Lord Gabriel congenial company, in different ways. Spending time with the two of them together was exhausting! Even when they were not engaged in open verbal sparring, she sensed there was more to their conversation than she could grasp.

Gabriel made a sincere effort to become better acquainted with her suitor. He'd asked all sorts of questions about Mr. Clarkson's family, education, pastimes and opinions and seemed genuinely interested in the answers.

With a twinge of shame, Moira realized how little she knew about the man she had promised to wed. That was her fault, of course. When they'd first met on the Isle of Jersey, Mr. Clarkson had been so sympathetic at a time when she'd desperately needed someone to confide in. He'd encouraged her to tell him about herself and she had poured out her heart to him without taking an equal interest in his concerns.

Privately she vowed to make up for her selfishness. She would start by paying close attention to the information he told Lord Gabriel. She might even ask a few questions of her own.

She soon discovered her suitor did not care to be the centre of attention. Though he did not refuse to answer Lord Gabriel's questions, he was quick to turn the conversation to less personal subjects or reply with inquiries about the duke's son.

"I sincerely hope my life has been good and useful, but I fear it has been far less interesting than yours, sir. Pray tell us about your travels. Where is the farthest place you've visited?"

It showed what a modest, unassuming man he was — more inclined to learn about others than draw attention to himself.

Lord Gabriel did not appear to share Moira's opinion. As the afternoon progressed, his imperturbable charm began to wear thin. Even the picturesque view of the surrounding countryside did not divert him.

"See there in the distance?" Moira pointed off to the west, eager to focus his attention in the opposite direction from Betsy Aubin's cottage. "That is Beckwith Abbey. Perhaps you might like to ride over and pay Lord and Lady Killoran a visit while you are in the neighborhood?"

"Perhaps ..." Lord Gabriel did not sound enthusiastic. "I cannot deny the Christmas I spent there was the most enjoyable of my life. But I did see the earl and countess only last week at Vauxhall. Besides, it might be my ill luck to pay a visit when her ladyship's brother is there."

Moira could not blame him for being reluctant to encounter the proud, disagreeable Lord Uvedale. Every time he had spoken to her that Christmas, she'd sensed he was wondering how an Irish upstart had come to be among his sister's guests.

"That would be a misfortune." She caught Lord Gabriel's eye and they exchanged reminiscing grins. "You would be wise not to risk it."

Suddenly she wished the two of them were alone on the crest of that hill, with the Surrey countryside spread around them, the breeze ruffling her shirts as downy clouds drifted above. There were so many questions she wanted to ask Gabriel, so many incidents she wanted to recall of their brief time together.

Mr. Clarkson spoke up. "The gentleman is not very agreeable company, I take it."

The comment reminded Moira of her suitor's presence. She had no business wishing to be alone with another man when she had just accepted a proposal from this one. Even if her romance with Lord Gabriel had not ended for the reasons she'd once believed, it *had* ended. She'd chosen to make a new beginning with Mr. Clarkson. Muddling the two would only lead to heartache.

She shook her head in response to the curate's question, not trusting herself to speak just then.

Lord Gabriel was more forthcoming. "That is a charitable understatement. Fortunately, Lord Uvedale has a high enough opinion of himself to offset any disfavour from others."

"Uvedale?" The curate murmured.

"Ah!" Lord Gabriel chuckled. "Have you had the misfortune of an acquaintance with the gentleman?"

"Indeed not!" Mr. Clarkson denied with rather excessive force. "For a moment I thought I recognized the name, but I was mistaken."

"To be sure." Lord Gabriel's grin did not waver, though Moira sensed an undercurrent of antagonism. "If you'd had the misfortune to encounter his lordship, I am certain you would recall it."

"I wonder if he has managed to snare a rich wife yet." Moira mused aloud. "I was afraid Miss Crawford might succumb to his charms, but she turned out to have better sense than I gave her credit for."

Once the words left her mouth, she wished she could take them back, knowing how sensitive Gabriel was on the subject of fortune-hunters.

But her remark did not fluster the gentleman. He continued to stare toward the Killoran's estate as if looking back in time. "That was an odd business between Captain Turner and the Crawford sisters. Engaged to the elder one until she broke it off, then he swiftly consoled himself with Miss Lily."

Moira remembered the Crawford twins, though she had not seen much of the younger one, who'd fallen ill not long after the house party began. She did recall how strangely opposite the sisters were in temperament, to the point that they scarcely resembled one another.

"Is that so?" she replied. "I had not heard. Society gossip seldom reaches the Channel Isles. I am surprised the captain was so quick to change his affections. He seemed perfectly besotted with Iris Crawford and determined to win her. What could have altered his feelings?"

Moira had liked Aaron Turner, whose brash frankness was a relief from Lord Uvedale's smooth arrogance. She would have wagered a tidy sum on the captain's constancy. This news made her question her judgment. Was it ever possible to know another person's true character, especially if they set out to deceive?

"Who knows?" Gabriel Stanford made a rueful face. "Perhaps his feelings for Miss Crawford were sparked by his rivalry with Lord Uvedale. Or perhaps he wanted to save her from an imprudent match. Once he accomplished his goal, success may have cooled his ardor."

Was he talking about Captain Turner's motives or his own? Moira wondered. In spite of Lord Gabriel's promise to help secure her father's consent to her betrothal, she'd sensed renewed romantic interest on his part. Was it only because the curate's claim upon her represented a challenge he could not resist?

For most of their walk, Mrs. Trimble had remained as silent and inconspicuous as any good chaperone. Now and then Moira had glanced over to find her smiling or stern-faced, depending on which of the gentlemen was speaking. For the past few minutes, her expression had grown darker.

Now she cleared her throat and addressed Lord Gabriel. To Moira's surprise, her companion sounded perfectly affable. "If you wish, sir, I would be happy to inquire whether Lord Uvedale is visiting at Beckwith Abbey."

"Why, thank you." He rewarded the lady with a smile that would have melted a harder heart than hers. "I would be very much obliged to you."

What had caused this sudden thaw in her companion's manner toward him, Moira wondered? Could her motherly companion be up to something?

As he headed down to dinner that evening, Gabriel found himself hoping Lord Uvedale *was* visiting his sister. That would give him an excuse to avoid calling at Beckwith Abbey. His absence would leave Moira with only Mr. Clarkson for company.

Did it truly matter? He stifled a sigh. After all, Miss Brennan and the curate were engaged now, subject to her father's approval.

Finding Moira alone in the dining room, and seeing the table only set for three, he regarded her with raised brows. "Will Mr. Clarkson not be joining us this evening? I hope our walk did not overtire him."

"Not in the least." Moira's delicate chin tilted in a defiant manner that Gabriel found curiously appealing. "If you must know, I did not invite Mr. Clarkson to dine with us tonight."

Before Gabriel had a chance to speculate about her motives, Moira enlightened him, "I was afraid too much company might tire Papa. Besides, I wanted to give you an opportunity to tell him your opinion of Mr. Clarkson and urge him to give our engagement his blessing."

She made it sound as if one would be a natural consequence of the other. Gabriel knew better, though that did not detract from his satisfaction in dining alone with the Brennans.

As he expected, the meal turned out to be much more congenial in the absence of Moira's suitor. It did not surprise Gabriel that he and Mr. Brennan were more at ease without Mr. Clarkson, but he sensed Moira felt the same. That did not bode well for a union between them, surely.

Yet the lady seemed determined to bring the match about.

After a spell of pleasant table conversation on a number of subjects, Moira found an opening to mention their walk to Hazel Hill. "Now that Lord Gabriel has become better acquainted with Mr. Clarkson, he can tell you how well suited we are, Papa."

Mr. Brennan directed a searching gaze at Gabriel. "Is that true, sir?"

Gabriel squirmed in his seat, keeping his eyes averted from Moira. "Not altogether, I'm afraid."

"I *beg* your pardon?" she demanded in a tone sharper than any knife on the table. "I thought ... you said ..."

Her father held up his hand for silence. "Let the gentleman speak, my dear. Go ahead, Lord Gabriel."

"Very well, sir." Gabriel chose his words with care. He did not want to aggravate Moira, nor did he wish to mislead her father. Most of all, he did not want to do anything that might hasten her marriage to Clarkson. "In truth I do not feel I know the gentleman any better than the moment we first met. All I learned about him today is that he is very guarded."

"What is wrong with that?" Moira demanded. "Surely it is better to be cautious of strangers than too easily trusting of the wrong people!"

Was she talking about herself and how unguarded she'd been when they first met? Did she repent her imprudence?

"I did not say it was *wrong*." He cast an apologetic glance her way, only to meet her livid glare. "But you must admit Mr. Clarkson's reticence makes it difficult to judge much about his character."

"I will admit no such thing!" Moira snapped. "Mr. Clarkson does not natter on about himself like a vain coxcomb. Some people might deduce a great deal about his character from that fact, all of it positive."

"I suppose they might," Gabriel turned his attention back to her father. "Yet I have not seen any particular interests he and Miss Brennan have in common. They might be very well suited for one another or they might not. At the moment, I cannot say which."

Mr. Brennan nodded slowly. "That sounds reasonable. I would have had trouble believing you, if you'd changed your tune too quickly."

He winked at his daughter as if she were a young girl he meant to jolly out of a bad temper. "Do not be cross with us, my love. Lord Gabriel and I only want what is best for you. We shall keep an open mind about Mr. Clarkson and he may win us over in the end."

"I'm certain he will, Papa." Moira's temper sounded as if it had cooled to a gentle simmer that might return to a furious boil at the slightest provocation. "If you knew his good qualities as I do, you would give us your blessing at once."

"Tell us, then," Gabriel urged her. "Perhaps if we know what to look for, we will have an easier time finding it."

The lady hesitated. Did her suitor have fewer virtues than she claimed? Or did she not know him as well as she believed?

"Very well." She tossed her head, making her auburn curls bounce. "I have found Mr. Clarkson to be attentive, considerate, thoughtful and understanding. He is a sympathetic listener who is genuinely interested in others."

As she spoke, Gabriel could scarcely keep from wincing. It was clear the virtues Moira Brennan described were ones she prized. He could not deny the curate might possess them, while he feared he did not. Were his suspicions about Mr. Clarkson based on sincere concern for Moira's happiness, or did they spring from flaws in his own character?

From that moment, Gabriel had little appetite for the meal or the conversation, though he made a brave effort to pretend otherwise.

His host did not seem to notice anything amiss.

After the final course, Mr. Brennan rose from his chair. "Let us retire to the music room where you can entertain me with a ballad or two."

Gabriel recalled the pleasure of singing duets with Moira at the Killoran's house party. Tonight he could not be certain which of them was more reluctant.

The lady drew a deep breath, as if bracing herself for a disagreeable task. But when she replied, her sweetly compliant tone betrayed nothing of her aversion. "Very well, Papa, though I am sadly out of practice on the pianoforte. Have you any requests?"

Mr. Brennan pondered his daughter's question as they strolled to the music room. It was a good deal smaller than the one at Cheviot House, but snug and inviting.

"Why not start off with something that you sang at the Christmas party?" He sank into a comfortable arm chair in the opposite corner of the room from the pianoforte. "They were all well received, as I recall."

"Gracious me, Papa." Moira glanced up from a sheaf of music she'd begun to examine. "That was months ago. I cannot recall what we sang."

Two bright spots blossomed in her cheeks, suggesting she remembered better than she was willing to admit.

Gabriel could not recall *every* piece they'd performed, but his impression was that most had been tender love ballads. When he'd praised the charms of Celia or Sylvia or Amaryllis in song, it was Moira who inspired his admiration.

"*Drink to me only with thine eyes.*" The song title burst from his lips before he could stop it.

Mr. Brennan clapped his hands with eager approval. "You see, my dear? Lord Gabriel remembers! That was one of your dear Mama's favorites. Start with that and it may help you think of others."

"Very well, Papa." Moira took her seat at the pianoforte. Without so much as a glance at Gabriel, she began to play the piece at a faster tempo than he was accustomed to.

"Are you going to sing or not?" she muttered after a few bars.

"As soon as you are finished the introduction," Gabriel responded with the teasing good humor he often used to defuse hostility.

It seemed to have the desired effect. Moira's pretty lips relaxed from their tight purse and the music slowed.

"*Drink to me only with thine eyes,*" Gabriel sang, "*and I will pledge with mine. Or leave a kiss within the cup and I'll not ask for wine.*"

The old song continued with more poetic references to wine and romance. In his experience, both could be sweet and intoxicating, yet sometimes lead to unpleasant consequences if overindulged.

At the end of the piece, Mr. Brennan applauded. "Well done, both of you! Give us another in that vein. You should sing along, Moira. As I recall, your voices go well together."

Before Gabriel could make another suggestion, Moira snatched up the top piece of music from the pile and began to play. The words of this song were not as familiar as the first, so he was obliged to stand close behind her and lean forward to make them out.

"*Sweeter than roses or cool evening breeze on a warm flowery shore,*" they sang together, "*was the dear kiss, first trembling made me freeze, then shot like fire all o'er.*"

While he might not recall every song he'd performed with Moira, Gabriel would never forget a single kiss they'd shared. The writer of these lyrics had described their delightfully contradictory sensations to perfection. What would he give for just one more kiss from her?

He had no business thinking that way about a lady who had accepted another man's proposal, Gabriel sternly reminded himself. But as they continued to sing, he found it increasingly hard to imagine how Moira could ever be anyone's but his.

"What next?" he murmured after several more pieces.

"I believe we may take a rest now." She nodded toward her father, who lolled in his chair, snoring softly. "Papa certainly is."

She turned on her stool and gestured for Gabriel to take a nearby chair. "Now that we have a moment in private, there is something I must ask you."

"There is?" The words came out in the quavering treble of an awkward schoolboy. Gabriel dropped onto the chair as if something had knocked his feet out from under him.

Moira nodded. "Before Mrs. Trimble interrupted us this morning, you claimed there was some truth to the insulting things I said when I refused your proposal."

"I did?" Gabriel had forgotten that part of their conversation, though clearly Moira must have pondered it the whole day. Could that be why she had accepted Clarkson's proposal with such distressing haste?

"I remember it distinctly," Moira insisted. "Now I want

to know what you meant. *Were* you only after my fortune?"

"Of course not!" What had he been trying to say? Gabriel cast his thoughts back to their earlier conversation. "I cannot deny I came to the party at Beckwith Abbey hoping to rescue myself from debt by securing an heiress. You must have noticed how Lady Killoran tried to promote certain matches among her guests."

"Her brother and Miss Crawford, you mean?" said Moira. "That one might have come about if not for Captain Turner."

Gabriel chuckled. "The captain's presence and Miss Lily's absence did rather scuttle her ladyship's plans. I could tell she wanted you to make a match with Rory Fitzwalter."

The memory sparked a bewildering rush of antagonism toward his friend.

Moira rolled her eyes. "I could tell Mr. Fitzwalter was equally determined to have nothing to do with me."

Though she tried to make light of the rebuff, Gabriel sensed it still stung.

"That was not because my friend found any fault with you," he assured her. "Rory has no intention of ever marrying. He prefers to amuse himself with a succession of wealthy widows. But that is neither here nor there. What I meant to say was that Lady Killoran had Miss Lily in mind for me. I had not exchanged more than a few words with the lady when I realized she did not like me nor I her, and no amount of money would induce me to pursue her."

Could he expect Moira to believe him? Perhaps not, but Gabriel hoped she would. Even if it changed nothing between them, he would be content if it improved her opinion of herself.

"When I became acquainted with *you*," he continued, "my feelings were entirely different. I liked you a great deal and wished you had no fortune at all, like Lady Killoran's companion, Miss Delaney."

"Why would you wish that?" Moira looked aghast. "I would not change places with that poor lady on any account."

"I did not want to see you poor and dependent." Gabriel longed to lean forward and take her hand in his, but he did not dare for a great many reasons. "But I did wish you could be certain the man who wooed you desired only your love, and not your fortune."

Moira's brows drew together and her blue-green gaze softened. "I never suspected otherwise."

The invisible bonds that had held Gabriel in his chair suddenly snapped. The force of his emotions propelled him to his feet and toward Moira. She rose to meet him.

The long months since they had first fallen in love melted away and with them all the resentment and suspicion, leaving nothing but pure longing. The air between them shimmered with it, like a far horizon on the hottest day of summer. It trembled on Gabriel's lips as well.

Chapter Eight

GABRIEL WAS GOING to kiss her! In that instant, it was the only thing Moira knew or cared about. When he surged to his feet, she rose without a thought, as if taking part in the most familiar dance.

Spurred by desire, their arms rose to enfold one another. Their heads tilted. Their lips parted.

Just as they were about to meet, her father yawned, stretched and declared, "Bless me, I did not mean to nod off!"

Those words drenched Moira and Gabriel like a bucket of cold water.

She pivoted away from his approaching embrace and bent down to rifle through the sheets of music. Enough of those foolish love songs! They had stirred up feelings she needed to keep safely buried.

"Do not take my dozing as an insult to your fine singing and playing," her father continued as if he had no idea what he'd almost interrupted.

What *was* that, exactly? Moira wondered now that she had come to her senses, more or less. Perhaps Lord Gabriel Stanford had no intention of kissing her at all. Her father's sudden waking might have saved her from bitter humiliation as well as wicked indiscretion. No lady with any claim to virtue would think of kissing a man when she had pledged herself to another.

"I blame it on our good dinner." Her father patted his waistcoat, which did not fit as snuggly as it had a year ago. "Nothing will lull me to sleep like a full belly."

"I quite agree, sir," Gabriel replied.

Was it her imagination, or did he sound winded? That thought made Moira conscious of her racing breath.

She struggled to slow it. "I am pleased to see you eating well and resting comfortably, Papa. Here is a song I believe you will enjoy: *O solitude, my sweetest choice.* Are you familiar with it, Lord Gabriel?"

Moira returned to the pianoforte and began to play.

"I have heard it, but never sung it that I can recall." Gabriel hovered behind her, so close she fancied she could feel his breath ruffling her hair. "Perhaps if you sing it through once, I might be able to join in."

"As you wish." Moira forced herself to concentrate her attention on the notes and words before her.

"Splendid!" Gabriel joined her father in applause when she finished. "Though I cannot endorse the sentiment. A little solitude is fine now and then, but I prefer good company."

"A young man after my own heart," Moira's father declared.

At his request, Moira and Gabriel sang a few more songs, though she was careful to avoid any more dangerous love ballads.

Was that what had put them both in an amorous mood? Or was it harking back to their old feelings for one another? It had been a reckless impulse to resume their conversation from that morning. She could scarcely blame Gabriel Stanford if he'd taken her request as some sort of encouragement.

Moira glanced at the pedestal clock near the door, surprised to realize how quickly the evening had flown by. She must get to bed soon, so she could rise early to see her baby. "Forgive us, Lord Gabriel. I expect you are accustomed to staying up much later, but Papa and I usually retire about this time. Please do not feel obliged to keep country hours on our account."

She hoped he would remain awake for several more hours and then sleep in late tomorrow morning. That way she could go to Betsy's cottage and return without rousing his curiosity.

But Lord Gabriel greeted her suggestion with a good-natured grin. "May I keep them on my own account? I believe country hours, fresh air and everything about this delightful corner of Surrey will do me good. I am grateful to you both for inviting me to stay and making me so warmly welcome."

Was he mocking her? Moira wondered. They both knew she had done little to make him feel welcome. His presence at Ardmore was neither comfortable nor convenient. And yet … she could not deny that she enjoyed having him around. It already felt as if he belonged here.

True to his word, their guest followed them as they retired for the night, maintaining a flow of lively conversation and pretending not to notice the effort it cost Moira's father to ascend the stairs. As they passed the door to his bedchamber, Lord Gabriel wished them both a good night.

Her father replied with fond familiarity. Would he ever treat Mr. Clarkson that way, no matter how long they were married?

"Goodnight, Papa." Moira kissed him on the cheek before leaving him to the care of his valet. "I hope the nap you had in the music room will not spoil your sleep tonight."

"Don't fret, dear child." Her father winked. "After a good meal and music with such congenial company, I shall sleep like a babe."

"Infants are not known to be the soundest sleepers," Moira jested, then realized what she had said. "At least, that is what I've been told …"

It was Betsy who sometimes complained of little Nora keeping her awake at night.

"That is true enough!" Her father gave a rumbling chuckle. It trailed off in bout of coughing that chilled Moira.

When her expression grew anxious, he waved her away. "Don't fuss, now. Off to bed with you!"

Reluctantly, she did as he bid and headed back to her own chamber. When she rounded the corner, she nearly collided with Gabriel.

Moira clapped one hand over her mouth to stifle an outcry.

"What are you doing up?" she demanded in a harsh whisper. "I thought you were eager to keep country hours."

"I am." He gave a carefree shrug that was almost as appealing as it was infuriating. "But, like you, I had a question I wished to ask in private."

"Could it not keep until morning?" Moira gave a furtive glance past Gabriel. "If we're seen together at this hour by any of the servants, there will be no end of tattle."

Would he remind her that she had not cared about servants' gossip when she'd slipped into his chamber at Beckwith Abbey that fateful winter night?

To her surprise, Gabriel did not allude to her shameful indiscretion. "I'll be brief. I would have waited for morning, but I feared we might be interrupted by your devoted fiancé."

Moira could not deny the possibility. "Go ahead then, but be quick."

Gabriel looked flustered, as if he had not expected her to agree so easily. Or perhaps he would have liked more time to lead gently into his question. "Why did you tell *me* you were planning to accept Mr. Clarkson before you told *him*? It's not much wonder the poor man suspected me of eavesdropping on you."

"*The poor man?*" Moira repeated in a strangled shriek. "When did you develop this sudden sympathy for Mr. Clarkson?"

"I don't suppose I have." Gabriel gave a shamefaced grin that was far too disarming for Moira's liking. "I only know I would feel slighted if our situations were reversed."

Confronted by his engaging candor, Moira found it impossible to respond with anything less. "I did not intend to tell you my answer before Mr. Clarkson. When we met at Vauxhall, I wanted you to stop pestering me about marriage. Telling you I was already betrothed seemed like the best way at the time."

Gabriel raked his long, nimble fingers through his dark hair. Suddenly Moira found herself ambushed by a memory of his fingers playing through her hair. Her cheeks tingled with a blush she hoped the flickering shadows would mask.

"It is *my* fault." He spoke in a stricken murmur.

Before she could ask what he was taking the blame for, Gabriel continued, "Once you told me you intended to accept Clarkson's proposal, you must have felt obliged to go through with it."

That was partly true, Moira acknowledged to herself.

"I have made such a dreadful hash of everything." Gabriel's soulful dark eyes brimmed with bitter self-reproach that Moira longed to relieve.

When he seized her hand, she could not resist. "Can you ever forgive me?"

"Of course." She struggled to keep the tremor of strong emotion from her voice. "But do not suppose that was the only reason I accepted Mr. Clarkson. Now, I have answered your question. Off to bed with you before someone sees us."

"Soon," Gabriel promised. "I have just one more query."

Part of Moira urged her to refuse or insist it wait until morning, but her lips stubbornly resisted forming a reply.

Gabriel clearly took her hesitation for consent. "I understand you must have felt you had no other choice. But did our conversation this morning not make you reconsider your decision, even briefly?"

What could she tell him? Moira's head spun. There was something very agreeable about the forthright exchanges she'd had with Gabriel recently. But the answer to his question was complicated. Besides, there was a limit to how much of the truth she dared tell him.

If he were still a gambling man, Gabriel would have wagered a great deal that Moira Brennan was not going to answer his question.

Her soft lips pressed together in a rigid line and she

refused to meet his gaze.

Yet when a reply burst from her lips, quiet but emphatic, it was not at all what he expected. "Why should our conversation have made me change my mind about marrying Mr. Clarkson? If anything, it furnished further proof that passionate attachment has no place in marriage. Feelings of that sort are too easily injured, leading to anger and hurt on both sides. Can you deny that is what happened between us?"

Hearing her describe her feelings for him as *passionate* brought Gabriel a rush of elation, even as her argument cast down his spirits. It might have troubled him less if he could insist it was not true.

Instead, he was obliged to shake his head. "I cannot deny it. I assumed you must think as ill of me as I did of myself. Because I craved your good opinion, that misconception hurt me deeply and provoked me to strike out at you. And that —"

"Made me believe you despised me." Moira completed his thought. "So I responded just as you had, creating a vicious cycle. The intensity of our feelings for one another heightened those destructive reactions, like throwing lamp oil on a bonfire. Surely it would be easier to remain on civil terms with one's spouse if emotions on both sides were less ... volatile."

"Perhaps." That notion was not so far from his long-held conviction that love and marriage must be mutually exclusive. Yet there was a subtle but important distinction. "But I have good reason to know that marriage without love does not guarantee happiness, or even contentment. My parents amply demonstrated that every day since I was born."

Moira's eyes widened. "You never told me that your parents were ... incompatible."

Her tone held a note of pity Gabriel could not abide. Chiding himself for allowing her to glimpse his true feelings, he responded with a careless shrug. "Love matches are rare among the *ton*, though I never witnessed such thinly-veiled animosity among any other married couples of my acquaintance."

He did not intend to say anything more on the subject, but Moira's anxious attentiveness seemed to draw it out of him. "The duke is as unloving and unlovable a man as ever drew breath — always finding fault. But at least I knew where I stood with him. My mother ran warm and cold, smothering me with affection one minute then turning frosty and formal the next. I should have guessed ..."

Discretion curbed his runaway tongue in the nick of time ... or perhaps not.

"Should have guessed what?" Moira prompted him with an air of beguiling sympathy that made Gabriel long to pour his heart out to her.

But how could he? Without his position in society or the respectability of legitimate birth, he had less to offer her than even a humble curate.

"Nothing of consequence," he lied, wishing he possessed Clarkson's ability to deflect intrusive questions.

Moira shook her head. "I believe it was of something of great consequence. Not to you now, perhaps. But very much to the small boy who grew up in such an unhappy home. Tell me, please."

Her whole being radiated tender compassion that tempted Gabriel to unburden himself. But he had seen how changeable her manner could be — one night burning with passion for him, the next morning spurning his proposal with icy contempt. In the past twelve hours she had gone from confiding in him to accepting another man's offer of marriage, then appearing to welcome his embrace.

The secret she begged him to reveal might only make her reject him again.

Moira was right about one thing, though. His mother's behavior had broken his young heart more times than he cared to recall, until anger and mistrust had come to his rescue, protecting him from further injury. Now they roused again in his defence.

"What does it matter to you?" he demanded. "There is

no point in discussing any of this if you have made up your mind to wed a man you do not love. Only bear in mind, even if you do not suffer for it, your children will. Is that what you want for them?"

Moira flinched, as if he had raised his hand to her. Fear and anguish twisted her lovely features into something distressing to behold.

It made Gabriel yearn to take her in his arms and tell her anything she wanted to know, consequences be damned. But vigilance still held his heart in its protective grip.

"N-no." Moira swallowed convulsively. "I ... no!"

If he continued to press her on that point, might she agree to break her engagement? Or might his tongue run away with him and betray his shameful secret? Gabriel dared not risk the latter.

"I will leave you to think on it." He gave a stiff little bow of leave-taking, as if she were a newly-met acquaintance. "You said yourself it would not do for us to be seen together at this hour. Good night."

With that, he spun away and marched off to his room.

Once he was out of Moira's presence, with a sturdy door between him and the rest of the house, Gabriel's self-control deserted him. His breath hissed in sharp, shallow gasps, racing to keep up with his speeding heart.

Had he just escaped a terrifying ambush of his own making? Or had he let a unique opportunity slip through his fingers? Gabriel could not decide.

He spent a restless night, beset by dreams that seemed so vivid and immediate until he opened his eyes. Then he could not recall them.

He rose and stretched then wandered to the window. The garden was dappled in bright floral hues and many shades of green. Morning sunshine glinted off drops of dew that clung to the leaves and flowers, making the entire scene sparkle.

Admiring the pastoral beauty, Gabriel remained at the window longer than he intended. He was about to ring for a footman to assist with his morning toilette when he spied a woman approaching the garden. Even from that distance, he recognized Moira.

Her gait was neither a purposeful stride nor a relaxed amble, but stiff, hurried movements followed by abrupt halts. Now and then she glanced back over her shoulder. Her manner was so furtive it reminded Gabriel of the mysterious woman who'd stolen down Bruton Street five months ago to deposit that fateful basket on Jack Warwick's doorstep.

Uncertain whether she would see him if she glanced toward the house, Gabriel took a swift step away from the window. Where was Moira coming from at such an early hour and how long had she been away? Could it be the same place she'd returned from the previous morning ... and perhaps the night before?

It was in the direction he'd gone yesterday when Moira and Mr. Clarkson had chased him down. He'd been flattered to suppose she might be worried about him getting lost. What if instead she'd feared he might stumble upon something she did not want him to see?

Gabriel could not imagine what that might be. He only knew that if Moira was so determined to conceal it from him, he was even more determined to discover what she might be trying to hide.

———•◆•———

Thank goodness she had been able to return from Betsy's cottage before Gabriel rose for the day! With a sigh of relief, Moira removed her bonnet and hung it on a peg in her dressing room.

She resented not having been able to stay longer, especially now that little Nora was growing accustomed to her presence and appeared happy to see her. But she could not risk being ambushed in the garden by Gabriel again. It had been bad enough when he'd confronted her last night on the way to bed.

She'd scarcely slept a wink for thinking over their conversation. Every step of the way to Betsy's cottage and back, she'd pondered what Gabriel had told her about his family.

During their brief courtship at Beckwith Abbey, he had only made occasional references to the duke's disapproval. When she and her father dined at Cheviot House, Moira had begun to suspect that Gabriel's past was even more troubled than he'd let on.

Her heart ached for the sensitive little boy who had grown up with a cold, critical father and a mother who'd failed to protect him. Of the two, the duchess's behavior had clearly done her son more harm. At least with the duke he'd known what to expect. His mother's inconsistent bouts of affection must have lured him to let down his defenses, so he would be hurt all the worse when she turned cold.

Had *her* behavior at the Christmas party reminded Gabriel of his mother? Moira silently questioned her reflection in the looking glass. One night she'd thrown herself at him. Then, when he proposed, she had refused him in the most insulting terms.

With good reason, her grieving heart protested. She'd been deeply hurt by his manner at breakfast after their tryst, rebuffing her when she'd expected tender glances and sweet, secretive smiles. If only she'd known she was getting a taste of the treatment Gabriel had received as a child, she might have reacted differently. Their future might have taken a much happier turn.

They could have been happily married now, with their daughter in her nursery, doted upon by her parents and grandfather. For a moment Moira allowed herself to fully imagine, and long for, the life they might have had. How she wished she could go back and urge her younger self to make a better choice!

That melancholy thought was followed by a more distressing one. Was it possible that, in a year or two, she might look back again and wish she'd taken a different path?

"No!" she cried aloud to the anxious-looking young woman in the mirror. "I gave Mr. Clarkson my answer. I cannot turn back now."

The wistful gaze of her reflection seemed to challenge her adamant words.

Fearing she might lose the argument with herself if she stayed, Moira spun away and raced to her door. Clearly she needed some distraction from the contradictory feelings that plagued her. Perhaps she would seek Mrs. Trimble's reassurance that marrying Mr. Clarkson was the proper thing to do.

But when she reached the spot where Gabriel had confronted her the previous night, his words seemed to echo around her. If she wed a man she did not love, they warned, her children would suffer for it. That had been Gabriel's experience, but must it be the same for their daughter? Moira could not bear the thought. Her reason for wanting to marry Mr. Clarkson was to secure her daughter's happiness.

A calm, comfortable marriage, unshaken by the treacherous tempests of passion had seemed very attractive after her disastrous romance with Lord Gabriel Stanford. But now she confronted the possibility that an absence of ardour could cause just as much unhappiness.

Could there be another way forward?

Pausing in the corridor, Moira sensed Gabriel's presence as clearly as if he were standing inches away from her. It forced her to reconsider her reasons for keeping their daughter a secret from him.

When she discovered she was with child, she had been so certain Gabriel would want nothing to do with her or the baby. Later she'd resented him for barging back into her life and for his attachment to some other woman's child. Perhaps her true reason for keeping silent had been a spiteful desire to punish him for breaking her heart.

Now she realized that she'd been as much to blame as he for what had gone wrong between them. And did their precious daughter not deserve to know her father as well as her mother?

The thought of telling Gabriel about their baby made Moira dizzy with dread. Once she shared her secret with him, she could never take it back. If only she could gain a clearer sense of how Gabriel might greet such surprising news, without revealing too much.

She rushed off to the breakfast room in search of him. Her heart sank when she found it empty except for a young footman.

He greeted her with a bright smile. "Can I fetch you something to eat, Miss?"

Though her stomach rumbled piteously, Moira shook her head. "No thank you, Samuel. I was hoping to speak with our guest. Has Lord Gabriel risen yet?"

"He has, Miss, and not very long ago." The footman appeared proud to share his information. "I could not tempt him to breakfast either."

"Not even coffee?"

Samuel shook his head.

What could that mean? Moira wondered. One of the first things Gabriel Stanford had told her about himself was how desperately he craved his morning coffee.

"Do you know where I might find him?"

"I'm not certain, Miss, though he did ask me where the footpath behind the garden leads. Perhaps he fancied a morning stroll?"

Not again! Moira's heart bounded into her throat, cutting off her air for a moment. Gabriel Stanford seemed to have an unerring instinct that drew him in the one direction she did not want him to go.

"Is something wrong, Miss? Not bad news for Lord Gabriel, I hope." Samuel seemed troubled by the possibility. Their guest did have a knack for winning the affection of everyone he met, even the servants. Was it a skill he had honed during childhood, seeking the love his father withheld and his mother dispensed in unpredictable bursts?

"Not at all," Moira reassured the footman. "I only wish he had waited for me. Perhaps I can join him."

She turned and walked away at a sedate pace until she was out of the breakfast room. Then her steps quickened.

The prospect of Gabriel seeing their daughter sent Moira scrambling along the familiar footpath, straining for a glimpse of him. Her pulse thundered. She dreaded how Gabriel might take the news, even if she broke it to him as gently as possible. For him to discover the truth some other way and realize she had kept it from him, did not bear imagining.

At last she rounded a turn and spotted Gabriel not far ahead. She had managed to intercept him, but they were within sight of Betsy Aubin's cottage.

It took every ounce of breath she could summon to call his name.

Fortunately he heard, stopped and turned toward her.

Moira slowed her pace and struggled to regain her composure as she approached him.

"What do you want? Do not pretend you are *worried I might get lost*." He spoke those last words with biting sarcasm that made it clear he had not believed her excuse yesterday.

"I need speak with you." Moira could not disguise her breathlessness.

"So urgently that you forgot your bonnet?" Gabriel's expressive dark eyes narrowed and one brow arched.

Moira nodded. "I want to finish the conversation we began last night."

He had ended it so abruptly. If the subject disturbed Gabriel, it might distract him, or at least make her feel at less of a disadvantage.

"You could not wait until I returned?" He scowled. "What are you trying so hard to hide?"

She must not let him see how much his question alarmed her, or it would fan his suspicion like a bellows blowing air over smouldering embers. But Moira could not conceal her distress.

"Hide?" Her fear exploded into anger. "You are a fine one to talk, Gabriel Stanford. I could tell *you* were trying to hide something from *me* last night when you broke off our conversation. Can you deny it?"

He might try, but his countenance would contradict him. Never had Moira seen tension etched so clearly on a man's features.

She might have savored a flicker of triumph at having put him on the defensive, but at that moment Betsy emerged from her cottage, carrying wee Nora in her arms. Invisible hands seemed to plunge into Moira's chest and squeeze all the air out of her lungs.

Worse yet, she could see that Betsy had spotted them and begun walking in their direction. In a moment her daughter's nurse might call out a greeting.

Moira braced for disaster.

A voice did ring out then, but it was not a woman's, nor did it come from the direction of the cottage.

"Gabriel Stanford? What a fine surprise! We were just on our way to pay you a visit."

Chapter Nine

RORY FITZWALTER'S VOICE was not one Gabriel expected to hear in the depths of the Surrey countryside. Surprise drove every other thought from his mind as he turned toward the sound.

He'd noticed that the path branched in two different directions at this point. One way skirted a small cottage and led eventually to a nearby village, or so the Brennan's footman had told him. The other short section opened onto the main road. It was there Gabriel spotted an open carriage in which Rory sat with Jack, Annabelle and little Sarah.

"Good Lord!" he cried. "What are you all doing here?"

He tried to keep an edge of annoyance from his tone. Not that he was displeased to see them, especially the child he'd come to think of as his daughter. But they had interrupted him on the verge of discovering Moira's secret.

On the other hand, they might have prevented *her* from digging deeper into matters he desperately wanted to keep private. Was he a hypocrite to expect Moira to be more forthcoming than he was willing to be?

"We're following your lead," Rory replied with a wry chuckle. "Taking advantage of having friends with country houses to escape the heat of the city. My brother is always after me to visit Beckwith Abbey, so I decided this would be the perfect time. Hospitable fellow that I am, I invited the Warwicks to join me."

Gabriel hoped Lady Killoran was happier to welcome these unexpected guests than she'd been when Rory appeared at her Christmas party with Captain Turner in tow.

"We knew you were visiting in the neighborhood." Rory smiled at Moira and doffed his hat. "A pleasure to see you again, Miss Brennan! You are looking very well."

Gabriel barely suppressed a sniff of derision. Clearly his friend was happier to see Moira than he'd been when his sister-in-law had tried to arrange a match between them.

She must have thought so too, for she replied in a bantering tone, "You flatter me, Mr. Fitzwalter, though I appreciate your kind words."

"They are quite sincere," Rory assured her. "Pray allow me to present my companions. This is Jack Warwick, who has been a more indulgent friend to Lord Gabriel and me than we deserve."

"Speak for yourself, "Gabriel protested, prompting laughter from his friends.

"This is Jack's wife, or should I say *bride*, Annabelle," Rory continued with cheerful ease, "and their young ward, Sarah."

Moira acknowledged the introductions with a graceful little curtsey as she approached the carriage. "Mr. and Mrs. Warwick, it is a pleasure to meet you at last. Lord Gabriel has spoken of you so warmly, I feel as if we are already acquainted."

Gabriel silently begged his friends not to inform Moira how much he had told them about her.

Fortunately, Jack seemed to sense his unspoken message. "I am delighted you feel that way, Miss Brennan, for we were on our way to pay a call at your home."

"You are all most welcome at Ardmore." There could be no doubt of Moira's sincerity. "Let us go there now, so I can offer you our hospitality!"

To Gabriel, she sounded excessively eager to entertain his friends.

"I should be grateful to accept, Miss Brennan." Annabelle cast Moira a warm smile as she soothed the baby, who had begun to fuss. "I believe Sarah may find it too hot in the sun."

Rory swung open the carriage door and climbed out. He

beckoned Moira and Gabriel. "Come aboard and we can all go together."

He scrambled up to perch beside their driver.

"Why, thank you." Moira did not hesitate to take a seat opposite Jack, Annabelle and the baby.

Feeling he had no choice, Gabriel followed.

As soon as the carriage began to move, Sarah settled down. Anabelle held the child on her lap facing Gabriel and Moira. The moment Sarah lavished him with a wide dimpled smile, Gabriel forgot about everything else.

"How did our little one manage on the journey from London?" he asked Annabelle.

"Surprisingly well," she assured him. "She seems to enjoy carriage drives. The bumpier the better. It is only when they stop that she expresses her disapproval."

Moira leaned toward Sarah, offering the baby her forefinger to grasp. "What a delightful little creature! No wonder you are all so devoted to her. Is she shy of strangers?"

"Sometimes," Annabelle replied in a tone usually reserved for old friends. Moira's praise of the baby had clearly won her approval. "But not of you, it seems."

Sarah had seized Moira's finger in her tiny hands and tried to draw it toward her mouth. When Moira diverted it to tickle her cheek, the baby let out an infectious chortle.

Jack regarded the interaction with a fond smile. "I see you have a way with little ones, Miss Brennan, much like my wife. Annabelle came to our rescue when Sarah first arrived, otherwise I don't know how we would have managed. Fortunately she had grown up with a tribe of young cousins. How did you acquire your knack with children?"

Though his question was addressed to Moira, Jack cast Gabriel a furtive glance that made him wonder if their visit to Surrey was intended to assist him.

Moira gave a self-conscious chuckle in response to Jack's question. "I have always been drawn to small children, Mr. Warwick, perhaps because I had no younger brothers, sisters or even cousins. I cannot claim any prior experience, other than befriending some younger girls at school."

Perhaps to avoid any further questions, she began to quiz Annabelle about Sarah's habits, abilities, likes and dislikes.

Nothing about Moira's manner toward the child suggested that she could be Sarah's secret mother. Perhaps his suspicions of her and Mr. Clarkson had been nothing more than an excuse to get close to her again.

Yet, as she spoke with Annabelle about the baby, Gabriel thought he detected a wistful note in Moira's voice.

Thank heaven Gabriel's friends had appeared when they did!

How many times had Moira thought so in the past few days? She could scarcely begin to count.

The presence of the Warwicks and Rory Fitzwalter seemed to have distracted Gabriel from his perilous curiosity about the path to Betsy's cottage. So much so that Moira had felt it safe to visit her baby this afternoon while Gabriel was paying a call at Beckwith Abbey.

"Now, remember," she urged Betsy as she was about to leave, "you must be careful. If the gentleman you saw me with the other day returns, you must stay inside and not open the door. If you see him coming, go back inside at once. If it becomes impossible to avoid him and he asks you any questions, tell him the same story you've told everyone else. Your husband is a soldier serving in Spain."

"I'm not likely to forget." Nora's nurse heaved an impatient sigh. "That's the third time you've told me."

"Because it is an important warning that bears repeating," Moira replied in a sharper tone than she'd intended.

Every time she thought back to the morning Gabriel had been within sight of the cottage, her stomach sank. While his attention had been focused on his friends, Moira motioned for Betsy to take Nora back inside. Only when she and Gabriel were in his friends' carriage heading back to Ardmore did she feel as if she could breathe properly.

"Who is that gentleman?" Betsy demanded. "And why must we be so wary of him?"

"He is the guest my father invited from London." Moira hoped her sudden blush did not give away more than she intended. "He is too inquisitive for his own good ... and ours."

"I will take extra care, then," Betsy assured her. "Though Baby does like to be out of doors in this hot weather. I could take her to the seaside until your father's guest leaves. I do miss the sound and smell of the sea."

Tempted as she was by the suggestion, Moira shook her head. "I have missed too much time with her already. I want both of you close by in case I get more chances to visit."

She gave her baby a soft kiss on the cheek, relieved when Nora did not object.

"One way or another," she promised Betsy, "all this secrecy will not go on much longer."

One way or another. As she hurried back to Ardmore, Moira mulled over her choices. Watching Gabriel with Sarah the past few days, she could not begrudge his fondness for the engaging little creature. Nor could she doubt he would make a doting parent, given the opportunity. As a mother who wanted only the best for her child, how could she deny Nora the love of such a father?

Was it only their baby for whom she wanted his love? Moira's heart quivered.

Since the arrival of Gabriel's friends, their time together reminded her more and more of the house party where they'd met. Those memories were beginning to rouse feelings she had tried so hard to forget. Caution warned her to mistrust those emotions. She knew how quickly they could turn from pleasant to painful.

Her feelings for Mr. Clarkson were safer, but far less stimulating. Could such a placid connection lead to the poisonous misery Gabriel had experienced in his family? Moira found it difficult to imagine.

Lost in thought, she wandered back to Ardmore only to find Mr. Clarkson in the garden.

"My dear Miss Brennan." He clasped her hands in his and beamed down at her. "Mrs. Trimble told me you would likely return soon, so I took the liberty of waiting. I wish I had come sooner, so I might have accompanied you on your walk."

Moira replied with a vague murmur that he might interpret however he wished. In truth, she had found Mr. Clarkson's attentions growing rather suffocating. Was she wrong to assume his feelings were as temperate as hers toward him?

"I came today hoping the two of us might speak to your father about our engagement." The handsome curate fixed Moira with a beseeching gaze that might have induced most women to do whatever he asked. "I feel certain if we join forces, we can persuade him to agree."

"But Lord Gabriel—"

"Lord Gabriel?" The curate gave a scornful sniff. "If we rely on his powers of persuasion, I fear we may never be united."

"That is not entirely his fault," Moira tried to withdraw her hands from Mr. Clarkson's, but he held them tight. "If you would only let him get to know you better ..."

Would that truly make a difference? She could not be certain.

"When would I have an opportunity to do that?" Mr. Clarkson's lip curled in a manner that quite spoiled his looks. "Now that those friends of his are constantly about."

Moira had never heard the word *friends* spoken in such a disparaging tone. For some reason, the mild-mannered curate seemed to have an aversion to the Warwicks and Rory Fitzwalter. He had scarcely been introduced to them when he remembered an obligation elsewhere and hurried away. Since then, his calls at Ardmore had not coincided with theirs.

Mr. Clarkson moderated his tone. "Please, dear Miss Brennan, let us take our destiny into our own hands, rather than rely on others who have less interest in our future happiness."

"I do not want to disturb Papa when he is resting," Moira replied, though she had no idea what her father might be doing just then.

"I can stay until he wakes," Mr. Clarkson offered.

"That may be awhile." Moira managed to disengage her hands from his with a sense of relief. "I told him to get a good long rest because we have been invited to a picnic tomorrow at the home of Captain and Mrs. Turner."

A sense of obligation compelled her to include her suitor. "Would you care to join our party? I am certain you would be most welcome."

"Another time, perhaps," he answered, almost before she finished speaking. "I shall be engaged elsewhere."

"You mentioned nothing about that before," Moira challenged him. "Do you not wish to mix with Lord Gabriel's friends? Why do you dislike them?"

"For the same reason, I do not care for Lord Gabriel Stanford." The curate's tone sharpened. "Because they are irresponsible, worldly and spoiled! I find nothing congenial about the company of such people."

There had been a time, not long ago, when Moira might have agreed with that harsh judgement of Gabriel and his friends. Now, his words provoked defensive impulses that surprised her with their intensity.

"On the contrary, I would say Lord Gabriel and his friends are quite responsible, giving a loving home to an abandoned infant when they might have turned her over to the Foundling Hospital! One has only to see him with her to know he has a caring heart."

"The man is a feckless rake!" Mr. Clarkson insisted.

"Once perhaps," Moira could not deny it. "But only because his birth and connections fitted him for little else. I believe there is a great deal more to the gentleman and he has only begun to discover it."

"You are blinded by your partiality for him." The curate looked angrier than Moira had ever seen him. "From the moment I met Lord Gabriel Stanford, I could tell he was determined to come between us."

That was a charge Moira could not deny, though she doubted it was for the reason Mr. Clarkson seemed to believe.

As she struggled to come up with a response, a nearby door opened and Gabriel strolled out.

"Did someone call my name?" he inquired with a cheerful smile.

Before either of them could answer, he greeted the curate with a polite bow. "Mr. Clarkson, you are just the man I was looking for. Will you join us for a picnic tomorrow? It promises to be a most amusing time."

The curate's nostrils flared and his lips compressed into a rigid line. For an instant Moira feared he might throttle Gabriel.

"There is more to life than *amusement*!" he snarled and stalked off.

As his footsteps retreated, Gabriel made a droll face. "Are you quite certain Mr. Clarkson is Church of England? The poor fellow sounds positively Calvinist!"

Moira knew she should not laugh at her fiancé's expense. Yet she could not help herself any more than she could regret that Mr. Clarkson would not be joining them tomorrow.

Why on earth was Moira's suitor so determined *not* to escort her to the Turners' picnic?

Gabriel pondered that unexpected but agreeable turn of events as he drove with Moira and her father toward the Turners' country house. Did the curate truly disapprove of such innocent pleasures? Until today, Mr. Clarkson had not struck Gabriel as particularly pious, in spite of his vocation. Or did Moira's suitor simply not wish to spend time with Gabriel's friends?

It had not taken the curate long to form an unfavorable opinion of Rory, Jack and Annabelle. Though Gabriel was no expert in theology, he felt certain the Scriptures did not sanction that sort of unwarranted judgment. When he'd overheard Clarkson pronounce his friends *irresponsible, worldly and spoiled*, it had been all he could do to keep from calling out the pompous prig!

Before he could do anything about it, Moira had risen to their defense, and his, with vigorous indignation.

Glancing across the carriage, Gabriel caught her eye and offered a grateful smile, since he dared not tell her he had eavesdropped on her conversation. Moira returned his smile with one that made his heart swell. She had not looked at him in quite way since the night of their Yuletide tryst.

He'd been surprised and touched to hear her extol his good qualities to the contemptuous curate. If his mother had ever defended him to the duke with such fierce resolve, might he have grown up to be a better man, more deserving of Moira's regard?

He heaved a wistful sigh.

"Curb your impatience, Lord Gabriel," Moira teased him. "We will soon be there."

"I am not impatient in the least," he assured her. "I shall be happy to see my friends and renew my acquaintance with the Turners. But I am not anxious to reach the end of such a pleasant drive with such agreeable company."

Mr. Brennan chuckled. "That is kind of you to say, sir. We could return your compliment most sincerely, could we not Moira?"

A faint blush crept into her cheeks, so subtle it might have been missed by anyone watching her less attentively.

"I believe we could," she agreed with a self-conscious smile.

Their journey came to an end sooner than Gabriel would have liked with their arrival at the Turners' house. A comfortable-looking place of generous proportions, it was not nearly as grand as Gabriel had expected given the combined fortune of their host and hostess.

No sooner had they alighted from the carriage than

Captain Turner appeared to greet them.

"Welcome to Linstead, Mr. Brennan, Miss Brennan, Lord Gabriel." Their host shook them each by the hand like old friends. "How good it is to see you again! Forgive me for not calling on you before this. I must confess, I had no idea you lived so near Beckwith Abbey."

"Do not fret, Captain," replied Mr. Brennan, who had been on congenial terms with Aaron Turner at Lady Killoran's house party. "My daughter and I have been travelling for the better part of a year and only lately settling back at Ardmore. Now that I know we are neighbours, I hope we shall see more of you and your family."

Their host beamed. "You may depend upon it, sir. Now come along and join the rest of our party. Most of them will be familiar to you, I believe."

He led them around the house and through a gated trellis hung with vines. They entered a large lawn, shaded by mature oak and chestnut trees. Beneath the trees, a long trestle table was spread with all the necessary service for an informal feast. Enticing aromas wafted on the summer air along with the perfume from several rose bushes.

Not far from the table, most of the Turners' guests were seated on low benches arranged in a half-circle. The exceptions were Lily Turner and Annabelle Warwick. The ladies sat on a picnic rug with the two babies, who seemed to be the center of everyone's attention.

Gabriel strode over and sank down beside them. "My word! If I did not know better, I should take these two young beauties for twins."

Not all twins resembled each other to such a degree, he remembered. Certainly not the Crawford sisters.

Lily Turner laughed. "The resemblance is partly due to their white gowns and bonnets. I suspect that even a boy of their age might be difficult for a stranger to tell apart."

"Perhaps so," he acknowledged. "Though on closer inspection, I have no trouble picking out our dear Sarah."

He pulled a face, making the child chortle and reach toward him.

"May I?" he asked Annabelle, who smiled and nodded.

He scooped Sarah up and blew a soft raspberry against her cheek, making her laugh even harder.

The other baby gave a soft bleat that threatened to escalate if ignored.

Before her mother could comfort her, Captain Turner came to his daughter's rescue.

"Never fear, Ella Rose," he crooned, hoisting her into his arms, "you shall not suffer for lack of a gentleman to admire you."

The rest of the company laughed as their host invited the Brennans to be seated.

Lily Turner shook her head. "I do not believe our daughter is jealous, my dear, but only missing her new little friend."

"Of course," Gabriel scrambled up with Sarah in his arms and approached Aaron Turner. The two babies reached toward one another, grinning and cooing.

Now that he looked closer, Gabriel could detect subtle differences between the little ones. Both were fair, but Ella Rose Turner had darker brows and her eyes were brown, like her father's. One similarity was impossible to deny — both babies were clearly the same age.

Not only were they a similar size, they also appeared to have only their four front teeth. By Annabelle's estimate, Sarah had most likely been conceived around the time of the Christmas party, which must mean the Turners' baby had too. But how was that possible when her mother had been bedridden at the time and her father in amorous pursuit of her Aunt Iris?

Gabriel glanced toward Moira and noticed she was watching both babies with pensive interest. Could she be wondering the same thing?

With no infant to tend, Annabelle Warwick rose from the picnic blanket and took a seat beside her husband.

"You would never believe it to look at Lord Gabriel now," she informed the others, "but when Sarah first arrived he was quite terrified of her. No worse than Jack and Rory, of course. She reduced the three of them to gibbering cowards."

The ladies of the party greeted her remark with laughter.

"We might have been rather *unsettled* at first," Gabriel protested, "but gibbering cowards? Hardly!"

Rory gave an emphatic nod, but Jack sided with his wife. "How soon they forget! The pair of you were so *unsettled* that first night, you went out carousing and left me to sink or swim on my own."

Now that Jack mentioned it, Gabriel did recall the incident with considerable embarrassment. He had let both Jack and Sarah down that night. Perhaps Mr. Clarkson had good reason to accuse him of being irresponsible.

"I say it was the best service Gabriel and I ever did you," Rory argued. "If we had stayed and tried to help, heaven knows what injury we might have done the poor child. And you might never have appealed to Annabelle for rescue."

"You make an excellent point," Jack conceded, his tone softening. "In hindsight, I cannot regret any event that helped bring us together."

"Quite right," Aaron Turner cast an affectionate glance at his wife. "I feel the same about Lily and me, which is why I shall be forever indebted to Lord Gabriel and Mr. Fitzwalter for asking me to spend Christmas at Beckwith Abbey. And Lord and Lady Killoran for making an unexpected guest most welcome."

"In that case," Lily Turner teased her husband, "it is the least we can do to provide *our* guests with some refreshment."

She signalled to a footman who stood quietly in the corner of the garden nearest the house. He hurried away but soon reappeared at the head of a small parade of servants, bearing trays of sandwiches, cold meats, cakes and fine fruit, as well as pitchers of cold drinks. Once the table was heaped with delicacies, Captain Turner invited everyone to be seated and partake of their hospitality.

Gabriel surrendered little Sarah to Annabelle. He soon found himself seated between Moira and her father. Mr. Brennan clearly relished the company of younger folk.

"Tell me, Captain Turner," he asked. "What have you been up to these days, besides raising a family?"

Before their host could answer, his wife piped up, "My husband has been keeping very busy running my late father's shipping company. Thanks to his capable management, the business is thriving. It is now worth a great deal more than it was when we married, much to my sister's delight. For my part, I would rather have him spend more time at home, even if means we must make do with a smaller fortune."

"I cannot argue with my wife." Captain Turner held out a tray of sandwiches to Mr. Brennan. "The business is taking too much of my time these days. I used to be an ambitious fellow, always anxious to overcome the next challenge. Now that I have my dear wife and our delightful daughter, I have discovered the joy of domestic contentment."

Gabriel could not deny that the Captain's description of family life sounded highly appealing. Like Jack and Annabelle, the Turners were obviously devoted to one another and their daughter, challenging Gabriel's long-held belief that love and marriage did not go together.

No doubt that was the problem with his parents — there never had been any love between them to begin with. Gabriel knew he must impress that point upon Moira. With Clarkson conveniently out of the way, this might be the best possible opportunity to persuade her.

Chapter Ten

WATCHING LILY TURNER and Annabelle Warwick cuddle their babies made Moira long to do the same with hers. After seeing the tender way Gabriel had interacted with little Sarah, she wished he could experience such a loving connection with *their* daughter. Could one of those desires only be achieved at the expense of the other?

The mellow rustle of Mrs. Warwick's voice broke in upon Moira's pensive musing. "Your Mr. Clarkson was not able to join us today, Miss Brennan?"

Her Mr. Clarkson? The reference made Moira bristle.

She shook her head with greater vigor than she intended. "Lord Gabriel extended an invitation, but I fear my friend was otherwise engaged."

Gabriel turned at the mention of his name. Moira caught his eye and silently pleaded for him not to reveal the curate's uncivil response to his invitation. He must have divined her thoughts, for he held his tongue.

"How unfortunate," Annabelle Warwick replied. "Ever since you introduced us, I have wracked my brains to think how we might have been acquainted in the past. If only I had a chance to speak with him a little longer, I might be able to recall. Or perhaps it is only that he reminds me of someone else."

"That is more likely." Moira inspected her plate and chose a dainty sandwich. "Mr. Clarkson has led a very retiring life. I doubt you would have moved in the same circles."

The lady's husband was heir to an earldom, after all.

Annabelle Warwick lowered her voice. "I did not travel in very exalted circles during my youth."

She seemed about to say something more when Moira's attention was drawn to Rory Fitzwalter and Captain Turner reminiscing about the Christmas party at Beckwith Abbey.

"Many of Lady Killoran's guests are reunited today," the captain observed, "with the exception of my wife's sister and aunt."

"Do not forget my dear brother," the countess reminded him.

"Forgive me," Aaron Turner replied. "How could I ever forget Lord Uvedale?"

A moment of awkward silence followed. Moira did not exchange a look with Gabriel for fear she might burst out laughing and offend the countess.

Lily Turner came to her rescue by steering the conversation in a different direction. "There is one other we are missing. I am sorry Miss Delaney was not able to accompany you today. I hope she is well."

Moira reproached herself for failing to notice the absence of Kitty Delaney, a young woman who served as Lady Killoran's companion. She had been pressed into service as a party guest when Captain Turner's arrival spoiled the countess's careful balance of male and female guests.

Lady Killoran shook her head. "I do not know whether Kitty is well or ill, but I fear the latter. She left us suddenly last summer and I have heard nothing from her since. Have you, Rory?"

"No." Rory sounded vexed at being asked. "Why on earth should I?"

"The two of you were once thick as thieves," Lord Killoran reminded his brother. "Back in Ireland before you went away to school."

"That was a lifetime ago," Rory snapped.

Why did the mention of Miss Delaney put him in such a temper? Moira wondered. As she recalled, the two of them had been on good terms at the Christmas party. She hoped Rory's mood would not spoil the cordial atmosphere of the picnic.

Perhaps Gabriel felt the same way for he quickly changed the subject. "I must compliment you on your hospitality, Mrs. Turner. These sandwiches are as toothsome as I have ever eaten, even at Carleton House."

"I agree," Moira hastened to support his effort, though she could scarcely recall anything she'd eaten at the Prince Regent's Ball. "The punch has a delightful flavor, too."

"Indeed." Annabelle Warwick chimed in. "It is most refreshing on a warm summer day."

After others offered more praise of the food and drink, the conversation moved on to other topics. Moira began to feel as if the past year and a half had melted away and she was back at the wondrous beginning to her acquaintance with Gabriel Stanford.

For Gabriel, their afternoon with the Turners was one of the most pleasant he'd spent in a very long time. Not only did he have the opportunity to enjoy the company of his friends and little Sarah. For the first time since he'd renewed his acquaintance with Moira Brennan, she seemed to welcome his presence.

On the drive home, the two of them chatted away like comfortable old friends, rather than foes negotiating an armed truce. As if by unspoken agreement, they both avoided any mention of Mr. Clarkson.

Mr. Brennan took little part in their conversation, but regarded them with fond approval.

As they pulled within sight of Ardmore, he shook his head and chuckled. "After that fine spread the Turners laid on, I fear I shall not have much appetite for dinner. But I suppose we must do our best so as not to offend our cook."

"That would never do," Moira agreed. "But perhaps I

will ask if we might dine a little later. That way you can have a rest, Papa. You seem wonderfully well today, but I do not want you tiring yourself out."

"I feel better every day," Mr. Brennan declared. "I credit the pleasant company I've been keeping. But I shall do my best to be an obedient patient until I am quite fit again."

Moira seemed satisfied with her father's answer.

Once they reached the house, the three of them went their separate ways until Gabriel was summoned by a footman for a word with his host.

"You wished to speak with me, Mr. Brennan?" Though he told himself it was foolish, Gabriel could not stifle a sinking feeling in the pit of his stomach.

Being summoned before the duke had always meant he was in for a tongue-lashing. Was it possible Mr. Brennan had learned of his disgraceful conduct at the Killoran's Christmas party?

Evidently not, for the older man beamed at him way that might have been described as *fatherly*. "I did, Lord Gabriel. I thought this might be a chance to ask you again about your opinion of Mr. Clarkson. I suppose you might feel able to be more candid without my daughter present."

Gabriel relaxed and dropped onto a chair toward which his host gestured. "I must admit, I found myself in an awkward position, wanting to give you my honest opinion, yet not wishing to offend Miss Brennan."

The older man nodded as he sank onto a sofa opposite Gabriel's chair. "I can understand that. You care for Moira's good opinion and do not want her to be angry with you."

"Quite so, sir." He could have stopped there, and probably should, but something made Gabriel continue. "She once thought better of me than anyone ever has. Her regard still means a great deal to me."

Mr. Brennan gave him a searching look. "More than her future happiness?"

Gabriel hung his head as if he had been chastised. "No sir."

"Good." His host leaned back. "Then let me hear what you truly think of Mr. Clarkson."

"I do not like him, sir." The words Gabriel had been holding back for days burst forth at last. "Nor do I trust him. I believe your daughter deserves a better husband — one she can love and who is worthy of her affection. I would not wish the blight of a loveless marriage on anyone, least of all her."

Perhaps Mr. Brennan had not expected him to be quite so blunt. Moira's father sat for a moment, taking in what Gabriel had told him. Then he gave a decisive nod. "I agree with you on every point."

He fell silent again then shook his head slowly. "I thought you and Moira might make a match after you met at that Beckwith Abbey. You seemed smitten with one another, but nothing came of it in the end. May I ask what happened?"

Mr. Brennan's question took the wind out of Gabriel. *This* was a question to which he dared not give an honest answer. And yet, his host deserved one.

"We … quarrelled," he confessed at last, hoping Moira's father would not press him for details, "and injured each other's feelings. I have regretted it ever since."

"I cannot say I'm surprised," Mr. Brennan replied. "I was worried about Moira after you parted. She tried to keep up a brave face for my sake, especially after I fell ill, but I could tell she was unhappy. I wished she would confide in me, but I reckon that is not the sort of thing a girl wants to tell her old father."

"Perhaps not." Gabriel lowered his gaze. "But if you knew I was responsible for your daughter's unhappiness, why did you invite me into your home and show me such uncommon hospitality?"

"I never thought you were to blame for Moira's unhappiness." The sympathy of the older man's tone settled over Gabriel's bruised heart like balm. "At least no more than she was to blame for yours. I know more about lovers' quarrels than you might imagine."

"You do?"

Mr. Brennan laughed at Gabriel's surprise. "Every old dog was a young pup once! Moira's mother and I were parted for a time before we reconciled and wed. We were both at fault, though neither of us meant the other any harm. When you care for someone that much, it softens your heart and leaves it far too easily bruised."

Gabriel nodded slowly. Mr. Brennan's wise words echoed the realization he and Moira had been groping toward in their recent conversations.

"I wonder," his host mused, "if sometimes young lovers need to lose one another for a time to understand how much they mean to one another."

Did they? The notion held an irresistible appeal for Gabriel.

"I agree that smarmy curate is not the right man for Moira," Mr. Brennan repeated, "but I believe you might be."

Much as Gabriel wished that were true, he felt compelled to disagree. "I cannot deny that I care very much for her, but your daughter deserves better."

"Better than you? Nonsense!" His host dismissed Gabriel's objection with a wave of his hand. "You come from a noble family, one of the highest in the land!"

Gabriel's heart sank. If noble blood was all he had to recommend him as a husband for Moira, his cause was lost. "Surely it takes more than breeding to make a man eligible. Think of Lord Uvedale — you would not want to see Miss Brennan married to a man like him."

Moira's father gave an exaggerated shudder. "I take your point. But at the end of the day what matters is who will love my daughter and make her happy? Lately, I have seen her happier than she's been since the two of you parted."

The words had scarcely left his lips when Moira's voice rang out from the doorway. "What were you saying, Papa? What are the pair of you up to?"

"Only enjoying a little chat before dinner," her father replied to Moira's second question, ignoring her first one.

"Isn't that so, Lord Gabriel?"

"It is." Gabriel rose. "Would you care to join us?"

"For dinner." She beckoned the two men. "Our food is ready, though I am still not certain I have much appetite."

As the gentlemen followed her, Gabriel pondered what Mr. Brennan had said. He might not have a drop of noble Stanford blood in his veins, but he *did* care for Moira more than ever. Surely he could make her happier than Clarkson … if only she would give him the chance.

Once they returned to Ardmore and left behind the company of Gabriel's friends, Moira had assumed her feelings for him would return to what they had been — a strenuous tug-of-war between attraction and wariness. Instead she remained relaxed and amiable in his company.

She enjoyed a pleasant dinner with Gabriel and her father, though she feared Mrs. Norris be offended by the amount of food that returned to the kitchen.

After they had barely touched an elaborate pudding, her father dabbed his brow with his handkerchief. "I wonder how much hotter this weather will get before it breaks. Shall we withdraw to the garden? It must be cooler out there."

Moira and Gabriel agreed readily.

On their way out, they met Mrs. Trimble, who asked if they wished her to join them.

Moira's father waved away her offer. "I believe we can get on quite nicely on our own, thank you."

For a moment Moira thought her companion might protest, but something cordially implacable in Mr. Brennan's manner seemed to persuade Mrs. Trimble otherwise.

"As you wish, sir," she murmured, though she did not look happy about it.

They strolled among the flowerbeds and herbaceous borders for a while, until Moira's father began to yawn. "Between the heat and our pleasant outing, I find myself weary. If you will excuse me, I shall retire for the night."

"Did our visit with the Turners overtire you?" Moira chided herself for not paying closer attention to her father that afternoon. "Shall I put you to bed and summon a physician?"

"Neither." He emphasized his answer with a vigorous head shake. "I am not overtired, only pleasantly drowsy. I expect I will sleep all the better tonight. And I will not hear of you exiling yourself indoors on my account."

Like Mrs. Trimble, Moira sensed it was futile to argue with him. Instead, she saw him off to bed with a kiss on the cheek.

"Do not fret," Gabriel whispered as they watched Mr. Brennan return to the house. "I suspect he is only trying to give us some time alone."

"Surely not," Moira protested. Then she remembered her father's firm dismissal of Mrs. Trimble. "Or perhaps you are right."

She feared their awareness of her father's ruse might make them self-conscious. But when Gabriel did not seem troubled by it, she allowed herself to relax. "I enjoyed seeing the Turners today. It felt like old times."

"Very much." Gabriel said. "Marriage appears to agree with both Captain and Mrs. Turner. He seems less driven by ambition and she has come forward to an astonishing degree."

Moira gave an emphatic nod. "Whatever Captain Turner might have felt for Iris Crawford once, I have no doubt he is very much in love with Lily now, and she with him."

A wistful note crept into her voice.

"Can you blame me for wanting *you* to experience that kind of happiness?" Gabriel's pensive murmur went straight to her heart.

Even as recently as yesterday, Moira might have answered such a provocative question with a sharp, defensive retort.

This evening, she could not summon up any such words. "I suppose not. But can you blame me for being afraid to seek it?"

She cast a sidelong glance at Gabriel in time to see him

shake his head. "Hardly. I have felt that dread myself. It is one of the reasons I gave up so easily on the hope of winning your heart. Now I believe there is more to fear from the prospect of a life without love."

It pained Moira to picture him suffering that fate. Yet, the thought of Gabriel happily wed to another woman brought her heart an even sharper pang. "Are you still determined to discourage me from marrying Mr. Clarkson?"

"More than ever." He infused the words with fiercer resolve than Moira had imagined him capable.

"How far would you go to prevent it?"

Gabriel rose to the bait. "I would do most anything."

Moira paused and turned toward him. She needed to see his face clearly to judge the truth of his answer. "Would you try to make me care for you again, so that I might break my engagement?"

His guilty wince immediately gave way to a look of ardent conviction. "That is what I told myself in the beginning, to overcome my doubts and protect my heart in case I failed. The truth is that my feelings for you made it impossible for me to accept your marriage to *any* other man, even one a great deal more worthy than Mr. Clarkson!"

Could she believe him? The part of Moira that had been devastated by the painful ending of their brief romance urged her to be wary. For months she'd been certain Gabriel Stanford had deceived and betrayed her. Lately she had begun to question that assumption, but she still could not dismiss it altogether.

In spite of her old doubts, she *wanted* to believe Gabriel truly cared for her. But could his feelings withstand learning the secret she had kept from him? If only she could be as certain of that as she'd once been of his selfish treachery.

"Perhaps I am not as deserving of love and happiness as you believe." She lowered her gaze. "You and I scarcely had time to become acquainted when we first met. No doubt we tried to reveal only our best qualities to one another. I certainly did."

After a pause for reflection, Gabriel nodded "I wanted you to like me, so I did everything in my power to win your good opinion. Fortunately, it was not difficult. I'd never met anyone who seemed so determined to see the good in me."

"I was," Moira agreed "As were you of me. We each tried to present an ideal image of ourselves, while the other turned a blind eye to anything that might contradict that picture of perfection."

A soft sigh escaped her lips. "I am far from perfect. I have faults I fear you would despise if you knew."

"Surely that might be true of any couple." Gabriel did not sound concerned by the prospect of learning unfavourable information about her. "I understand why one might hesitate to confide in a person they cared about for fear of losing their regard."

He truly seemed to comprehend her feelings, perhaps even share them. The notion filled Moira with a volatile mixture of trepidation and hope.

"But," Gabriel continued in an earnest tone that sounded somehow wistful, "if the one they love cannot sympathize and forgive if need be, would it not be better to know first as last?"

"Perhaps." Moira caught her lower lip between her teeth.

If Gabriel had a secret he was reluctant to confide in her, she would want to know. Agreeable as it might be to see oneself reflected in a lover's eyes as the paragon of every virtue, she would prefer to be with someone who recognized her faults and loved her in spite of them. Was that the sort of bond Aaron and Lily Turner had found with one another? From what Gabriel had told her about Jack and Annabelle Warwick, Moira felt certain it was the basis for their devotion.

If she could persuade Gabriel to confide in her then offer him acceptance and compassion, might he respond in kind when she told him about their daughter?

"Is there anything you were reluctant to tell me for fear I would turn against you?" Moira asked in a soft tone that she strove to keep free of suspicion or judgment.

Gabriel did not answer right away. When he did reply at last, he avoided meeting her gaze. "There is."

"I thought so." She recalled his flash of defensive anger when she had pressed him about his parents' unhappy marriage. "Would you be willing to tell me now?"

Again he hesitated. She sensed he was asking himself that same question.

"I want to." He met her gaze now, perhaps hoping she would recognize the sincerity in his dark eyes. "I wish I could be certain you care enough to give me a sympathetic hearing. Not only for what I have to say, but for keeping it from you until now."

His words so perfectly mirrored her dilemma, they took Moira's breath away.

"Can you begin to understand what I mean?" His clouded gaze conveyed a plea.

"Better than you can possibly imagine," she whispered.

"Is there something you wish to tell me?" Gabriel asked. "I cannot conceive of anything that would diminish the … esteem in which I hold you."

Was esteem all he felt for her now? It horrified Moira how much that mild threat distressed her. She doubted he could guess her secret, though it had once been a firm certainty in his mind. Having accepted her assertion that she was not little Sarah's mother, he seemed incapable of imagining the closely related truth.

"I wish I could be as confident as you are." Moira found it difficult admit even that much. "Perhaps I need to be persuaded that you care enough to give me a sympathetic hearing."

Gabriel nodded. "Perhaps we should keep our own counsel for now and concentrate on persuading one another that our feelings are strong enough to withstand whatever we might confide."

Moira's heart fluttered, though whether from anxiety or anticipation, she could not be certain. "How do you suggest we accomplish that?"

A slowly blossoming smile spread upward from Gabriel's lips, kindling a warm glow in his dark eyes.

He was about to answer when Mr. Clarkson's voice rang out. "Miss Brennan? Mrs. Trimble told me I might find you out in the garden."

At that moment Moira could not think of anyone she was *less* happy to see than the man she'd promised to wed.

Chapter Eleven

THE ONLY THING that tempered Gabriel's resentment of Clarkson's intrusion was the unmistakable flash of annoyance he glimpsed in Moira's eyes when the curate called out to them. If only Clarkson could have delayed his arrival by a few more minutes. Gabriel sensed that he and Moira had been on the verge of a new, favorable understanding.

Now she cast him an apologetic glance, as if she were to blame for the interruption.

"Over here, Mr. Clarkson," she called in tone that did not contain even a hint of enthusiasm.

Yet it stirred a quiver of hope in Gabriel's heart.

Brisk footsteps signalled the curate's approach and betrayed his eagerness ... at least until he caught sight of Gabriel. He halted abruptly and his ardent smile faltered. "I was not aware you had company. Pardon my intrusion."

If he expected Moira to be intimidated by his air of disapproval, the curate was in for a disappointment.

"You are not intruding." Her tone remained cool and her posture stiff. "But surely it can come as no surprise to find Lord Gabriel here. He has been a guest at Ardmore for some time now."

Gabriel strove to conceal his satisfaction that she was annoyed with someone other than him.

The curate must have realized that he was sailing into dangerous waters, for he quickly changed tack. "You are angry with me and no wonder after my churlish behavior when we last spoke. That is why I came to see you this evening — to beg your pardon most humbly and pray that you can find it in your heart to forgive me!"

As he spoke, Clarkson rushed toward Moira, grasped her hand and sank to his knees before her. "I should not sleep a wink tonight knowing I had offended you without making a sincere effort to explain myself and beg your pardon!"

The force of his contrition took Gabriel by surprise. Anger was like a fire — antagonism made it burned hotter. A show of remorse, especially one so intense, acted like a douse of cold water.

Moira seemed lost for words.

"P-please, Mr. Clarkson," she sputtered at last. "Do get up. There is no need to take on so."

Her suitor did as she bid him, though with obvious reluctance. "Even if you can excuse my conduct, I fear I cannot forgive myself. You offered me the kindest of invitations and I spurned it with the meanest incivility. I am heartily ashamed of my behavior!"

Though Gabriel resented the clergyman's intrusion, how could he begrudge Clarkson's willingness to apologize? If only he had been so quick to beg Moira's pardon after their quarrel at Lady Killoran's party, he might not have lost her.

Yet Moira seemed somewhat repelled by her suitor's excessive remorse. Did it make her feel obliged to dismiss his earlier rudeness as a trifle or even take some undeserved blame upon herself?

"I cannot deny, I was . . . bewildered by your response," she admitted. "Our picnic luncheon in the Turner's garden was as respectable a gathering as one could hope to find. I know it can feel uncomfortable to mix with a group of strangers who are all well acquainted with one another, but you would have known at least three of the others there, and perhaps more."

Was that the reason Clarkson had refused the invitation with such violent disapproval? If so, it was a motive Gabriel could understand. No doubt Moira could too, or she would not have suggested it.

A clever man might recognize that and seize upon it as a way back into his sweetheart's good graces. But Mr. Clarkson did not seem to recognize the opportunity Moira had presented him.

"More?" he sounded almost alarmed. "I do not understand. Who would I have known apart from you, your father and Lord Gabriel?"

His tone made it clear the latter would have been no comfort.

"Mrs. Warwick believes she may have met you before." Moira explained, with more patience than her suitor deserved. "She'd hoped to speak with you and perhaps discover how the two of you might be acquainted."

"I fear the lady is mistaken," Mr. Clarkson insisted with greater certainty than Gabriel could have claimed about almost anything. "I have no doubt I would recall if we had met before."

"I told Mrs. Warwick you were not accustomed to mixing with the sort of company she must keep. She assured me she came from humble beginnings."

"That is true." Gabriel felt compelled to speak on Annabelle's behalf. Clarkson's adamant denial seemed to question his friend's sincerity. "Her parents died when she was young and she was taken in by wealthy relations who had disapproved of her parents' marriage. Her aunt and uncle treated her as an unpaid nursery maid to her younger cousins."

"Most charitable of them," Clarkson replied in a dismissive tone. Clearly he did want Gabriel to take any part in his conversation with Moira.

"Charitable?" Gabriel bridled. How could a clergyman of all people say such a thing? "Her relatives' treatment of Annabelle was anything but charitable! They felt free to put upon her and criticize her, while her loutish cousins were free to torment her. The only advantage of her situation was finding friends in Jack Warwick and his cousin Lord Southam who lived nearby."

The curate flinched at the indignant rebuke. "I fear I misspoke. I only meant it does not alter my certainty that I have never met the lady."

Pointedly turning his back on Gabriel, Clarkson lowered his voice and appealed to Moira. "Perhaps if we could speak in private, I might better convey my remorse."

"I cannot see what difference it will make," Moira also spoke softly, as if to shut Gabriel out. "There is nothing you could say to me that our guest should not hear."

Tempted as he was to voice his agreement, Gabriel feared it might have the opposite effect.

The curate's voice fell to a murmur that Gabriel could not make out. Whatever he said clearly persuaded Moira.

She glanced up at Gabriel with a beseeching look he was helpless to resist. "Would you be so kind as to excuse us?"

The last thing he wanted to do at that moment was to surrender the field to his rival. But if he imposed his presence upon Moira, how did that make him any better than Clarkson?

"If that is your wish, I am yours to command." Gabriel emphasized his words with a gallant bow.

"I am certain. Thank you."

Reluctant but resolved, Gabriel turned and walked away.

Behind him, he heard Moira sigh. "Go on then Mr. Clarkson. What more do you have to say?"

The curate might believe he had won the battle, but Gabriel was not so sure. He was tempted to linger in the garden in case Moira changed her mind and summoned him back. But as he approached the house, he found Mrs. Trimble hovering near the side door.

"Good evening, Lord Gabriel." The lady acknowledged him with a complacent little smirk that raised his hackles. It reminded him of the way the Duke had looked at him when he got into trouble.

If he hoped to prevent Moira from wedding the curate, Mrs. Trimble could prove a troublesome obstacle. Why did she dislike him so? He had long prided himself on being able to gain favor with any new acquaintance he'd wished to cultivate.

For Moira's sake, he could not allow himself to be daunted by her companion. Rather than circling around the lady to reach the door, he strode directly toward her until she was compelled to retreat a step or two. Her smirk faltered.

Gabriel confronted her with a direct gaze. "I care a great deal about Miss Brennan, you know."

Mrs. Trimble gave a start, perhaps dismayed that he had divined her thoughts so accurately.

She swiftly marshalled her composure to answer his challenge with one of her own. "If that is true, you will do nothing more to stand in the way of her making a steady, respectable marriage. That is what she deserves, surely."

Moira's companion was a formidable opponent indeed. Gabriel tried not to flinch when she found the weakness in his defenses. For years he had gone out of his way to reject the steadiness and respectability Lord Cheviot so prized.

"Miss Brennan *does* deserve those things," he admitted, to her companion's obvious surprise. "But not at the expense of her happiness. I assure you, I will do nothing to stand in the way of that. I hope you can promise me the same."

The lady's eyes widened and her jaw went slack.

Before she could mount a counterattack, he gave a respectful bow. "I bid you good evening, Mrs. Trimble."

As he strode away, Gabriel's thoughts returned to his earlier conversation with Moira. What could it be that she feared to tell him? He found it difficult to imagine anything that would alter his growing feelings for her. If only he could be certain she felt the same. How could he risk confiding the scandal of his parentage when it might push her straight into the respectable arms of Mr. Clarkson?

———•◆•———

When Gabriel left her alone with the curate, as she'd asked, Moira sensed his reluctance. Knowing he was going against his own wishes to oblige her fanned the glowing embers of her regard for him. She hoped he knew that she was just as unwilling to part from him.

She'd scarcely been able to conceal her impatience at the curate's latest intrusion. But how could she refuse his apology, especially such a fervent one? Besides, she wanted to understand what had made Mr. Clarkson take such umbrage at her invitation. His apology did nothing to enlighten her. Though he admitted the error of his ways and begged her pardon most humbly, he'd offered no reason for his behavior.

When Mr. Clarkson first asked to speak with her in private, she'd resisted. But when he murmured, "I have a confession to make, for you alone," Moira found it impossible to refuse.

Her suitor was offering to confide in her, something she wished Lord Gabriel could bring himself to do. Perhaps this might be the explanation she'd hoped for.

"We are alone now," she prompted him, though she could hear a distant murmur of conversation from the direction of the house. "What is this confession you wished to make Mr. Clarkson?"

"Henry."

"I beg your pardon?"

"Please call me Henry," he entreated her. "Surely now that we are on the verge of matrimony we my address one another by our Christian names."

"Of course … Henry." The familiarity made Moira uneasy. "Your confession?"

For a moment his brow furrowed, as if he did not understand her. Could it have been a ruse to get her alone? Moira chided herself for entertaining such a suspicion. She might not *love* Mr. Clarkson … Henry … with the dizzying, breathless rapture she had once experienced, but she could *trust* him. Surely that was more important to her future happiness.

"My confession. Of course." The curate hung his head. "I am ashamed to confess the true reason I refused your invitation with such a regrettable show of temper. I fear I have been guilty of a deadly sin ... jealousy."

Moira's thoughts had run ahead of his words, anticipating something different.

"*Is* jealousy one of the seven deadly sins?" she asked, though she knew it was beside the point.

"Of course it is," the curate snapped. All appearance of humble contrition vanished. "I mean, it must be, surely."

Religious instruction had been a rigorous part of her schooling, particularly those principles aimed to mold Moira and her fellow pupils into virtuous wives and mothers. She could scarcely imagine the horror of her teachers if they knew she borne a child out of wedlock.

Now she counted off the Seven Deadly Sins on her fingers. "Pride, greed, gluttony, sloth, lust." She blushed and hurried on.

"Wrath." That had been the one she'd expected him to name. "And envy."

"Yes!" Mr. Clarkson stabbed his forefinger toward her. "You see. Just as I said!"

"You said jealousy," Moira ventured, suddenly reluctant to contradict him. "I'm not certain they are quite the same."

"Of course they are," the curate insisted. "And I have been guilty of it. Ever since Lord Gabriel Stanford came to Ardmore, I have feared you prefer his company to mine. The appearance of his friends with their wealth and taste for amusement only increased my feeling of inferiority. Every moment you spend in their company, I sense you slipping further away from me. I could not bear to witness it first-hand nor to place myself in a situation where I must compete for your attention and favor, conscious of my disadvantages."

Her suitor's distress intensified with every word, as did Moira's remorse. He had bared his heart to her but all she could do was quibble. Little wonder he felt jealous or envious of Gabriel and his friends. She could not deny the appeal of their genial, stimulating company. But where had they been when she'd desperately needed the support of a sympathetic friend?

"Oh my dear Mr.... Henry!" Moira clasped his hand and gave it a sympathetic squeeze. "I regret that I have grieved you in that way. Please believe it was never my intention!"

She wanted to insist that his worries were groundless, but she feared it was not true. Perhaps she *could* assure him that her feelings for him had not changed. That was correct, but only because those feelings had never been what he appeared to believe and desire.

"What can I do to set your mind at ease?" she asked, hoping he would not request a passionate declaration of her love.

She shrank from the idea of rejecting Mr. Clarkson after the kindness he had shown her. Besides, she might be happy to wed him if her hopes for a reconciliation with Gabriel were dashed, as they well could be. Moira tried to dismiss that shamefully selfish notion.

Her offer acted as a powerful tonic upon the curate's spirits. His shoulders straightened out of their dejected hunch and his eyes sparkled with hope. "There is one thing that would quell my fears entirely."

"What might that be?" Moira resolved to do what he asked, if it was at all within her power.

"Let us elope!" He urged with eagerness that verged on desperation. "All these delays are driving me to distraction. I cannot bear to wait for Lord Gabriel to secure your father's consent, when I fear he is trying to do the opposite."

She wanted to deny his suspicions, but how could she? What had Gabriel and her father been discussing before dinner? Something that had made them look guilty when she appeared.

"E-elope?" The suggestion left her breathless. "But Scotland is so far away. And the scandal would disgrace my father."

Both those statements were true, yet Moira knew her resistance sprang from another source. The prospect of an imminent, irrevocable union with Mr. Clarkson made her realize that she could not imagine a future with anyone but

Lord Gabriel Stanford.

Her reticence must have betrayed her thoughts.

A livid flush suffused the curate's face and his mild blue eyes flashed with fury. "You would not object if *he* asked you to run away with him!"

There could be no doubt who he meant. Moira longed to deny the charge, but her conscience was already overburdened.

"I thought not!" The words rasped out between gritted teeth in a voice that sounded like another man entirely.

She tried to withdraw the hand she had extended to him in sympathy, but his fingers closed around her wrist with the violent swiftness of a sprung trap. A cry rose in her throat but stuck there, throttled by his next accusation.

"You did not wait to leap into bed with him, either, did you?" Mr. Clarkson's meaning was brutally clear.

He had guessed that Gabriel was the father of her child.

Though her arm throbbed, Moira could not summon the breath to tell him he was hurting her. Especially not when part of her believed she deserved it.

"Which do you suppose will shame your father worse," he demanded in a menacing murmur, "hurrying the wedding to your betrothed or being exposed for bearing a bastard brat?"

The insult galvanized Moira like nothing else he could have said. *She* might deserve contempt and disgrace, but Nora was entirely innocent.

"*Never* speak of my child in that way!" Maternal outrage gave her the strength to break free. "I was prepared to marry you because I thought you would be a good father to her. But jealousy has maddened you — perhaps it *is* a deadly sin after all."

Rather than being chastened by her reproach, Mr. Clarkson narrowed his eyes. "I am tired of dancing to your capricious tune. Make up your mind what you want — a home with me and your daughter or a scandal that will ruin you."

"You would blackmail me into marriage?" Moira could scarcely believe her ears.

She had trusted this man, confided in him, defended him to her father and Lord Gabriel. It horrified her to realize how vulnerable her naiveté had left her. Could she ever trust herself to see a man for who he truly was, rather than who she wanted him to be?

"Blackmail?" The curate dismissed her charge with a derisive snort. "I am only advising you to weigh your options carefully. What will you choose, a mild scandal or certain ruin?"

Moira longed to tell him he was now the last man on earth she would consider marrying. She wanted to call the servants and have him thrown out. But what price would she pay for that momentary satisfaction? Others would pay too — her child, her father, and Gabriel.

"If you expect me to consider carefully, you must give me time." It was not a plea or a request, but a demand. If he forced her to act immediately, the outcome might not be to his liking.

The curate hesitated, perhaps grasping the peril of *his* situation. As long as he held his tongue, he had power over her. The moment he exposed her secret, he would lose it.

"Very well," he growled. "You have three days to come to your senses and make preparations for our journey. But only because I have matters I must attend to in London."

Clarkson took a step toward her but Moira hastily backed out of his reach.

His features settled into a scowl of icy menace that chilled her to the bone in spite of the evening's sultry heat. "Do not entertain any romantic fancies about Gabriel Stanford. Much as he may covet your fortune and enjoy an illicit frolic, he will never risk disgracing his family by wedding the daughter of an Irish tradesman!"

Having delivered that brutal jab, the curate turned and stalked off.

All the resolve Moira had mustered to confront him drained away, leaving her wilted and trembling. She had three days reprieve, but what could she do in that time other than fret?

The sound of approaching footsteps made her heart hammer until she realized they were too light to belong to either the curate or Lord Gabriel.

Mrs. Trimble appeared, fluttering like an agitated hen. "What on earth did you say to poor Mr. Clarkson? He stormed past me just now without a word."

"*Poor* Mr. Clarkson?" Moira responded with a burst of bitter laughter. "Do not talk to me of your poor, precious Mr. Clarkson!"

Before Mrs. Trimble could demand an explanation that might trigger a storm of desperate tears, Moira fled to her bedchamber as fast as her feet would carry her.

Her only hope of escaping Mr. Clarkson's trap was to forestall him by confessing her secret to Gabriel and her father. At least then she might have an opportunity to explain herself and break the news as gently as possible. Her recent conversations with Gabriel had kindled a spark of hope that he might be able to forgive her.

But Clarkson's words, "*He may covet your fortune,*" rang in her ears. Could she trust her own judgment of Gabriel when it had proven so disastrously wrong in the past?

Chapter Twelve

SOMETHING WAS WEIGHING on Moira's mind. Gabriel sensed it from the moment he saw her that morning. He wanted to ask her what was the matter but Mrs. Trimble had hovered around them like a persistent fly, evading every effort to swat her away.

Fortunately, deliverance came in the shape of Jack and Annabelle Warwick.

"Would you care to join us for an afternoon of boating?" Jack inquired as his wife fanned her flushed face. "Captain Turner knows of a well-shaded stream nearby. A gentleman whose land it flows through hires out little boats to holiday-makers."

Gabriel glanced at Moira, seeking her reaction. Might a quiet afternoon on the water lift her spirits? Her expression looked brighter than it had so far that morning.

"It sounds like an agreeable way to spend a hot afternoon," he replied, "though I cannot claim any skill at boating."

"Nor can I," Jack chuckled. "But Captain Turner assures me the stream is narrow and the current strong enough to float us along at a leisurely pace without much effort on our part."

"Enjoyment without effort." Gabriel made a droll face. "Who can resist such an invitation? Count me among your party!"

"And you, Miss Brennan?" Annabelle asked. "I hope you will be able to join us. Mr. Clarkson as well, if you would care to invite him."

For the first time in their acquaintance, Gabriel found

himself annoyed with Jack's wife. He knew she was anxious to quiz the curate about where and when they might have met, but did that matter? Surely it was more important that he and Moira have as many opportunities as possible to spend time together without her suitor.

Much to his relief Moira shook her head. "Mr. Clarkson has gone up to London for a few days."

She did not sound as if she regretted his absence any more than Gabriel. Was that what the curate had wanted to tell her in private last evening?

"Your father, then?" suggested Annabelle. "Or perhaps your companion?"

They relayed the invitation to Mr. Brennan, who thanked the Warwicks but made his excuses. "I have had enough of boats to last me a lifetime."

Mrs. Trimble said she would be happy to go along but Mr. Brennan would not hear of it. "I am quite satisfied that my daughter will be well-chaperoned by Mrs. Warwick and Mrs. Turner."

Moira's companion did not look pleased with her father, but Gabriel could have shaken his hand most warmly.

"If only two from Ardmore will be joining us," said Jack, "you might as well come in our carriage."

He consulted his time piece. "We had better not dally. I promised the Turners and Lord and Lady Killoran that we would meet them in an hour's time."

Gabriel hoped that being in the company of his friends would lift Moira's spirits, but it did not work as well as he would have liked. He doubted anyone else in the party noticed. When Annabelle or Lily Turner engaged her in conversation, she seemed lively and at ease. But when she thought no one was watching, Gabriel noticed how quickly she slipped into anxious abstraction.

Whatever was troubling her, Gabriel doubted it had anything to do with him, for Moira seemed to welcome his company.

As the two of them settled into their little boat, he could scarcely contain his curiosity. He made certain theirs was the last to push off from the bank. Rather than using his oars to propel it along, he slowed the light craft until they lagged some distance behind the others.

Moira scarcely seemed to notice. She reclined in the bow, holding a parasol with one hand, while she trailed the other through the lazily moving water.

Gabriel drew in a deep breath of warm summer air, faintly scented with clover. "What did Mr. Clarkson have to say last evening that was so private?"

She flinched so hard it made the small boat rock.

Gabriel used the oars to steady it. "Did he say something to upset you? Is that what has been troubling you all morning?"

"What makes you suppose I've been troubled?" Moira sat up straighter and made an obvious effort to look carefree.

He shot her a challenging look. "From the time I was very young I learned to discern the moods of those around me from their looks and bearing. It is a kind of language without words."

Moira responded with a slow nod. "I suppose it is. That ability must have been quite an asset to you growing up."

"At times." Gabriel pulled back on the oars to maintain their distance behind Jack's punt. "It helped me make myself scarce when the duke was in a particularly vile temper. Later I put it to good use at the gambling tables. But it can have its disadvantages as well."

"What might those be?" She no longer looked lost in thought, but deeply attentive to him.

A rueful sigh escaped his lips. "While it is possible to tell *how* another person may feel, it can be far too easy to mis-understand *why* they feel as they do. Am I wrong to assume you are troubled by your conversation with Mr. Clarkson last evening? Or is it something to do with me?"

"Not at all!" she insisted, rather too forcefully.

"Are you certain?" His tone and searching gaze warned her that it was futile to pretend otherwise with someone who possessed his particular skill.

"Perhaps a little," she admitted, "but only as it relates to what Mr. Clarkson said. He told me that he is jealous of the time I have been spending with you and your friends. He fears it is luring me away from him."

None of that surprised Gabriel. "Is he right?"

For some reason his question seemed to rile Moira.

"He needs no help from anyone on that score!" she muttered.

"I beg your pardon?"

Moira put her hand back in the water and directed her gaze that way as well. "I only meant that I am not very pleased with Mr. Clarkson at present."

Gabriel strove to conceal his satisfaction. "For any particular reason?"

She did not answer at once, making him wonder if she had heard his question.

He was about to ask again when a reply burst out of her. "He claims you covet my fortune!"

The charge made Gabriel wince. His oars jerked out of the water and fell again with a splash.

It took a moment to contain the volatile emotions that accusation ignited.

"Do you believe him?" His heart hammered, as if he was taking a grave risk by asking that question.

Moira's lips pursed and her fine brows drew together. "Would I be cross with *him* and spending the afternoon here with *you* if I did?"

Her answer should have set Gabriel's mind at rest. It did not, entirely, because she hadn't given him a clear denial. Could that be the reason for her pensive air? Had his rival managed to sow doubt in her mind about his motives? If so, how could he tell her that he was not the son of duke after all, but an unknown man? Could she ever believe he was *not* after her fortune?

His heart sank like a stone hurled into the stream. For a

moment it came to rest at the bottom, in a state of hopeless surrender. The duke had been right about him — he would never amount to anything, never be worthy of a woman like Moira. She would be better off without him.

Rubbish! Gabriel fancied he could hear the word bellowed by an insistent chorus of his friends: Jack, Rory and Annabelle. They believed in him. So did Mr. Brennan, little Sarah and especially Moira. He could not let them down. Nor could he give the duke and Mr. Clarkson the satisfaction of being proven right.

Tightening his grip on the oars, he began to row with brisk determination. By the time they reached the spot where the carriages awaited and the boats were to be retrieved and carted back upstream, Gabriel had a plan in mind. After years of aimless drifting, it felt invigorating to have a clear purpose.

As they drove back to the Turners' for tea, Moira remained preoccupied, as did Gabriel, working out his plans.

At first he did not fully attend to what Jack was saying … something about a magnificent estate that had been all but abandoned by its owners. "The old Earl of Tandridge came back from his Grand Tour wild to recreate the beauties of the Classical world. He ran through his own fortune and two of his wives' to make Farleigh Park the showplace of the county."

Gabriel winced at Jack's reference to the earl squandering his wives' money.

"When he died, twenty years ago," Jack continued, "the grounds were still not perfected to his satisfaction but his heirs were heartily sick of the place. They have been trying to sell it ever since, to no avail. They occasionally allow visitors and I have managed to secure an invitation for tomorrow. I hope you will all be able to accompany Annabelle and me. I believe the place is well worth seeing."

The others were quick to accept Jack's invitation, including Moira. His description of Farleigh Park seemed to entice her out of her brooding. For the first time that day she looked truly engaged.

"Miss Brennan," said Jack, "I hope your father will be able to accompany us. He is a capital fellow, not stiff and stodgy like so many of his generation."

Gabriel nodded. He knew Jack's uncle had been just as stern and disapproving as the Duke of Cheviot.

"Papa would be pleased to hear that, Mr. Warwick," Moira replied with a grateful smile. "I shall relay your kind invitation."

While the rest of the company made plans for their expedition, Gabriel drew Captain Turner to one side. "I have concluded it is long past time I made my own way in the world. I would be grateful if you could let me know of any situation for which I might be suitable. I cannot boast great experience in anything useful, but I can read and write a tolerable hand and I know how to get on with people. What is more, I am eager to learn and determined to become independent."

Aaron Turner's initial look of surprise settled into one of increased respect. By the time Gabriel finished speaking, the captain had begun to nod. "Those are important qualities for success in any endeavor. Would you be willing to come and work with me to learn the shipping business? When you are ready, I can give you more responsibility."

"That is a most generous offer." Gabriel extended his hand. "I am honored that you consider me worthy of such an opportunity."

The captain clasped his hand and shook it warmly. "This may be the very thing we both need. For me, a chance to spend more time with my family and for you … a chance to prove yourself to Miss Brennan?"

Gabriel shook his head. "I suspect what I need is an opportunity to prove myself to … me."

———◆———

Why had she squandered her chance to confide in Gabriel? Moira chided herself bitterly as they drove to Farleigh Park with her father the next day. Fate had given her an ideal opportunity as they'd floated down that peaceful stream, yet she had failed to take advantage of it. If she could not bring herself to tell him about their child, at least she might have urged him to unburden his heart to her.

Instead, she'd allowed Mr. Clarkson's accusation to revive the anguish she had suffered the first time she placed her trust in Gabriel Stanford. Lately those wounds had begun to heal, but she'd been a fool to suppose they were fully mended.

When Gabriel had pressed her about her conversation with Mr. Clarkson, memories of past suffering and fears of more to come fused into an instrument of torture. Instead of soothing her afflicted spirits, the gentle babble of the water crooned a siren's song about escaping her troubles in its peaceful depths. When Gabriel had asked if she believed the curate's charge that he coveted her fortune, she could not give him the whole-hearted reassurance he must crave.

She knew him well enough to sense how her tepid response stung, yet she could not bring herself to amend it. The pain inside her cried out to be shared, as if any hurt she caused him might diminish hers. But that was a false promise — it had only added a taint of guilt to the bitter brew that churned within her.

The worst of the pain had drained away, but dregs of anxiety and self-reproach remained. She had squandered her chance to share her secret with Gabriel, and who knew when or if she might get another.

He and her father chatted away now, oblivious to Moira's silent distress, or perhaps hoping to distract her.

"I recall hearing of Farleigh Park when I was looking to settle in this part of the country," said her father. "The asking price was too dear for my pocket at the time. If I'd known it was such a spectacle, I might have taken a look at least."

Gabriel glanced out the carriage window at the overcast sky. "I hope it will not rain until after our tour. I thought the sun's absence might make for a cooler day, but I fear it is quite the opposite."

Moira's father pulled out a handkerchief and mopped his brow. "That is often the way before the heat breaks. We may be in for quite a storm, once it starts."

Was that how it would be when Mr. Clarkson returned from London? A weight of suffocating oppression settled over Moira. Would this sense of dread give way to a violent tempest capable of destroying her life?

"I recall once," her father continued, "when we were sailing to the Nova Scotia colony ..."

Talking about the weather often reminded her father of his years at sea, perhaps because ships were so much at the mercy of the elements.

As he launched into a familiar tale, Moira found herself preoccupied again. How long would Mr. Clarkson's business keep him in London? He might return tomorrow for all she knew, demanding she make a terrible choice.

She scarcely heard another word her father spoke until the carriage took a sharp turn off the main road and Gabriel said, "I believe we have reached our destination."

"This?" Moira peered out the carriage window at the tall evergreens that crowded the lane, leaving scarcely enough space for a single carriage to squeeze between them. "I see nothing remarkable except the height of those trees."

Gabriel gave a cheerful shrug. "Lord Killoran said the place has long been neglected. I have tempered my expectations accordingly."

"A wise course, young man," Moira's father chuckled. "In my experience setting your hopes too high generally leads to disappointment. Did your father teach you that?"

"In a manner of speaking," Gabriel replied with jaunty composure, though Moira sensed darker emotions stirring beneath his cheerful façade.

Their carriage came to a brief halt then continued on through an impressive archway of pale stonework with wrought-iron gates. In the center of each gate the sturdy metal bars had been fashioned into an emblem of exquisite delicacy.

"A lyre surrounded by laurel leaves," Gabriel mused aloud as if he had overheard Moira's thoughts. "Fitting indeed, since Jack claims its owner intended Farleigh Park as tribute to the Greek Muses."

Once through the gates, the press of evergreens gave way to wide meadows, smaller stands of lofty oaks and elms, and clusters of shrubbery. At last their carriage pulled up beside Lord Killoran's elegant equipage. The earl and countess had just alighted with his younger brother.

"This way, everyone," Lord Killoran beckoned the party, "and try not to dawdle. We have a good deal of ground to cover, though I trust it will be worth the exertion."

Moira followed the example of the other ladies, opening her parasol though the sky was too overcast for them to need much protection from the sun.

Gabriel emulated the other gentlemen by offering her his arm.

She cast her father a questioning glance, which he answered with a nod and a doting smile.

Slipping her gloved hand into the crook of Gabriel's elbow, Moira found her senses overcome by his nearness and the physical contact between them, proper as it might be. That heady sparkle of awareness chased away the dark shadows of regret and distant rumbles of anxiety that had consumed her thoughts, like a stray sunbeam piercing the clouds to gild every surface it illuminated.

"My word," Gabriel breathed in a tone Moira could only describe as *reverent.*

She followed his gaze. The view that stretched before them took her breath away as completely as if Gabriel had swept her into a passionate embrace.

A frame of verdant woodland encased broad meadows of tall waving grass studded with wildflowers in bright shades of yellow and pink. The grassland rose on either side to cradle a perfect blue gem of a lake, fed by a slender waterfall that Moira could scarcely wait to view at closer range. But there were other sights to take in first — exquisite miniature temples on either bank of the lake and a third on a small island. A delicate stone bridge connected the island to the bank, while another traversed the narrow stream that trickled from the base of the lake. A lofty white tower stood guard over the head of the waterfall.

She might have stood there all afternoon drinking in the pastoral beauty of their surroundings, but Gabriel tugged her toward the nearest temple.

"I feel as if I've fallen into a painting by Poussin," he murmured, "or a Spenserian sonnet. *Come live with me and be my love and we will all the pleasures prove that valleys, groves, hills and fields, woods or steepy mountain yields.*"

Sweet, reckless yearning took possession of Moira and threatened to run away with her.

"I beg your pardon?" Her words emerged high-pitched and breathless.

"A quote from Marlow's *Passionate Shepherd to His Love*," Gabriel explained with a self-conscious chuckle. "This seems the sort of place that might have inspired him to write those words."

Moira hoped if he noticed her flushed cheeks, he would blame the heat of the day. "Perhaps your poet drew inspiration from a particular lady rather than the scenery."

Gabriel turned his admiring gaze upon her. "You may be right, Miss Brennan. The natural beauty of the countryside would only serve as an ideal setting for the object of his affections."

What would her father make of such a flirtatious exchange? Moira wrenched her gaze away from Gabriel only to discover her father absorbed in an agreeable conversation with Rory Fitzwalter.

Rory gestured toward the miniature temple they were approaching. The main structure looked round from a distance, but as they drew nearer it proved to have eight sides with a domed roof and an impressive pillared portico over the entrance that was half the size of the rest of the building.

The party entered to discover what had clearly meant to be a fine library. Empty bookshelves lined the lower portion of the lofty walls. Above them, tall, slender windows let in plenty of light for reading, even on such a dull day. In the centre of the great room stood a female statue carved from marble so white, it fairly glowed. The lady was dressed in classical robes, her hair bound with a circlet of laurel leaves.

"Clio," Gabriel whispered. The place had an air of restrained contemplation that inspired everyone in the party to speak softly. "The Muse of history."

Moira dared not disturb the sacred tranquility with anything louder than a murmur. She turned toward Gabriel and leaned in close so he might hear her question, "How can you tell?"

He angled toward her to offer an equally soft reply. But Moira did not turn quickly enough to lend her ear. For an instant his lips hovered near hers, barely a kiss away.

They arched into a smile that appeared self-deprecating, yet strangely tender. "Classics was one subject I enjoyed at school. Notice the scroll she is holding in one hand and the quill in the other. Most of the other Muses would have musical instruments or dramatic masks."

With considerable difficulty, Moira shifted her gaze back to the statue. "The sculptor was very skilled. The folds of her gown look as if a gust of wind might ruffle them. Not to mention the feather of her quill. I can scarcely believe it is stone."

Their companions milled about, quietly admiring the excellence of the statue and her temple, until Lord Killoran reminded everyone that there were other wonders awaiting them. They set off again, following a path that wound through meadows of tall grass that swayed in the breeze.

Moira cast a wistful gaze toward the island, the tower and the waterfall, but the path took them in another direction, toward a copse of trees.

"Who do you suppose we will find there?" she asked

Gabriel, nodding toward the grove.

"I could make a guess out of seven," he replied with a chuckle that rustled like the wind in the leaves, "but a guess is all it would be."

"What do you mean, *out of seven*?"

"Well, there are nine Muses," Gabriel explained, "and we have visited one already."

"Which leaves eight," Moira responded in a bantering tone. "I may not *enjoy* cyphering, but I am capable of doing sums."

"I do not doubt your capability for a moment." Gabriel pointed toward the tower that seemed to stand guard over the head of the waterfall. "But I should be very much surprised if that is not the abode of Urania, the Muse of astronomy."

"Of course." Even from a distance, Moira could make out a walkway circling the roof of the tower. "How clever of you to work out! Imagine the view of the heavens from up there on a clear night."

She pictured the two of them stargazing from atop Urania's tower.

By this time they had reached the grove. It appeared overgrown after years of little tending. Yet that did not detract from its charm — quite the contrary. They followed the path to the heart of the little wood where they discovered the statue of another Muse. This one was not as pristine as her sister, Clio. Small patches of lichen speckled her skirts, while vines of ivy curled around her slender form.

"Now do you recognize her?" Moira prompted Gabriel.

His brow furrowed in an expression she found dangerously attractive.

"This one presents more of a challenge. Though it would be very apt if she turned out to be …" He reached up and pulled away an ivy creeper that obscured the statue's left hand to reveal a broadly grinning mask. "Thalia, the Muse of comedy. Ivy is one of her symbols."

The other ladies applauded while Jack Warwick cried,

"Well done, Gabriel! I had no idea you were such a scholar."

Though he acknowledged his friend's praise with a droll grimace, Moira sensed he was pleased. She and Gabriel lingered in the grove after the rest of the party had moved on.

"Lady Thalia looks quite at home here," he said. "This grove puts me in mind of the Forest of Arden in *As You Like It*. Or the Athenian Woods where the faeries frolic in *A Midsummer Night's Dream* and the lovers suffer all their amorous confusion under Puck's spells."

Moira nodded. The whole estate seemed removed from ordinary life, with all its complications.

"I fell under *your* spell," Gabriel murmured, "from the moment I met you. I tried to break free but I never could."

He reached up to caress her cheek with the back of his fingers. "Now I cannot imagine why I would want to."

Nor could she. All the heartache she'd suffered on his account suddenly seemed like a bad dream.

Though his caress exerted no more pressure than the flutter of a moth's wing, some irresistible force urged her toward him. Slowly their lips approached, though without a trace of hesitation. Instead, they seemed to savor the anticipation of what was to come.

As their lips met, the hand that stroked her cheek opened to cradle her face. It felt like an enchantment, this kiss, making her forget everything else, including the need to breathe. Outwardly she might seem as still as a statue, but inside her flesh hummed with powerful currents of sensation. How could so soft a touch unleash such a powerful response?

Perhaps the way a single ember could ignite a bonfire.

From a distance that seemed even greater than it must have been, Moira heard Rory Fitzwalter call their names.

"We had better catch up," Gabriel spoke in a ragged whisper, "Or they will come looking for us."

He sounded as if he would cheerfully do away with his dearest friend. At that moment, Moira would not have lifted a finger to stop him.

Chapter Thirteen

As he and Moira responded to the summons, Gabriel sensed his friend knew exactly what he was interrupting. There was scarcely a torture so gruesome he would not have wished it on Rory Fitzwalter at that moment.

His arms ached to enfold Moira and never let her go. His lips tingled with kisses he yearned to impart. As for the rest of him . . .

Gabriel strove to curb his arousal.

Perhaps it was just as well Rory had interrupted them.

"There you are," his friend called when they emerged from the grove. "I was beginning to wonder how you could get lost among so few trees."

Rory and Mr. Brennan were standing on a decorative stone bridge that led to a small island on the lake.

Gabriel was tempted to dive into the water. Perhaps it might extinguish the bewitching flames that raged through his flesh. A sidelong glance at Moira made him doubt it would be enough.

"This is an extraordinary place." He tried to keep his voice from betraying his agitation. "We should savour our time here, not rush through it."

"Far be it from me to stand in the way of anyone *savouring the pleasures* of life," Rory replied in a suggestive tone that Gabriel resented. "But, that sky is looking more threatening by the minute. The others have already visited the island and moved on."

He gestured toward the other branch of the path that

wound up the broad slope. In the distance Gabriel could make out the other three couples as they approached a magnificent fountain. "We were about to follow, but I promised I would chivy you along."

"You have discharged your duty." Gabriel could not keep an edge of annoyance from his voice. "Miss Brennan and I will pay a brief visit to the island then follow as quickly as we can."

"No doubt you will catch up with us soon enough." Mr. Brennan beamed at Moira and Gabriel as he and Rory headed up the hill.

"Take your time, Papa," Moira called after him. "Do not tire yourself out."

Without looking back, her father raised his hand. Whether the gesture was meant as a sign of agreement or dismissal, Gabriel could not be certain.

He gave Moira's arm a reassuring pat. "Rory will look after him. The sooner we stroll around the island, the sooner we can join them."

They crossed the dainty arched bridge to the island, which was barely large enough to hold a few trees and a small open rotunda. This was clearly the temple of another Muse.

Moira gave an admiring sigh. "She is the most beautiful we have seen so far."

The statue was most attractive indeed, her hair adorned with a coronet of flowers. Over a simple flowing gown she wore a belted robe with voluminous sleeves. Her left hand was pressed over her heart, while her right one held a lyre. She looked as though the sculptor had captured her in mid-step.

"Which of the Muses is she?" Moira ran her fingers over the statue's trailing sleeve as if she expected to touch fine linen rather than marble.

"Erato," Gabriel replied, "the Muse of love poetry."

He could understand why many might pay homage at her shrine, though the only inspiration he needed to wax poetic was the living, breathing lady at his side.

"How do you know this time?" The harmonious notes of

wonder and admiration in her tone were the sweetest music to his ears.

Gabriel gestured to the floor of the temple, a mosaic of tiny tiles. He could scarcely imagine the skill that had gone into creating it. In a semicircle around the base of the statue was a Latin quotation. "It is from the poet Virgil, who must have been inspired by Erato. *Love conquers all, so let us all yield to love.*"

"Love conquers all," Moira mused, staring up at the sculpture. "Do you believe that?"

"I *want* to believe it." A sigh escaped Gabriel's lips in spite of his strenuous effort to contain it. "And I want to persuade you of it as well. But I have had considerable experience to the contrary. I idolized my mother as a child and wanted nothing more than to be certain she cared for me. So many times I convinced myself she did, only to have those hopes dashed."

Moira nodded. "I can see how difficult that might make it to believe in the power of love. Though I am not certain Virgil meant that we can win the affection of someone else with the power of our love for them."

When he heard the proposition spoken aloud, it did sound unlikely. "What do you suppose he meant then?"

Moira's brow furrowed as she sought to clarify her thoughts on such a vital subject. The soothing sound of the nearby waterfall seemed to wash over the island temple.

"I am no scholar of the classics like you," she said at last, "but I wonder if Virgil might have meant that love can win out over other feelings that might rule our hearts in its place: anger, fear ... shame. Or perhaps he meant that when two people love one another truly and deeply, nothing can overcome their devotion."

Her quiet, thoughtful declaration staggered Gabriel, as if his world had suddenly tilted. "You may not be a classical scholar, but I would say you are a perceptive philosopher when it comes to matters of the heart."

He wanted to take her in his arms again, as he had in

Thalia's grove. But this time he would kiss her with as much tenderness as desire.

Perhaps sensing his intent, Moira replied it with a subtle, regretful shake of her head. "I could happily spend hours here — days, even. But we promised Mr. Fitzwalter we would not linger."

"So we did, dash it all." Gabriel strove to disguise his wistfulness with banter. "Let us go then, for every moment I spend here makes it harder to leave."

When he took a halting step, Moira followed, though it felt to Gabriel as if they were walking through a swamp of deep, sucking mud rather than over smooth stone tiles.

Crossing the bridge, they finally seemed to break free from the bewitchment had sought to keep them on the island. They hurried up the path to the fountain, anxious to make up for the time they had lost, though Gabriel did not begrudge a moment of it.

He and Moira had not gone far before they met her father and Rory coming back down. Mr. Brennan's face looked very flushed as he fanned it with his wide-brimmed hat.

Letting go of Gabriel's arm, Moira dashed toward her father. "Papa, what is the matter? Are you unwell?"

Gabriel heard a harsh note of self-reproach in her voice. Would she reproach him, too, for neglecting her father?

"Only a little winded," Mr. Brennan insisted, "and over-heated. I fear I am not yet in condition to climb such steep ground on a hot day."

"Then we must get you home at once." As Moira took his arm, she cast a fleeting glance toward the fountain and the tower beyond it.

"Do not leave before you have seen the rest of the park, Miss Brennan." Rory addressed his words to Moira but his gaze was directed at Gabriel. "Your father and I have agreed that I will escort him home. I am certain the Warwicks or the Turners would be only too happy to offer you a drive back afterwards."

"It is a kind offer," Moira replied, "but I could not impose upon you, Mr. Fitzwalter. Besides, it is still quite a distance back to the carriages."

"All of it downhill." Her father detached his arm with gentle insistence. "And we will take our time. Now go along with Lord Gabriel and catch up with the rest of the party. I refuse to spoil your tour of Farleigh Park."

Moira glanced from her father to Gabriel. It was clear she felt torn between duty and inclination.

Rory sought to tip the scales in Gabriel's favour. "I promise you it would be no imposition, Miss Brennan. Your father is very good company and I have had my fill of classical follies for one day. I do not believe you can truthfully make that claim, can you?"

Gabriel had never felt deeper in Rory's debt. He regretted his earlier harsh thoughts about his friend.

"I suppose not," Moira confessed with obvious reluctance. "But —"

"That settles it then," Rory dismissed any further objections with a breezy wave. "Now I suggest you not waste any more time if you hope to catch up with the others and see the rest of the park while the weather holds."

Mr. Brennan gave a decisive nod. "Off you go."

He and Rory headed off while Moira stared after them.

"What would you like to do?" Gabriel asked her.

"I cannot decide." Moira's gaze swept over the captivating panorama around them then returned to the retreating figures of her father and Rory. "I want to stay and see the rest of the park ... with you, but I also want to go home with Papa. Since I cannot do both at once, I feel as if I am frozen in place."

Gabriel gave a sympathetic nod. "I am well-acquainted with that sensation. After we parted, I found myself torn between my desire to see you again and the urge to get as far away from you as possible. I shall always regret allowing myself to be ruled by fear rather than ..." A remnant of that fear made the word stick in his throat. "Love."

Though the word emerged scarcely louder than a whisper, it had the power to break Moira's deadlock.

"I am far too well-acquainted with regret. It is a tiresome companion." She held out her hand to him. "If we hurry, perhaps we can outrun it."

She spoke as if that emotion was an unwelcome third party intruding on their time together, like Mrs. Trimble ... or Mr. Clarkson.

"I am in favour of that." Gabriel clasped her hand and set off up the path toward the fountain, running as fast as he could while still allowing Moira to keep pace.

Something about their headlong scramble sparked a child-like sense of freedom and adventure. He let out a whoop of glee which prompted a merry shriek from Moira, followed by a trill of breathless laughter. Gabriel's heart leapt as he sensed they had left regret plodding so far behind them it might never catch up.

They were both gasping for air by the time they reached the fountain.

"We must not tarry," Gabriel panted, "if we hope to overtake the others."

"I know." Moira wilted onto the grass, still chuckling. "Only long enough to catch our breath."

Gabriel sank down beside her. "And cool off a little."

He released her hand long enough to pull a handkerchief from one of the pockets and wet it in the fountain. His forehead cried out for an application of cool water, but seeing Moira's flushed cheeks he offered it to her first.

"Thank you." She pressed the damp linen to her face, then to her neck and lower.

A fresh wave of heat broke over Gabriel that had nothing to do with their recent exertions or the sultry summer air. How he longed to follow the path of his handkerchief with his lips!

Moira glanced up and must have seen the desire that flickered in his eyes. Quickly she looked away as if searching for some distraction.

She gestured toward the statue. "Who have we here?"

On the top tier of the fountain perched another marble Muse. This one held a pair of long slender pipes.

Gabriel strove to master his wayward yearning. "I believe this must be Euterpe, the Muse of music."

Moira nodded. "This is a fitting home for her. The splashing water makes a kind of melody."

"So it does." Gabriel agreed. "And not just *any* melody. I reckon it is enchanted music."

"Enchanted? In what way?"

"Like the tune played by the Pied Piper," Gabriel suggested. "Only, instead of luring listeners to follow, it holds them captive."

"Nonsense!" Moira gave a chuckle more bewitching than any music. "You are being fanciful."

"Am I? Then tell me, do you not feel compelled to linger when you know we should go?" he asked, not entirely in jest.

"Perhaps." Moira plunged his handkerchief into the fountain then held it out to him. "Though I do not believe it is on account of enchanted music. Our legs are weak and we are out of breath from running, nothing more."

"*Nothing* more?" Gabriel's question came out in a husky tone.

The roses in Moira's cheeks intensified from innocent pink to fiery scarlet. "You know what I mean."

She swatted at his hand with the wet handkerchief, but he was too quick for her. His fingers encircled her delicate wrist and drew it toward him. When he pressed his lips to the tender flesh below the heel of her hand, Gabriel could feel the rapid flutter of her pulse keeping time with his.

Encouraged when Moira made no effort to pull away, he looked up at her. "I believe we understand one another very well indeed."

Did Gabriel understand how very much she wanted him at that moment? Moira wondered. There was not enough water in Euterpe's fountain, or indeed the whole lake, to quench the ardor he roused in her.

Experience warned her that such flames could quickly blaze out of control, consuming everything in their path and leaving nothing but a trail of bitter ashes.

"Then you must know as well as I that we cannot stay here." Her words emerged in a strangled squeak as if an invisible hand had caught her by the throat. "We must catch up with the others or we will have no way home."

Gabriel replied with a sigh that seemed to expel every particle of air from his body. It spoke more eloquently than words of his reluctance to leave this place, which felt so removed from the rest of the world.

Beyond the gates of Farleigh Park lay all the complications of life — regrets from the past, fears for the future. Here, the Muses held those at bay allowing every moment to shimmer with the clarity of a single perfect drop of water. Who would want to leave that behind?

"You are right, of course," Gabriel admitted in a wistful murmur.

He struggled to his feet like a puppet resisting the pull on its strings. Then he hoisted Moira to her feet. "Let us press on before I lose my willpower completely."

Hers was sipping from her grasp, though she dared not admit it to Gabriel.

"No running this time," she warned him, pointing with the tip of her parasol toward the steep grassy slope that led to the tower. "Or we may collapse halfway up and roll back down."

"That sounds quite amusing." Gabriel continued to clasp her hand as they started up the hill. "When I was a child, I liked nothing better than a good roll, much to the horror of my nursemaid. Something about it felt so wild and free. I would laugh until I could scarcely breathe."

Moira pictured the scene so vividly she could not help

but chuckle. A warm tide of tenderness rose in her heart for that small boy who had known too little freedom and too little affection. No wonder he'd seized any opportunity to do things that brought him momentary pleasure, no matter the risk of torn clothes or even injury.

"If I had done anything like that, I would have been sent down from school," she mused, shaking her head. "Most of my teachers and some of the other girls would have expected no better from an Irish child. I was always afraid of committing some infraction that might bring disgrace upon my father."

She had never told anyone about the worry that had governed her every word and action for so many years. Not Mrs. Trimble and certainly not her father. But she sensed Gabriel would sympathize. Besides, she wanted to share more of herself with him, not only the appealing façade calculated to make a favorable impression.

He gave her hand a gentle squeeze. "It can be exhausting, always trying to do and be what we believe others expect of us. Meanwhile, the urge to rebel grows stronger and stronger until it takes all our energy to resist."

Something deep inside her resonated to Gabriel's words.

"Perhaps rolling down a hill was my way of letting that rebellion out," he continued, "without doing much harm."

Was it necessary to indulge in a little rebellion now and then, Moira wondered, to keep the pressure from becoming unbearable?

She was so preoccupied with their conversation that she scarcely noticed they were climbing the hill until Gabriel paused at the crest to catch his breath.

He looked toward the tower and beyond it to an ornate bridge over the stream which fed the lake by way of the waterfall. "I'd hoped we might catch up to the others by now. Clearly they are not taking enough time to properly appreciate such an extraordinary place."

"Perhaps we have taken too *much* time," Moira teased him.

"Impossible." One corner of Gabriel's generous mouth

arched and his dark eyes twinkled with merriment. "A whole day would not be too long to spend with each of the Muses in turn. Come. Let us climb to the top of the tower. From there we should be able to see the whole park and discover how far ahead our friends have gotten."

Would that be worth further delay? Moira wondered, though she did not protest. She could not bring herself to hurry away from this enchanting place, nor from Gabriel's enchanting company.

As she stepped under the columned rotunda that surrounded the lower floor of the tower, Moira felt a drop of moisture on her neck. Could it be spray from the nearby waterfall borne on the increasingly strong breeze?

Gabriel held open the door and ushered her inside. Despite the many narrow windows that ringed the tall room, it took a few moments for Moira's eyes to grow accustomed to the shadowy interior. When they did, she could make out a long spiral staircase that wrapped around the interior wall.

As she headed toward the base of the steps, Gabriel motioned toward the pale statue in the center of the room. "Just as I predicted, this is the tower of Urania."

Moira might not have known the Muse's name, but one glance at the globe she held in her hand proclaimed the branch of science she inspired. Urania's chin tilted upward, her gaze directed toward the heavens.

They had climbed halfway to the second story of the tower when Gabriel paused and pointed back toward the lower floor. "I never noticed until now. It required a little distance to properly appreciate."

Looking down, Moira could now see the intricate mosaic that covered the floor around the sculpture of Urania. It depicted the night sky with various familiar constellations iridescent against a blue-black background.

"Magnificent," Gabriel pronounced in a reverent murmur. "I would not have wanted to miss this for the world."

Though she knew they should keep going, Moira lingered

there, staring down that the mosaic of the heavens, lost the beguiling illusion that she and Gabriel were all alone in the universe.

Then suddenly the dim interior of the tower lit up in a swift, blinding flash. A deafening crack of thunder followed, so loud it seemed to shake the sturdy stone building to its foundations.

A wave of panic sent Moira dashing up the steps, though reason told her she would find no refuge there.

Bursting through a door at the top of the stairs, she found herself on a balcony that ringed the second floor of the tower. Heavy drops of rain struck her as if they were being hurled down by the angry clouds.

But even the storm could not entirely distract from breathtaking view spread before her. A stream flowed past the tower, cascading over a ledge of rocks into the lake below. On the left-hand shore of the lake, Moira saw all the spots they had visited on their way here — the temple of Clio, Thalia's grove, Erato's island and Euterpe's fountain. On the other side, still awaiting them, was a statue overlooking the waterfall and a set of large flat stones that led into some manner of cavern. Beyond that lay another temple and a sunken garden.

But she saw something else too. Tiny in the distance, a group of people were running toward a stone bridge that spanned the stream at the other end of the lake. Moira knew it must be the rest of their party, moving in pairs, the ladies with their parasols open in a futile effort to protect themselves from the rain.

She glimpsed all that in an instant, then let out a startled shriek when a firm hand gripped tugged her back inside the tower.

"Come in at once!" Gabriel cried. "It is not safe to be up so high in this kind of storm!"

Another flash of lightning stressed the truth of his warning. The booming clap of thunder that followed sounded as if the heavens had broken apart.

Never before had Moira experienced a thunderstorm so near and so violent. A scream stuck in her throat for lack of breath while her heart pounded in a vain effort to drown out the thunder.

She threw her arms around Gabriel's neck and clung to him. Her whole body quaked with terror and her knees threatened to buckle.

"There, there. You're safe now." He held her in a firm yet tender embrace that offered her a haven from the storm and any other trouble that might ever threaten her. "I'm sorry I frightened you."

"Not you, the thunder!" Moira managed to gasp, cleaving to him with every ounce of strength she possessed. "I have never heard it so loud."

"It makes quite a racket." Gabriel spoke in a soothing tone as he began a gentle, rhythmic sway. "But it poses no danger, unlike the lightning."

One of his hands began to move over her back in a soothing circular caress. Just as Moira's breathing grew easier and her tense muscles began to relax, another flash of lightning and roll of thunder made her cling tighter than ever to Gabriel.

"It will be alright, I promise you," he crooned. "Your father said there was a storm brewing. I know it may sound even louder up here, but we were fortunate not to be caught out in it. Our friends may not be so lucky."

"I ... saw them," Moira replied with some difficulty, "just before you pulled me ... back inside. They were making ... a run for the bridge."

"The bridge? I never imagined they would be so far ahead of us. Surely they will have reached the carriages by now."

"How will *we* get home?" Moira cried. "When they see Papa's carriage is not there, they will think we have all gone back."

"Quite likely." Gabriel did not sound much troubled by the prospect. "But when they reach Beckwith Abbey, Rory will tell them what happened and they will send someone to get us. In the meantime, we can wait out the storm here and be none the worse for our little adventure."

The storm! Moira tensed again, anticipating the next clap of thunder. Instead she heard the softer drumming of rain on the balcony outside. The sound reminded her of her damp sleeves and bodice. She shivered.

Gabriel responded at once. "You are wet and cold, poor creature."

He released Moira just long enough to remove his coat and wrap it around her. She tried to protest, but he would not hear of it. Besides, the garment, still warm from his body, enveloped her like a soothing embrace. She inhaled his scent in a way she had not done since that distant winter night when she'd stolen into his bed.

Her slowing pulse began to race again and her knees once more grew weak. This time her reaction had nothing to do with fear of the storm.

Chapter Fourteen

USUALLY WHEN A storm broke with such violence after a long hot spell, it brought in cooler air. If that was the case this time, Gabriel could not tell.

Wrapping Moira in his coat was not as chivalrous a gesture as she might believe. He had selfish motives as well. He'd hoped that shedding a layer of clothing might cool the fever that swept through him like wildfire. But it did not abate.

He had been a fool to suppose it might.

This fire had been building for some time. The first spark had been struck innocently enough when Moira first took his arm to explore Farleigh Park. Their flirtatious conversation had fanned the glowing embers until they'd blazed into that kiss in Thalia's grove. Rory's summons had acted like a dash of cold water, but it had not extinguished the flames. After Rory and Mr. Brennan had headed back to Ardmore, only the urgent need to overtake the rest of the party had kept Gabriel's ardor in check.

Holding Moira so close for the past several minutes had ignited an inferno he was powerless to control, let alone extinguish.

Gabriel's pulse roared in his ears, rivalling the heavy rain and rumbles of thunder outside. In his rush up the stairs after Moira and his effort to soothe her fright, he had scarcely noticed their surroundings. Now his rapid scan of the room revealed a steep spiral staircase in the center, no doubt leading to an observatory above. A series of tall, narrow windows lined the rounded walls of the tower. Unlike the chamber below and the other shrines they'd visited, this room was furnished, though sparsely, with a pair of broad upholstered benches.

When he felt Moira collapse against him, Gabriel drew her toward one of the benches. "We may be here for a while. Might as well make ourselves more comfortable."

She sank down with soft sigh that sounded grateful. Gabriel followed, not certain how much longer his legs could hold him.

Another flash of lightning lit up the tower, making Moira gasp and seek the comfort of his embrace again.

"Shhh," he whispered, his lips grazing her brow. "The worst of the storm is moving away. Hear how the thunder is delayed."

A muted rumble followed, confirming his reassurance.

"Thank goodness," she breathed, lifting her face until her lips found his.

If a bolt of lightning had struck him just then, Gabriel doubted it could have electrified him with such raw, feral power. He seized the kiss she offered without restraint and Moira responded with answering passion. The fearful damsel of a moment ago had transformed into a potent goddess, one who welcomed worship and carnal tribute. There could be no doubt she wanted him as much as he wanted her.

That assurance unleashed the fervid desire Gabriel had struggled for so long to suppress. It had been an exhausting effort, he realized now as he imbibed the exquisite nectar of her kisses, and it had been going on far longer than he'd realized. After they parted he had used his hurt and anger as shackles to restrain his fierce yearning for her. Otherwise it would have tormented him beyond bearing.

Now those bitter feelings gave up the fight they could never hope to win. The result was an intoxicating sense of liberty!

As profoundly sweet as Moira's kisses tasted, they were not enough to satisfy his yearning. With awkward eagerness, he fumbled the ribbon of her bonnet until it fell away, exposing her silken curls to his caress. The ripple of those lustrous locks through his fingers was even more delightful than he remembered.

With a soft gurgle of enjoyment, Moira reached up, tipped off his hat and plunged her fingers into *his* hair. Gabriel responded with a deep, quivering sigh.

His breathing gathered speed again when her hand trailed down his cheek and began to tug at his neck linen. The cloth suddenly felt far too tight around his throat. In fact, all his clothes seemed to shrink, constricting his body unbearably!

To his relief, Moira proved far more adept at untying his cravat than he had been when struggling to remove her bonnet. The stifling bands of linen yielded to the deft persuasion of her fingers, falling open to let him breathe with greater ease. Yet when those same delicate fingers fluttered over his bare neck in a provocative caress, he inhaled sharply. For a dizzying instant he could not recall how to release his breath again.

That was only one of many things he could not remember. His mind refused to entertain any thought that was not of *her* or *them*. Space contracted to this one room and even smaller, until no place had any reality for him beyond reach of her body. The flow of time grew languid. A soft impenetrable cloud enveloped the past while the future was impossible to imagine and therefore of no consequence. Nothing mattered beyond this moment. The feelings set free from his heart found expression in tender caresses, murmured endearments and rapturous kisses.

Every instant of contact between them produced sensations of overwhelming pleasure that were more than physical. They seemed to soothe all the injuries his heart had suffered over the years. They nourished a deep hunger in his soul. Yet for every longing satisfied by the feel of her skin against his, an even more urgent desire ignited.

He did not want to caress her here or there, but everywhere at once. He wanted to wrap himself around her, at the same time losing himself in the loving warmth of her embrace.

He knew with wondrous certainty that Moira felt the same. The way she clung to him, molding the contours of her form to his, assured him of it.

Clothing presented a series of impediments to the fulfillment of their desire. But he and Moira were only too eager to remove those obstacles as each presented itself. Every conquest bared new parts of their bodies to be explored until not even the flimsiest barrier remained between them. The delight of pressing against her like that was almost more than Gabriel could bear, yet he longed to commune with her in a way that was even more intimate.

When she welcomed him closer still, he could not have resisted her alluring invitation for anything in the world!

———•◆•———

Moira heaved a deep sigh of satisfaction as she and Gabriel joined together in the most intimate manner possible.

She was scarcely aware of their precarious perch on a bench that had never been designed for such use. If the storm had returned with even greater fury, she could have ignored the blazing lightning and deafening thunder from the impregnable shelter of Gabriel's embrace.

Intense as her desire for him had grown, she'd never intended for matters to go this far. But once she lowered her guard enough to permit his kisses and his touch, she found it impossible to stop short of complete surrender. It was not a matter of giving her lover *his* way, but also of allowing herself to take what she wanted so urgently.

During the months of fear, worry and grief after their parting, she'd often thought back to that fateful night she had shared his bed. She'd been aflame with innocent yearning and too tipsy to give any thought to the consequences of her carnal adventure. Motivated by infatuation, curiosity and reckless ignorance, she had offered Gabriel her body and heart.

The giddy haze of intoxication that led her into his bed

had made the events of that night feel somehow unreal. Apart from a hazy impression of great pleasure, she had not been able to recall their Twelfth Night tryst in much detail. Though she could not admit it to herself until now, she'd regretted that lapse at least as much as the shocking impropriety of her behavior.

She would not make the same mistake this time. She roused all her senses to savor her communion with Gabriel to its fullest. Her admiring gaze drank in the lean, masculine perfection of his naked body, superior to the finest sculptures she had ever viewed. The velvet rasp of his breath and his low sultry moans of pleasure fell on her ears like the most stirring music. Greedily she inhaled his scent and imbibed his kisses, both with a vintage entirely unique to him.

Her entire body was alive to his touch, aching with hunger in its absence, quivering with delight when he dusted a string of feathery kisses down her arm from shoulder to fingertips. Profound contentment enveloped her when his weight came to rest upon her, his warm, smooth skin pressing and rubbing against hers. Gabriel's lovemaking was a feast for her senses, which had been starved for him. A gurgle of appreciation and enjoyment rolled in her throat, the only voice she could give to emotions that ran too deep for words.

Her passion for him found expression in touch and movement. How many ways could her lips respond to his? From grazes softer than a whisper to deep, hungry kisses that went on and on. She clasped him to her, moving by ancient instinct in a quest for something she could not imagine. That quest took on greater and greater urgency until it seemed to become a race. They did not compete *against* one another, with one seeking to win at the other's expense. Instead, she sensed this was a mutual pursuit and neither would taste the full sweetness of victory unless the other did as well.

Sensations of pleasure intensified, growing more powerful, pulsing faster until they overwhelmed her, cascading through her body in a torrent of unbearable delight. Only after she had drained the cup of rapture to its depths did Gabriel partake of his. He gasped for breath and cried out her name, shuddering as pleasure surged through him.

His release sent answering ripples of delight through Moira. Her heart ached to contain the deluge of tender emotions that gushed from an untapped spring. It cleansed her of all the hurt, bitterness and shame that had tormented her for far too long, poisoning her hope for the future.

Now she had something better than hope. As she clasped Gabriel in her arms and ran her fingers through his hair, she savoured the joyous certainty that all would be well for them.

———◆———

He could tell her now, without the slightest fear of Moira's reaction to the truth about his parentage.

They lay tangled in each other's arms, the king and queen of a secluded realm of enchanted beauty. Perhaps one day, with hard work and good fortune he might amass enough capital to purchase Farleigh Park and present it as a fitting tribute to his beloved. Basking in warm ripples of bliss, his imagination spun a hundred lofty fancies, each grander than the last, but none that would be too fine for Moira.

But gradually the real world began to encroach upon their idyllic tryst.

"It sounds as if the rain has stopped." Gabriel pressed a soft kiss to Moira's brow, silently begging her pardon for breaking the spell.

"So it does." She gave a wistful sigh, which he understood fully. "We had better make ourselves presentable before anyone comes looking for us."

"I suppose we must," Gabriel agreed reluctantly. "Though I would not be sorry if our friends forgot us here for several days at least."

Fighting a powerful urge to linger in her arms, he sat up and began to gather his hastily discarded garments.

"Several days?" Moira chuckled as she began to dress. "You would be so hungry by then, you might sell me to a baker for a loaf of bread."

"Never!" he protested with outrage that was not entirely feigned. "I would bargain for half a dozen pork pies at least, which I would share with you."

"I suppose that would be alright." Moira cast him a sidelong glance with twinkling eyes and a pert little smile that made him want to make love to her all over again. "Provided the baker was very handsome and charming ... and well-informed about the classical world."

"That might be rather a lot to ask, don't you think?" Having buttoned his breeches, Gabriel sank onto to bench beside Moira and kissed her again, though he knew it risked a renewal of greater intimacies. "Besides, I haven't seen any sign of a baker or butcher at Farleigh Park. We could always try our hand at fishing from the lake or foraging for mushrooms. I might even be able to snare us a rabbit if the occasion demanded."

Their affectionate banter eased what might have been an awkward postscript to their passionate encounter. So Gabriel kept it up as they departed Urania's temple and followed the wet path to cross another ornate stone bridge that straddled the stream. Fed by the recent deluge, the placid waterway had swollen to a furious torrent.

As they peeped over the bridge's parapet, Gabriel spotted an oak leaf that must have blown down from a nearby tree. Caught by the current, it raced toward the falls, no more able to resist than he and Moira had been able to resist the force of their desire for one another.

Across the bridge, the path led them near the top of the waterfall, overlooked by the statue of yet another Muse.

"Terpsichory," Gabriel raised his voice to carry over the rumble of the rushing water, "the Muse of dance."

Moira might well have guessed that for herself, by the way the Muse's flowing skirts were gathered up to reveal a pair of dainty bare feet poised in mid-step. Her flowing garments and hair had been skillfully sculpted to suggest movement.

"Very fitting, once again." Moira nodded toward the falls. "See how the water bounces from one outcropping of stone to another on its way down. It is like dance, though rather a hectic one at the moment."

They descended the steep ground on this side of the falls by a series of large flat stones that created a natural staircase.

"What is this, I wonder?" asked Moira as the steps led down below the level of the ground. "A tunnel of some kind?"

"I believe it is a grotto," said Gabriel as they entered a rustic chamber, the walls, floor and ceiling of which were studded with seashells.

He pointed to an alcove in the rear wall of the chamber that housed another statue. This one's upper face was covered with a gauzy veil that looked as if a breeze might waft it back at any moment to reveal her face in sharper detail. "If I am not mistaken, this must be Polyhymnia, the Muse of sacred poetry."

As Moira surveyed the intricate patterns of seashells, her eyes widened. Her delicate lips parted in a look of wonder that Gabriel wished he had the skill to capture and preserve for all time. "There *is* something sacred and unearthly about such beauty."

He raised her hand to his lips in a gesture of homage as his gaze drank in every detail of her features. "I quite agree."

"I *meant* the beauty of this grotto."

She nodded toward something behind him. Gabriel glanced back to discover an opening in the wall that faced the lake, just above the level of the water. It created a rough-hewn window that lit the shadowy grotto and framed an exquisite vista of the opposite shore. The island and its temple were mirrored in the glassy surface of the lake. It was a sight capable of making the heart ache with admiration.

"That is very fine," Gabriel allowed with a soft chuckle. "Though none of the wonders I have seen today stirred my senses as powerfully as the sight of you."

"I find that hard to believe." The dimness of the grotto concealed a blush that Gabriel sensed had risen to warm her cheeks. "Except that I could say the same about you."

There was bashful quality to her confession that touched Gabriel's heart, even as that organ seemed to swell in his chest. How could it contain the surge of joy and tenderness as now flooded it, like the thirsty stream after a deluge of life-giving rain? Clearly the secret was not to dam such feelings up, but let them flow.

It was all he could do to keep from dropping to his knees then and there, to beg one last time for her hand in marriage.

What held him back? There could be no more ideal spot for a romantic proposal than the exquisite seclusion of a Muse's grotto. Surely he could have no doubt of Moira's answer after she had given herself to him with every sign of passionate desire.

Even as he yearned to secure her at last, a countering force restrained him. He did not want Moira to pledge herself to him because she'd been enchanted by the magic of this place or the potent current of desire that had swept her into his arms. Nor could he bear to have any more secrets between them. When she agreed to marry him, Gabriel wanted her decision to be informed by cool, constant reason as well as warm regard and searing desire.

This was not the proper time to look toward the future by asking for her hand nor to revisit the past with revelations of difficult secrets. This was a moment to be savoured here and now, like a cup brimming with delight.

The best way of doing that was to take Moira in his arms and let his lips acquaint her with his feelings, not by the words they spoke, but by the way they lingered upon hers. The kisses they bestowed and received in the quiet depths of the grotto were different than the urgent, consuming ones they'd shared in the tower. Fitting to the Muse who ruled this realm, their kisses conveyed the blessings of kindness, patience and faithful devotion each offered the other and hoped to find in return.

How long they lingered in tender communion, Gabriel could scarcely tell. But at length, by unspoken consent, their embrace melted into a twining of arms and hands and they drifted on, emerging from the grotto to follow the path to another temple and from there to a sunken garden.

It was there they heard Rory Fitzwalter calling their names. In unison they heaved a soft sigh and reluctantly unclasped hands.

"Over here!" Gabriel called out to his friend, striving to keep his tone from betraying a lack of gratitude to Rory for coming to fetch them.

As they emerged from the sunken garden, careful to keep a decorous distance between them, Gabriel felt as if he was wading in deep water against a strong current. Every step demanded far greater effort than it should have. He wondered if Moira felt the same.

They crossed the other bridge that spanned the lake's outgoing stream. On the other side, Rory awaited them. He sported a grin of devilish amusement that Gabriel resented on Moira's behalf.

"I feared I might find you half-drowned from the recent deluge," he greeted them with hearty glee, "but you appear to have weathered it better than the rest of our party. I take it you found shelter to wait out the storm?"

From the impudent twinkle in his friend's eye, Gabriel sensed that Rory knew exactly how they had spent the time.

———◆———

She must not blush! That would only confirm what Rory Fitzwalter obviously suspected. But Moira could no more keep the guilty colour from flaring in her cheeks than she could have held back the raging water that poured over the falls.

Fortunately Gabriel answered, drawing his friend's attention away from her. "We had the good fortune to be in the tower when the rain started. We could see the others rushing to reach the carriages, so we knew there was no hope of overtaking them. We decided the safest course was to take shelter there until the storm passed."

His tone was perfectly matter-of-fact, with an edge of severity that seemed to suggest his friend curb his mischievous inquiries.

"How very prudent of you." A suppressed chuckle seemed to bubble beneath Rory Fitzwalter's approving words. "The others did not fare nearly so well. Jack and Annabelle looked quite bedraggled when they called at Ardmore to collect me."

To Moira's relief, he said no more on the subject but led them toward the spot where they had parked the carriages earlier that day. Could it have been only a few hours ago? It felt so much longer.

"How did they know to find you at Ardmore?" Gabriel asked.

Rory let out the chuckle Moira suspected him of suppressing earlier. "Even in their mad scramble to reach the carriages, our friends noticed that Mr. Brennan's had already gone. They assumed that all four of us had been sensible enough to turn back when the storm first threatened. To their credit, they were half right."

"My father!" Moira cried. How could she have forgotten him in her selfish indulgence? "Was he well after you returned to Ardmore?"

"Well enough, once we were no longer trudging uphill in the heat. I certainly felt a good deal improved. The worst thing that ailed your father was his concern for you and Lord Gabriel. Once he sees that you have taken no harm from your *little adventure*, I expect he will be in fine fettle."

Would he, though? Guilt nagged at Moira as she quickened her pace. The sooner they returned to Ardmore, the sooner her father's anxiety would be put to rest and she could judge if the day's exertions had done him any harm.

Their excursion to Farleigh Park had been an escape from

all the responsibilities and complexities of her life. It had felt as if she'd been conveyed out of the modern world entirely, to classical times when people believed in the power of Muses and the dictates of Fate. She had lost herself in the enchantment of the place and Gabriel's company, the way she had once become immersed in the pages of a book where there could be no doubt of a happy ending.

Rory's arrival had reminded her there was a very different world awaiting them beyond the gates of Farleigh — one where actions had consequences and joyful outcomes were not certain by any means.

On the drive back to Ardmore, Gabriel and his friend kept up steady banter. Though Moira found it impossible to concentrate on what they were saying, she welcomed it all the same. It spared her the obligation to join in and pretend all was well.

Every rotation of the carriage wheels drew them closer to home, where her father might be suffering the ill effects of an outing she should never have let him undertake. Meanwhile her little daughter's attachment to Betsy Aubin was growing stronger by the day. Finally there was Mr. Clarkson, determined to have her as his wife regardless of her wishes, threatening to expose the secrets she'd guarded so desperately and endanger everything she held most dear.

Her pulse gathered speed as if desperate to catch up with the time that had slowed so perilously during her excursion to Farleigh. She'd wasted precious hours trying to hide from her fears, like a child hiding her face in her hands in the foolish belief that if *she* could not see approaching danger, *it* could not see her. In truth, it made her more vulnerable, not less.

Lord Gabriel seemed heedless to her growing distress, chatting with his friend about trivialities while her whole world wobbled like an egg on the edge of a tall table. Could he behave in such a carefree manner if their tryst in the tower had meant half as much to him as it had to her?

Perhaps it had not. The possibility made Moira positively bilious.

Had she made a fool of herself once again, succumbing to Lord Gabriel Stanford's boyish charm? With far too little effort, she had persuaded herself that he'd come to Surrey and tried to win her heart once again because he truly cared for her. But what if it had only been a challenge the bored aristocrat could not resist? Was it possible he'd contrived this whole romantic excursion with the help of his friends to get her alone and seduce her?

He could not have summoned that summer storm at just the right moment, a faint whisper of reason protested, but it was drowned out by a thunderous chorus of suspicion. *Gabriel Stanford had seduced her and abandoned her once before!* it howled.

They'd discussed what had taken place between them at Lady Killoran's house party and Moira thought it had been resolved. But clearly the ordeal had left some injuries that were slower to heal. Now it felt as if those wounds had reopened.

Rory smothered a yawn. "Between the exertions and alarms of the day, I shall sleep soundly tonight. Not to mention the relief from that deuced heat. The past few nights I felt like I was drowning in a Turkish bath."

With no more ado, he leaned back in his seat and tipped the brim of his hat down over his eyes. If he meant to take a nap, he would not enjoy a long one. Moira glimpsed enough landmarks from the carriage window to know they were nearing Ardmore.

Now that he no longer had Rory's conversation to divert him, Gabriel seemed to recall Moira's presence. He caught her gaze and flashed a captivating smile that might have set the marble hearts of the Farleigh Muses aflutter. Moira could not keep her lips from mirroring his expression, even as she wondered how many other women had been disarmed by it.

He looked as if he wanted to say something but could not bring himself to speak while his friend might overhear. Moira was reminded of the day they'd driven from London and confronted one another in harsh whispers while her father and

Mrs. Trimble slept. Her feelings had undergone such a reversal since then, it felt as if that day belonged to the distant past. Yet she knew it was no more than the length of the holiday party where they'd met. How could she trust emotions that had sprung up in such a short time?

When the carriage reached Ardmore, she did not wait for Gabriel to assist her. Instead she pushed the door open, scrambled out and dashed into the house calling for her father.

He emerged from his study, his arms open to her. Mrs. Trimble followed, her motherly features clenched in a disapproving scowl.

"Dear heart!" cried her father as Moira cast herself into his embrace. "I am happy to have you home safe and sound, though I trusted Lord Gabriel would see you came to no harm."

Mrs. Trimble muttered something under her breath. It was clear she did not share Mr. Brennan's confidence.

"What about *you*, Papa?" Moira pulled back for a better look at him. "I hope today's excursion has not done you any harm."

His face still seemed flushed and his features drawn.

"Not in the least," he protested, though his voice sounded hollow and his breathing too fast. "I shall improve further now that the infernal heat has broken."

"I tried to persuade him to lie down," Mrs. Trimble complained, "but he would not hear of it until you were safely home."

"Well, I am back now," Moira took her father's arm, "and perfectly safe, as you can see. That should put your mind at ease."

He nodded.

"Then you must ease mine by having a good rest while I summon a physician to examine you."

Her father had not built a successful business without learning how to bargain. "I will lie down if you promise not to send for a doctor right away. Wait until after I have rested. If you do not find me improved, then I will submit to being examined."

"Very well." Moira edged toward the nearest staircase, drawing him with her.

During their exchange, Gabriel and his friend had hung back, uncharacteristically subdued.

Now, as Moira led her father past them toward the staircase, Mr. Brennan raised his free hand to the gentleman. "Thank you for all your help today, Mr. Fitzwalter, both in seeing me home and going back to fetch Lord Gabriel and my daughter."

Rory acknowledged the thanks with a genial bow. "I am happy to have been of service, sir. I hope a rest will see you entirely restored."

"I'm certain it will," her father replied, though he sounded winded. "As for you, Lord Gabriel, I am in your debt for looking after my daughter."

Gabriel flushed a guilty scarlet and lowered his head as if under a stern rebuke.

"It was m-my pleasure," he stammered, then lost his composure entirely. "That is … I meant to say … I was happy to be of service … er … to help."

Moira's father gave no sign that he found anything suspicious in the gentleman's awkward response. But perhaps he was not paying attention. He leaned more heavily on Moira with every step. When they reached the staircase, he gripped the bannister with his other hand.

Had this one day cost him all the progress he'd made since his illness? The twinges of guilt that had begun to plague Moira intensified.

"If you will excuse us, gentlemen," she murmured, unable to bring herself to look at Gabriel.

"Of course," Rory answered for both of them in a carefree tone that irritated Moira. "I should get back to Beckwith Abbey and let the others know that all is well that has ended well."

Had this day ended well? Moira might have begged to differ, but she did not want to upset her father or permit any delay in getting him to bed.

Step by laborious step, she helped him up the stairs while Mrs. Trimble followed close on their heels. When they reached the top and Mr. Brennan no longer had the bannister for support, she insisted on taking his other arm.

He hardly protested at all, which fuelled Moira's worry.

Fortunately it was not many steps from the head of the stairs to his bedchamber.

"Mr. Clarkson called while you were out," Mrs. Trimble announced as she and Moira settled her father in bed. "He was disappointed to find you gone, but asked me to tell you he would return in the morning."

The news sent Moira's already rapid pulse into a frantic gallop. Disaster of her own making was bearing down on her and she had nowhere to run.

Chapter Fifteen

Dɪᴅ Moɪʀᴀ ʀᴇɢʀᴇᴛ giving in to their desire for one another? Gabriel feared so as he waited to see if she would dine with him that evening.

She had been ominously quiet on the drive home from Farleigh. Meanwhile he had done his best to fill the uneasy silence and distract Rory from inquiring further about their time alone at the park. Did Moira feel responsible for her father becoming unwell ... or did she perhaps blame him?

More than anything, Gabriel did not want a repeat of what had happened at Beckwith Abbey after their previous tryst. Fate had already given him one more chance than he deserved. He did not want to impose on its generosity by bungling this opportunity.

His spirits rose when Moira appeared for dinner, though it grieved him to see her looking so weary and anxious. He asked after her father, to show his concern and offer her a sympathetic ear.

"At least he is resting." She heaved a sigh. "And he does seem more comfortable now that the heat has broken. But you saw for yourself how weak he is. I fear it will be a battle to get him to consult a physician."

"I could speak to him," Gabriel volunteered, "if you think it would do any good. Sometimes people are more receptive to advice from those who are not as close to them."

"Would you?" Moira glanced up from her plate, where she had been pushing pieces of food around with her fork. "I believe Papa might heed you better than he would me or

Mrs. Trimble."

"Of course." Gabriel wished they were seated closer, so he could clasp her hand. "I shall always be happy to do anything I can to assist you."

He tried to infuse his smile with all the sympathy and affection that swelled in his heart. "About this afternoon …"

When he hesitated, trying to decide what he should say, Moira gave a subtle shake of her head. Her gaze flickered to the footman standing still and silent, ready to remove their plates and serve the next course.

Gabriel had grown up surrounded by so many servants, he'd felt more comfortable with them than with members of his family. Often it did not occur to him to hold his tongue in their presence.

Now he responded to Moira's silent warning with a barely-perceptible nod. He lowered his voice to a murmur that would reach no farther than her ears. "We do need to talk."

"Perhaps we could go for a stroll after dinner," she suggested.

Clearly she was prepared to talk, but did not want to risk being overheard.

Gabriel agreed completely. "That sounds like an excellent idea."

They finished their meal mostly in silence. Moira continued to toy with her food, while Gabriel ate as quickly as good manners allowed. He could not wait to clear the air between them and make his feelings for her perfectly clear.

Once the last course had been removed, Moira went to check on her father, while Gabriel paced in the garden, rehearsing what he would say to her. When he found it only made him more anxious, he decided to trust to the moment and took a series of slow, calming breaths.

They were beginning to take effect when Moira appeared, glancing behind her nervously. "I managed to elude Mrs. Trimble. We had better not linger here or we may find ourselves chaperoned with a vengeance!"

Smothering a grin at her choice of words, Gabriel gave an emphatic nod. Quickly he followed her out of the garden to the path that ran parallel to the main road with a hedge-row between.

Once they were out of sight of the house, Moira's steps slowed.

"Is your father any better?" Gabriel asked.

"He was still sleeping when I went to check on him. I hope that is a good sign." She did not sound optimistic.

Gabriel reached for her hand, as he had longed to do all through dinner. "I know how worried you must be, but I hope you do not blame yourself for his condition. Your father insisted on coming today and he is a strong-willed man. He showed good sense in returning home when he began to feel unwell."

Something in Moira's expression told Gabriel she longed for all the reassurance he could provide.

"I should have gone with him," she reproached herself, "instead of . . ."

When her words trailed off, Gabriel finished the sentence for her. "...instead of staying behind to dally with me?"

She hung her head. "I did not give Papa a moment's thought until Mr. Fitzwalter came to fetch us. I was too wrapped up in my own enjoyment."

Gabriel raised his free hand and brushed it down her cheek in a tender caress. When he reached her chin, he nudged it upward until her gaze met his. "I am delighted to hear that you enjoyed our time together. Those hours were some of the happiest of my life."

"And mine." She tightened her grip on his hand. "But it feels wrong to have been so happy while my father was unwell. When he needed me, I was not there!"

"He insisted you stay," Gabriel reminded her. "He wanted you to enjoy yourself."

"Perhaps so, though I doubt in quite *that* way." Her lips twisted into a self-conscious grin, which she swiftly suppressed.

Gabriel could not stifle a chuckle. "I regret with all my heart that your father is unwell, but I cannot regret the feelings we have for each other or the way we acted upon them today. I only hope you do not, nor will ever have cause to!"

When she shook her head, a wave of relief swamped Gabriel. Gathering Moira into his arms, he pressed his cheek to her soft auburn curls. "I have lost count of how many times I've asked you to marry me. I still want that more than anything, but before I propose again there is something I must tell you."

The tension in her stance seemed to melt away. Moira subsided deeper into his embrace. It was all the reassurance Gabriel needed that the secret he was about to reveal would not lessen her feelings for him. "Before I answer, there is something I must tell *you*."

"Of course." He released Moira so he could look her in the eye. "If we mean to spend the rest of our lives together, there must be no more secrets between us. Will you walk with me? It will make it easier for me to say what is on my mind."

"By all means, let us walk this way." Then, more to herself than to Gabriel, she added, "It is only fitting."

What did she mean by that? Gabriel could not be certain, nor did he ask. Could this secluded path have something to do with the secret she intended to reveal? He would find out soon enough and it would come as no surprise. For now, it was more important to unburden himself.

He offered her his arm, as he had done at Farleigh. As they set off, Gabriel inhaled a deep breath and kept his eyes fixed on the path ahead. Somehow it was easier to speak about painful subjects when he did not have to meet Moira's gaze. "You may recall what I told you about my family, how I was treated by my mother and the duke and their loveless marriage."

"Every word," she murmured. "It was not a pleasant conversation. You told me things I did not want to hear. Yet somehow it made me feel closer to you."

Her reply encouraged Gabriel to continue even as a qualm

of fear threatened to silence him. "What I could not tell you then was that I recently discovered what was behind their unhappiness and their behavior toward me."

"I cannot imagine any excuse for parents to treat their child in such an unfeeling manner!" Moira's passionate indignation on behalf of his younger self eased the ache of old wounds.

"I did not say that my discovery *excused* their conduct, but it did provide a reason other than the one I'd always believed."

"Which was ...?"

"That it was somehow my fault." The words caught in Gabriel's throat like sharp little fish bones. "That I had done something wrong. That I was unworthy of their affection."

"That is *not* true!" She gripped his hand so hard that it hurt his fingers, even as it relieved a different kind of pain.

"Thanks to you, I have begun to believe it is not." Gratitude and deep affection warmed Gabriel's tone. "That is why I was reluctant to confess the truth. I know your father favors me as a suitor for you hand because he believes I am the son of a duke."

"But you are." Moira sounded bewildered. "Everyone calls you *Lord* Gabriel. We dined with you at Cheviot House."

"My mother was married to the Duke of Cheviot when I was born." Gabriel's jaw tightened as he spoke. "So I bear the Stanford name, though not a drop of his blood flows in my veins. I am the unfortunate result of my mother's adultery with another man."

"Who?" Moira sounded dazed and breathless, as if she had been ambushed. Her reaction sent a chill through Gabriel.

"I have no idea." The words fell from his lips like chips of flint. "A servant, perhaps. Some unscrupulous scoundrel to whom she owed a gambling debt."

Now that the truth was out, he felt compelled to suggest the worst possibilities.

"Perhaps a man she loved, who loved her," Moira countered in a tone that sounded maddeningly sympathetic to his errant mother, "in a way her husband could not."

"Why didn't she elope with him, then?" Gabriel demanded. "I can understand why she might not have been faithful to an unfeeling man like the duke, but why did she stay with him, especially when she knew she was with child? Why did she deceive me my whole life and force me to grow up in a family where I was not wanted?"

Long-suppressed resentment broke free, determined to vent itself at last.

"Your mother may have had no choice." Moira paused and turned toward him. "Perhaps her lover could not marry her or the duke might have refused to grant her a divorce. What sort of life would you have had then, not to mention your brothers? Your mother might have been cut off from all contact with them. Perhaps she sacrificed her own happiness for the sake of her children."

How could Moira stand there and make excuses for his mother's conduct? Did she not care what he had endured or how he had been deceived?

As if she had not said enough to inflame old wounds, Moira continued, "Perhaps her husband agreed to raise another man's child because he *did* care for her and would do anything to keep her?"

Her plaintive tone seemed to appeal for understanding, perhaps even forgiveness. But Gabriel was not in a forgiving mood.

"You do not understand!" he wrenched his hand from her grasp. "She deceived me in the most vital way. If my very identity is a lie, what *can* I believe? If I cannot trust my own family, who can I trust?"

Gabriel struggled to rein in his outrage, but he might as well have been trying to curb a runaway stallion. Every word Moira had uttered in the Cheviots' defence stabbed him like a deliberate betrayal.

Could she not see that their lies had hurt her as well? "That is why I refused to believe you at first, when you told me you were not Sarah's mother. It is why I was so suspicious of your motives. Deception like that is poisonous!"

That was why he could not ask her to marry him until he'd told her the truth about his parentage. Surely Moira would understand now and stop trying to excuse his mother and the duke.

"*I* do not understand?" Her misty, beseeching gaze turned stormy. "Perhaps it is you who do not understand a woman's straits. A man may follow his desire wherever it leads without the consequences a woman might suffer. *He* does not stand to lose his reputation — quite the contrary. *He* will not be responsible for a child without the means to provide for it."

Her challenge sounded like a direct attack on him and his friends. "Any honorable man would take responsibility for the consequences if his indiscretion compromises as lady!"

"Are you certain of that?" Moira's voice rang with indignation.

Only when a carriage rattled past on the other side of the hedgerow did Gabriel realize how loud their quarrel had grown and how easily someone might overhear them.

"I *am* certain of it!" He lowered his voice to a fierce growl. "If you are not, then we have nothing more to say to one another."

With that Gabriel turned and strode back toward Ardmore. It was some time before he grew calm enough to reflect on what had happened and wonder how his intended proposal had gone so disastrously wrong.

As she watched Gabriel storm away, Maura's knees grew too weak to bear her weight. A choked sob caught in her throat as she wilted to the ground. The grass was still a little damp and muddy from the earlier rain, but she did not care if it ruined her gown. That was the least of her worries at the moment.

She'd been buoyant with relief when Gabriel began to confide in her. Whatever he meant to confess, she was certain it would make no difference to her feelings for him. If that secret had weighed as heavily upon his conscience as hers did, surely he could understand and forgive her. His revelation had the opposite effect to what she'd expected, though not because she cared about his aristocratic connections.

As Gabriel spoke so bitterly of his mother's indiscretion and the desperate steps she'd taken to conceal it, Moira knew that he would never be able to forgive what *she* had done. She'd concealed his daughter from him just as his mother had concealed the secret of his paternity. Both women had compelling reasons for their actions, but clearly Gabriel had no compassion for them.

Perhaps they did not deserve his forgiveness. They had made terrible choices based on fear rather than having the courage to do the right thing. Those choices had harmed the people they cared for most and there seemed no way to make amends.

Burying her face in her hands, Moira wept for the bright hope that had seemed within her grasp, but now lay shattered in a thousand sharp fragments. Her wretched sobs were loud enough to drown out the soft rustle of approaching footsteps.

"My, my. What have we here?" The sound of Mr. Clarkson's voice startled Moira. "A damsel in distress?"

The curate's tone of mocking menace sent a chill through her. Moira scrambled to her feet and backed away from him.

"Please leave me alone." She sniffled. "That is the kindest thing you can do for me just now."

She tried to wipe her tear-stained face dry with her hands, humiliated that anyone should see her like this — him in particular.

Mr. Clarkson gave a heartless chuckle, as if her misery was the most amusing thing he had witnessed in some time. "Did I say I wanted to do you a kindness, you daft chit? You must have misheard me."

"On second thought." He pulled out a handkerchief and thrust it at her. "Take this and wipe your nose for God's sake! I have no intention of going anywhere or letting you out of my sight until we are safely married. After that, you can suit yourself."

His scornful tone struck a dangerous spark to Moira's volatile emotions.

"Then you will be seeing a great deal of me." She hurled the handkerchief back at him. "For I have no intention of *ever* marrying you. You can save your threats to tell Lord Gabriel about the baby. I mean to tell him myself!"

For an instant, Moira could scarcely believe those words had come out of her mouth. Yet when that bold declaration rang in the air, she knew it was true. She'd intended to share her secret with Gabriel when she had reason to hope he might understand and forgive her. Now she could see that was impossible, yet more than ever Moira knew she owed him and their daughter the truth, no matter what it might cost her.

Summoning as much dignity as she could muster, considering her soppy, bedraggled appearance, Moira turned to walk away.

"*Lord* Gabriel, is it?" The curate's taunting words stopped her before she could take a step. "I wonder that you still call him that after what we both just heard. Not Lord Cheviot's son after all, but the spawn of an adulterous affair. Won't the scandal magazines have a fine time with that juicy bit of tattle? Think of the lurid caricatures in every print-seller's window in London."

How could she have been taken in by this horrible man? Moira struggled to keep her legs from giving way beneath her. She'd believed his deepening antagonism sprang from jealousy of her feelings for Gabriel. Now she realized that, in spite of his determination make her his wife, Mr. Clarkson despised her.

"How much do you want," she demanded, even as she quailed inside, "as payment for keeping quiet? I have some money of my own … jewelry …"

His lip curled in a chilling smirk that was almost a leer. "What would I want with a pittance when I can have control of *all your worldly goods*? Not to mention the *worship of your body*?"

He taunted her by twisting sacred wedding vows into a lewd threat.

"You aren't a clergyman at all, are you?" Moira's gorge rose at the thought of this scoundrel touching her.

He pulled a face. "The most tiresome role I've ever had to play. Fortunately you were too gullible to suspect anything. If only you hadn't brought that meddling fool Stanford from London, it wouldn't have come to this. But all's well that ends well. That's Shakespeare, by the way."

The only person Moira loathed more than him at the moment was herself. "How is it you see any of this ending well?"

"The way all good romantic comedies do, of course," Clarkson replied with such an odious air of smugness that Moira wished there was a ripe cow pat on the ground that she could hurl at his head. "With a wedding. Unless you want the world to know about your secret and Stanford's, you will come with me to London. Tomorrow morning we will be married by Special License, which will be worth all the trouble and expense it took me to procure."

Moira longed to defy her tormenter, the way she had only a few days ago. But the scandal he threatened would destroy Gabriel and their daughter's future and possibly be the death of her father. Whatever it cost, she must protect those she loved from the consequences of her folly.

"How will we get to London?" She mounted a pitifully feeble protest. "You don't have a carriage."

"No." He waved her objection away. "But *you* do. And once we are married, my dear heiress, it will be as good as mine."

Gabriel's temper was still blazing by the time he reached Ardmore. He might have left Moira behind, yet in his mind their argument continued to rage, growing ever more hostile. He thought of all the things he could have said to refute her preposterous defense of his mother. No sooner had the words formed in his mind than he imagined Moira firing back an even more provocative reply.

Reason tried to tell him that those derisive taunts were not the sort of things Moira would say. But his anger burned far too hot to be quenched by a small bucket of water. He knew he must get it under control somehow, or he might do something he would bitterly regret.

That flicker of rational thought led him to the stables where he began to saddle a fine roan gelding.

"I can do that for you, sir," one of the stable boys offered.

"Thank you," Gabriel replied in courteous tone quite at odds with the fury smouldering inside him, "but I need the distraction."

"Just as you say, sir." The boy sounded puzzled, as if he did not understand what the gentleman meant.

Gabriel was not certain he did either. He only knew that the calm, sturdy presence of the horse quieted the imagined argument in his thoughts. Concentrating on the mundane routine of placing the saddle on its back and cinching the girth properly helped too. By the time he mounted and rode away, his temper had begun to cool.

The steady beat of the gelding's hooves and the easy rhythm of its gait sapped the rigid tension from his body. The peace of the surrounding green countryside soothed his overwrought emotions.

Gradually he began to reflect, with some detachment, on what Moira had said about his mother and the duke. *Was* it possible his mother had chosen to remain with the duke in order to protect her sons from the scandal and family separation? He tried to imagine himself in Lord Cheviot's place, raising another man's child, one who would always remind him of his wife's betrayal. Would he have acted any more charitably under those circumstances?

Much as he hoped so, Gabriel could not be certain. His conscience reminded him how he'd lashed out at Moira when her actions had opened old wounds.

She'd forgiven him before, the way he had once forgiven his mother after she ignored or rebuffed him. But when the duchess reverted to her old hurtful behavior time and again, it had chipped away at his feelings for her until nothing remained. He must not make the same mistake with Moira.

Reining his mount to a halt, he let it rest and crop a mouthful of tall grass from the roadside. Then he turned the gelding back toward Ardmore.

"Thank you for your help sorting that out." He stroked the horse's neck. "I owe you a bunch of carrots, or perhaps a sack of apples."

The gelding tossed his head and gave a whinny that sounded like laughter. Without any particular urging from Gabriel, it galloped back to Ardmore at a swifter pace.

The young stable boy had kept busy during Gabriel's absence mucking out the gelding's stall, putting down fresh straw and filling the water trough.

Gabriel greeted him with a smile. "I'd be obliged if you could unsaddle this fine fellow and rub him down." He dug a sovereign out of his pocket and tossed it to the lad. "I would do it myself, but I need to speak with Miss Brennan on a rather urgent matter."

He headed away so quickly that he was almost out of earshot when the boy called after him. "You won't find her in the house, sir."

"I won't?" Gabriel rushed back to the gelding's stall. "How do you know?"

"Right after you left," the boy replied as he reached up to remove the horse's bridle, "she came with that priest and said to harness the travelling coach. Then they drove away in it."

Had Moira eloped with Clarkson? It certainly sounded that way. But how could she after what had happened between her and Gabriel only that afternoon?

"How long ago?" He demanded. "Heading which way?"

Had his confession about his scandalous parentage persuaded her that a respectable clergyman would make a better husband after all? Or was it his furious outburst that had pushed her into the arms of another man?

"That way, sir." The boy pointed in the opposite direction from the one Gabriel had taken — the road that led north. "Not more than a quarter hour ago. I heard the priest say something to the coachman about London."

Whatever had made Moira go with Clarkson, it was clear she wanted nothing more to do with Gabriel ... and on reflection, he could not blame her. Dejected, he thanked the stable boy for his information and offered him another coin. Then he trudged back to the house to pack his belongings.

To his surprise, Mrs. Trimble descended upon him in a state of violent agitation. For a change, he did not appear to be the cause of her distress.

"Lord Gabriel, whatever shall we do? Miss Brennan has eloped with Mr. Clarkson!"

"Forgive me." Gabriel did not attempt to hide his surprise at her flustered greeting. "But I thought it was your fondest wish to see them wed."

"Wed, of course," she snapped, "but properly in front of friends and family at the parish church. Not run away to who knows where with her poor father lying ill. I fear the scandal will be the end of him!"

Surely Moira would have seen the danger of that. Gabriel wondered if he had made her too angry to think straight.

"I am bitterly disappointed in Mr. Clarkson!" Moira's companion wailed. "I never expected a man of the cloth would think of eloping. He refused to let me go with them when I asked. He looked very severe — not like himself at all."

Clarkson, severe? That sounded odd as well. Gabriel had often seen the curate annoyed at him, but now that Clarkson was about to get what he wanted, shouldn't he have appeared happy, or at least satisfied?

"Moira ... Miss Brennan ... how did *she* look?"

Mrs. Trimble shook her head. "Not well. She tried to hide it, but I could tell she was troubled. I thought you might have done something to upset her. But when I asked, she said she was not unhappy on her own account, but yours and ... she did not know how she could ever make it up to you. Please, Lord Gabriel, is there anything you can do?"

Moira hadn't been vexed with him after the things he'd said to her? She'd regretted *his* unhappiness and felt responsible in some way? Gabriel's view of the world shifted with a dizzying lurch. He recalled how he and Moira had misjudged each other after their tryst at the Killorans' house party. He must not give up on her again until she clearly told him they had no future together.

He met Mrs. Trimble's pleading gaze and for once did not detect disapproval. *Was* there anything he could do?

"I can try." He sought to assure her and himself. "Please do not say anything about this to Mr. Brennan yet. No need to upset him any sooner than necessary."

Moira's companion nodded emphatically. "Of course, sir. Just as you say."

When he turned and strode back toward the stables, Mrs. Trimble called after him, "God go with you, Lord Gabriel!"

"If he will," Gabriel called back, "I should be grateful for his help."

Whether he deserved Divine assistance, Gabriel had his doubts, but he was not too proud to accept it. There was another source of aid he knew he could always call upon — deserving or not.

"Can I trouble you again?" he asked the now-familiar boy once he reached the stables.

"Another horse, sir?" The lad led out a big bay mare all saddled and ready to ride. "I reckoned when you asked which way Miss Brennan went that you must mean to go after her. Zephyr is a good horse for a long ride."

"Clever lad!" Gabriel lost no time climbing into the saddle.

"I shall thank you as you deserve when I return."

He rode off at as swift a pace as possible that would not exhaust the mare's reputed stamina. He did have one brief stop to make before he focused all his effort on pursuing Moira and the curate.

A short while later he strode into Lady Killoran's drawing room, where the family and guests were enjoying their evening amusements.

"Please excuse the interruption," he begged the countess, "but I have an urgent matter to discuss with my friends."

"What is it, Gabriel?" Jack jumped up from his place at the card table. "We were planning to ride over to Ardmore in the morning with some information."

Desperate to get back on the road, Gabriel scarcely heard a word his friend had said. "Moira eloped with Clarkson less than an hour ago. I fear she may have been coerced!"

"Oh no!" Annabelle cried. "We should have wasted no time getting word to you. I recalled how I know that scoundrel who calls himself Clarkson."

Gabriel's stomach sank.

Before he had a chance to inquire, Annabelle rushed on. "Herbert Stuart-Clark is his real name. He was a school friend of my odious cousins and he came to stay at my aunt's house one holiday. That was years ago and he has lost a good deal of weight since then. He fancied himself quite an actor, but the last part I could imagine him playing was that of a priest."

"Stuart-Clark," Gabriel muttered to himself. "How do I know that name? And why did I not recognize him?"

Rory abandoned the card table to join the conversation. "Perhaps because you only know him by reputation, as I do. And a notorious one it is. He never belonged to our club, thank heaven. He hung about the Madras Club and used to fleece all the nabobs. When his luck turned foul, he ran up gambling debts he could not pay. Finally he was caught cheating and called out for a duel. He disappeared and rumor had it he'd done away with himself."

As his friend recounted the story, Gabriel recalled hearing about it. "Instead he must have been hiding out on the Isle of Jersey, until he crossed paths with a pretty heiress."

Suddenly his quest became more urgent than ever. "I must track them down and get her out of his clutches before it is too late!"

"I'm coming with you," Jack announced, before Gabriel could ask.

"And I," Rory insisted. "Come, we haven't a moment to lose!"

His friends' support buoyed Gabriel's spirits and steadied his nerves. Surely with the help of Jack and Rory he could find Moira and rescue her from a true fortune hunter.

As the three men rode north, the sun set and a pale moon, nearly full, rose to light their way.

With every mile of their journey, Gabriel's anxiety for Moira grew, along with the weight of guilt upon his conscience. Who knew what a desperate scoundrel like Stuart-Clark might do to her? If only he had not stormed off and left her all alone she might not be in danger now. Having lost her once before, through his own folly, he could not bear to lose her again.

This time, he feared their parting might be irrevocable.

Chapter Sixteen

A ROUGH HAND on her arm shook Moira out of an exhausted but restless doze.

"Rise and shine, my sweet," Mr. Clarkson urged her in a tone of mock affection. "You do not want to be late for our wedding."

Moira kept her eyes resolutely shut. This was the first time she'd ever woken *to* a nightmare, rather than *from* one. Every instinct urged her to retreat into the peaceful haven of sleep rather than face this day.

At first she was confused to find herself lying on a bed. Then she recalled being dragged out of the carriage in the waning hours of the night to a room in some coaching inn.

"Wake up!" the curate demanded. "If we do not get the deed done by noon, we shall have to wait another day and it is half-past ten already."

Stubbornly ignoring his order, Moira rolled over and continued to feign sleep. She doubted he was fooled, just as she knew it would make no difference if she managed to postpone their dreaded nuptials for one more day. Her fate had been sealed the moment Clarkson overheard Gabriel confess the truth about his parentage. Still, some obstinate part of her refused to take those enslaving vows a moment sooner than necessary.

"Very well then," the scoundrel crawled onto the bed behind her. "Perhaps this will *rouse* you!"

The next thing Moira felt was his arm slung over her and his hand groping at her breasts. Meanwhile he rubbed his thighs eagerly against her backside. His ragged breath hissed in her ear.

"Let me go, you brute!" Pushing his hand away, she thrashed and kicked until she managed to wriggle out of his grasp. She retreated to the corner of the bed, sitting up with her back to the wall and the coverlet pulled in front of her like flimsy armor.

Clarkson staggered up from the bed, rubbing his belly where she had landed a sharp jab with her elbow.

"Suit yourself." He scowled. "I would rather wait until tonight when I can take my time."

Moira shuddered.

"You will not be able to deny me then," he taunted her. "And if you try, I shall be just as happy to take my *marital rights* by force."

Never in her life had Moira felt so helpless.

"Now get out of that bed," Clarkson ordered, "and make yourself presentable for our wedding."

Though she knew she had no choice, Moira could not make herself move.

Muttering a very unclerical oath, Clarkson approached the bed again, clearly determined to haul her out.

A loud knock sounded on the door of the room.

"Go away!" Clarkson shouted. But the knocking continued more insistently.

Cursing again, he left Moira and strode to the door. "What is it? I did not order any food!"

He lifted the latch and opened the door a crack. An instant later it burst open, sending Clarkson staggering backward as Gabriel barreled in.

Paying no attention to Clarkson, he approached the bed with open arms. "Moira, has he harmed you?"

The invisible bonds that had restrained her shattered. She dove into the shelter of Gabriel's embrace. She had never been so happy to see anyone in her life. After the way they'd parted, she had not expected him to care what became of her.

In answer to his question she shook her head. "Not

much ... yet."

"Please, Moira." Gabriel ran his hand over her tousled hair. "You cannot marry this man. He is an imposter who is only after your fortune!"

"I know that now." She clung to Gabriel, drawing strength from his embrace. "But I have no choice. It is the only way I can atone for what I've done."

"Atone?" Gabriel's dark brows drew together. "What for? I don't understand."

Clarkson gave a scornful laugh. "I can be quite persuasive."

When Moira glanced toward her captor, she could see that he had regained his menacing assurance. "I would advise you to be on your way, Stanford, and not delay our wedding."

"I will do nothing of the kind." Gabriel's arms tightened around Moira.

"No?" It was clear from his gloating tone that Clarkson enjoyed baiting them. "Then I shall have to make certain everyone knows the sordid little secret of your paternity."

Moira felt Gabriel flinch.

Thrusting her out at arm's length, he confronted her with an accusing, wounded gaze. "You told him?"

That was what dismayed him? Not the fear of his scandalous parentage being revealed, but the suspicion that she had betrayed his secret?

"No. Never!" Moira willed Gabriel to believe her. "He was behind the hedgerow and overheard us talking."

Gabriel's dark eyes widened. "You agreed to marry him in order to protect me?"

His gaze glowed with such intense gratitude and trust that Moira could not bear to sustain it. There had been more to her decision than that. But how could she tell him when he looked at her as if he would willingly place his life in her hands?

"Yes, yes. All very touching." Though Moira refused to look at him, she knew Clarkson must be rolling his eyes. "Now that you understand I have it in my power to ruin you, your mother and the entire Cheviot family, I assume you will do the sensible thing and leave us to get on with our wedding."

Moira braced for Gabriel to let her go. She must not cry out or make any appeal to his chivalrous nature for fear it would make him do something he would surely regret.

"Very well," he replied though he made no move to release her. "On one condition."

"You are in no position to dictate terms!" Clarkson snapped.

"Perhaps not." Gabriel gave a careless shrug, as if his reputation and future were not at stake. Was this some desperate gambler's bluff? "But if you intend to wed today, time is running out."

"What is it then?"

"I will leave you in peace," said Gabriel, "if Moira can look me in the eye and swear she wants to wed you because she does not love me."

"Go ahead," said Clarkson. "Tell the man what he wants to hear."

In spite of everything at stake, that was a lie so profoundly false Moira knew she could never force herself to utter it.

She buried her face in Gabriel's shoulder. "Please do not make me!"

He pressed a kiss to the crown of her head. "That is all I need to know."

He addressed his next words to Clarkson. "I refuse to let you take Moira anywhere, least of all to a church."

"You are making a very dangerous mistake!" Clarkson's cold, confident mockery deserted him. "Are you certain you want to take so much trouble over a woman who concealed your child from you?"

Those words struck Moira like a bullet in the back — one that blasted through her to imbed itself in Gabriel's chest. A powerful spasm convulsed him and his arms fell slack.

The pain that pierced Moira's heart could scarcely have been worse if Clarkson *had* shot her.

The scoundrel's accusation left Gabriel barely able to speak.

"Liar!" In denial, he sought protection from the pain that threatened to destroy him.

"Am I?" Clarkson demanded, his vicious bravado returning. "Perhaps *that* is a better question to ask the lady."

Gabriel was not certain he could bring himself to. "Moira? It is not true, is it?"

She raised her tear-streaked face to him. Guilt and sorrow were etched so deeply on her features that he did not need to hear her speak the damning words.

Still somewhat numb, he struggled to hold the agonizing truth at bay. "But you assured me repeatedly that you were not Sarah's mother. How could you do that?"

He'd given her every opportunity to tell him the truth. He had struggled with his doubts and in the end he'd believed her. Had she taken him for a fool? Had she laughed behind his back at how easy it was to charm him into trusting her?

Moira caught her trembling lip between her teeth to still it. Her wide blue-green eyes seemed to hold an ocean of anguish.

She shook her head and for a preposterous moment his heart lifted.

"Not Sarah." Her voice was so muffled with tears that Gabriel wondered if he'd heard her correctly. "I named *our* daughter Nora, after my mother."

He had a daughter, a child Moira had kept from him in spite of all the opportunities he'd given her to confess. So many conflicting emotions tore at Gabriel's heart that he feared it would be ripped into bleeding pieces.

Now that those first true words had breached the barrier, more poured from Moira's lips as if she could not contain them. "I never thought of giving our baby away as Sarah's mother did! I only encouraged *that man* because he made me believe he was good and kind and might let me raise Nora in our home."

If she thought that part of her confession would appease Gabriel, she could not have been more disastrously mistaken.

He imagined his daughter, a child he had never met but whom he loved immediately with all the paternal affection Sarah had inspired in him. How could Moira have planned to raise her in the same poisonous atmosphere he had endured, with a man a hundred times worse than the grim but honourable Duke of Cheviot?

Overcome with revulsion, he struggled to his feet, dumping Moira off his lap onto the floor.

Before he could escape, she seized his hand and clung to it with desperate strength. "Gabriel, I know you cannot forgive me, but please listen! I did not tell you about the baby at first because I thought you wouldn't want anything to do with either of us. By the time I discovered my mistake, I had other reasons that seemed important at the time. Now I see they were cowardly and selfish."

The last thing Gabriel wanted just then was for his disgust and righteous wrath to be weakened by pity.

"I wanted to tell you." Moira bent under the weight of remorse. "I *tried* to tell you."

Much as it complicated matters, Gabriel could not deny either of those things. Moira had confessed to harboring a secret she was afraid to tell him. He knew what that was like. If he had not stormed away from her yesterday, she might have finally been able to admit the truth.

"I only ask one thing of you." The words sounded as if they were being ripped out of Moira's heart. "Please take our daughter. I know you will love her and your friends will help you care for her. I could not bear to see her raised anywhere near *that* fiend!"

A wave of certainty engulfed Gabriel. Everything Moira had done these past months, good and bad, had been to protect their child and keep her near. Would he be willing to surrender their daughter entirely if the circumstances were reversed?

"No need to call names!" Clarkson snapped at Moira. "It is not of the slightest interest to me what you do with the brat. Now, we have a vicar waiting and I doubt Stanford has any further interest in detaining us unless he wants his face plastered all over the scandal sheets."

That was the threat Clarkson had used to make Moira come with him. She was prepared to sacrifice her freedom and future happiness to protect Gabriel and their daughter. It did not excuse the hurt she'd caused him, but neither was it a truth he could ignore. Moira wanted to atone for her mistakes, but this was a penance far beyond any he would ever wish upon her.

He glared at the other man. "Moira is not going with you, Herbert Stuart-Clark. If I were you, I would think carefully before spreading any gossip about us. If I see or hear so much as a hint of such tattle, I will make certain the members of your club know that rumors of your demise were rather premature."

Gabriel's counter-threat wiped the insolent sneer from the blackguard's face. For an instant his features went slack with the shock of losing the prize he had connived so hard to secure. Then they clenched in feral rage, like those of a wild beast cornered.

With a frenzied bellow, he lunged.

Before Gabriel could prepare to defend himself, Moira thrust out her foot, sending his assailant sprawling to the floor.

The next moment the door burst open and Jack and Rory rushed in.

When they saw their friends unharmed and Stuart-Clark writhing on the floor, Rory began to laugh.

Jack swooped down and hauled the scoundrel up by the back of his collar. "We heard every word of your threats. I expect the authorities would be delighted to prosecute you for abduction, impersonation and blackmail!"

With every word he shook the villain until there was a shriek of tearing cloth and Stuart-Clark broke free. He staggered to the door and fled before anyone could stop him.

The three friends exchanged a look, silently debating whether to give chase.

Rory shrugged. "He isn't worth the bother."

"I doubt he will cause you any further trouble," said Jack. "Scavengers like him only prey upon the weakest victims. I wish he would run afoul of Clarissa Reynard. Those two deserve each other!"

He stooped and offered Moira his hand. "Come, Miss Brennan. Let us get you home. Your ordeal is over."

Gabriel saw and heard everything going on around him, yet none of it seemed real. During the past half-hour his heart had been lobbed back and forth between extremes of emotion like a tennis ball in fiercely contested match. It had left him numb to every feeling except relief that he could feel nothing else.

When Jack hoisted Moira to her feet she immediately hurled herself toward Gabriel and burst into turbulent sobs. He had not felt so overwhelmed and ill-equipped since the day little Sarah had begun wailing on the steps of Jack's townhouse.

Gently but firmly he passed her off to his friend. "I trust you will see Miss Brennan home safely."

"Of course." Jack sounded bewildered.

"If that is what you wish," Rory added.

Gabriel could not summon the words to reply. Instead he gave a wooden nod and stumbled away, not certain where he meant to go or what he meant to do.

———

Gabriel's friends made all the necessary arrangements to get Moira back on the road to Surrey. She did whatever they bid her without reply or even much thought, like a wooden puppet responding to the pull on its strings. The past hours seemed like a nightmare that had left her exhausted and overwrought, yet profoundly relieved to have escaped its clutches.

She was free of Mr. Clarkson's machinations — after all this time, she could not think of him by any other name. For better or worse, Gabriel knew the truth about their daughter.

As she huddled in the corner of the carriage opposite

Jack Warwick and Rory Fitzpatrick, Moira wondered where Gabriel had gone and what his abrupt departure could mean. Nothing good, surely.

He had ridden to her rescue and saved her from Clarkson in spite of the scoundrel's threats to broadcast his scandalous secret. Even after he learned about their daughter, he had not abandoned her to the fate she deserved. Tempting as it was to interpret those actions as signs of his love for her, Moira feared they had more likely been motivated by chivalry.

"Thank you for coming to my assistance," she murmured to the weary looking men slumped on the other side of the carriage. "I was a fool to have trusted such a wicked scoundrel."

"Do not reproach yourself too severely," Mr. Warwick replied. "I know what it is to be blinded by desperate circumstances."

He told her how he had nearly been hoodwinked into marriage by Madame Reynard, only to be rescued at the altar by his friends and Annabelle.

Knowing someone understood soothed her guilt a little. "I doubt Lord Gabriel will view my errors so charitably."

"Do not jump to conclusions," Jack Warwick advised, "until you have had a long, frank discussion of the matter with our friend."

"How can I do that when I have no idea where he has gone?"

She could tell from his expression that the gentleman had his doubts. "I am only asking you not to give up hope. Let your emotions settle and his likewise."

As Moira pondered his advice, Rory Fitzwalter spoke up in a hoarse, drowsy voice. "I have never seen Gabriel so distraught as when he realized you were in danger. Take hope from that."

She gave weary nod. "I will try."

It was a kind thing for him to say. Moira had never thought of Lord Killoran's brother as being especially kind. He had impressed her as an amusing but cynical libertine with little interest in anything beyond his own pleasure. Yet he had ridden through the night to assist his friend in finding her. Perhaps there were greater depths to all three gentlemen than anyone suspected — even they themselves.

After Jack and Rory delivered her home as they'd promised, Moira gave herself over to Mrs. Trimble's care like a helpless child. Her motherly companion did not ask a single question about her ordeal, but put her straight to bed with a posset of hot sweetened milk, liberally laced with brandy.

After she woke many hours later and assured herself that her father was recovering well, Moira gathered her courage to broach a conversation she had long dreaded and done so much to avoid. As she'd expected, her father looked very downcast after she told him about her tryst with Gabriel and the baby she had borne out of wedlock.

Shaking his head, he heaved a deep sigh. "I cannot deny, I am disappointed that you did not feel you could confide in me until now, my poor dear girl."

His words were so contrary to what she'd expected Moira wondered if she had heard him correctly.

"As I told Lord Gabriel," he continued, dispelling her doubts, "I recall very well being young and in love, when amorous feelings cannot always wait upon vows before the vicar. If I'd suspected the truth, you may be certain I would have summoned him at once and urged the pair of you to make up your quarrel, for both your sakes and the sake of my grandchild."

"Oh Papa," Moira bent to kiss the hands that held hers. Though his understanding had lifted a great burden from her heart, there was still plenty left to weigh it down. "I have been such a fool and caused everyone I care about so much grief!"

"You have made mistakes, to be sure." Her father detached one hand to run over her hair, the way he had comforted her as a child. "But few folks get through life without committing a great many errors. Those paragons of sense and virtue who manage it, I wonder if they were too cautious to have truly lived at all. What matters is learning from those mistakes and doing our best to make right what we have done wrong. You have taken a great step by confiding in me just now. I know that cannot have been easy."

His words brought her comfort enough that she was able to manage a subdued chuckle. "That is an understatement if ever I heard it."

Her father laughed at her quip, but soon grew sober again. "There is something more you can do to make amends for keeping me in the dark all this time. I doubt you will find it as difficult a task as this confession of yours."

"Of course, Papa!" she cried without hesitation. "What would you have me do?"

He looked surprised that she did not guess. "Fetch my granddaughter to Ardmore at once and bring her up here where she belongs."

When Moira seemed bewildered by his request, her father continued, "You are not a poor servant girl who must give her child up or farm her out. You have a good home and fortune enough to keep you both in comfort as long as you live."

"But the scandal, Papa …" Surely her father must know it would mean the end of his dreams of social advancement for their family.

"Oh there will be tattle, I have no doubt." He did not try to hide his disappointment. "But perhaps I have been a vain old fool to care so much about trifles that might have cost your happiness and my chance to know my grandchild."

Her dream of making a home with her daughter beckoned, too good to be true. "This is so much more than I deserve."

"Nonsense." Her father gave her hand a final pat then let it go. "This is what we all deserve. Now go and fetch your babe to meet her grandpapa!"

His hearty order loosened the bonds of disbelief and remorse that held Moira back. She sprang to her feet with a truly lighter heart than she had known in many months.

As she headed away her father called after her, "I should

have asked before. What is the child's name?"

When Moira told him, he broke into a broad smile that quite outshone the misty glint in his eyes.

Moira had not gone far before guilt and worry began to nag at her. Why had she not gone straightaway to check on her daughter the moment she returned from London? What if Gabriel had gone to see the baby as soon as he learned about her? What if he had persuaded Betsy to let him take Nora away?

If that was what he'd done, Gabriel might believe he had Moira's permission. After all, she had begged him to take their baby, rather than let Nora fall into the hands of the scoundrel who was blackmailing her mother into marriage. Thanks to the timely intervention of Gabriel and his friends, that calamity had been averted. Would he understand that changed her wishes in the matter entirely? By the time, she reached Betsy's cottage, Moira was in such a state she could scarcely breathe.

The sight of her small daughter, safe and content, brought a surge of relief so intense that she dropped to her knees and burst into passionate tears.

"Whatever is wrong, Miss?" Betsy seized the baby, perhaps to comfort if Moira's outburst upset her. "That man you warned me about, did he harm you?"

"N-No!" Moira struggled to contain her tears, but she might as well have tried to hold back the water behind a broken dam. "He s-saved me from harm!"

Seeing the baby begin to fuss, Moira forced herself to take several deep breaths until she grew composed enough to speak calmly. "Has he been here?"

Betsy shook her head. "Not since that day I saw the two of you together. Why? Did you expect her would be?"

"I was afraid he might." Moira summoned the strength to rise. "It is a long story, but I promise I will tell you all of it. I am done with keeping secrets. Now I need you to come with me."

Now it was Betsy's turn to look alarmed. "Come where, Miss?"

Moira smiled, hoping to reassure her. "To Ardmore. I told my father about Nora. He is eager to meet her and give her a place in our home."

"What about me, Miss?"

"That will be entirely up to you, Betsy." Moira restrained the powerful urge to take the baby into her arms. "I am grateful beyond words for the wonderful care you have given my daughter all these months and the sacrifice you made in coming so far from your island home. If you wish to remain with us, I should welcome your help with Nora. But if you would rather return to Jersey, you will be handsomely rewarded for all you have done."

Betsy's dark brows knit together and she gnawed on her lower lip. "How soon must I make up my mind?"

"Take as long as you need," Moira replied in a tone of quiet resolve tempered with sympathy. She knew how conflicted Betsy must feel, yet she could not let anything prevent her from seizing this opportunity to make a life with her daughter.

As she began to absorb the sweet certainty of a future with Nora, Moira questioned why Gabriel had refrained from claiming the child he must long for as much as she did. She should have known him better than to suppose he would deprive her of the baby, no matter how deeply she had wronged him. Yet he must know that if he was to have a place in their daughter's life, Moira would always be a part of his. After everything she had done, did he now consider that too high a price to pay for fatherhood? If he did, she could hardly blame him.

At that moment, her heart had never felt so full ... but at the same time, so very empty.

Late on an overcast afternoon in the waning days of summer, Gabriel stood in the yard of Crawford's Wharf with Captain Turner. The two men were looking over a bill of lading from a ship that had docked the previous day with a cargo of spices from the South Seas.

Though this business of working for a living required more effort and discipline than Gabriel had ever dreamed he might possess, it had proven unexpectedly rewarding. Perhaps more gentlemen ought to try it for themselves before turning up their aristocratic noses at *trade.* In the short time he had been working with Aaron Turner, Gabriel often felt far out of his depth with so much to learn. Yet none of his studies at Eton or Oxford had ever challenged and stimulated him to such a degree.

In the past he had taken for granted the supply of so many items of necessity and comfort. Now he knew where many of them came from, what they cost and how they reached England's shores. It made him appreciate the whole complex process and the many people who played their part in it.

Keeping his mind occupied with business for hours a day calmed his emotions so he could reflect on recent events with welcome detachment. It also helped him ignore a persistent gnawing ache in his heart.

"What does the symbol before this number mean?" Gabriel pointed out the unfamiliar notation, pleased that the rest was beginning to make sense to him.

Captain Tuner glanced at the bill. "That shows the cost of the cargo in guilders. Many merchants in the South Seas still insist on payment in Dutch money. Others demand Spanish dollars. It complicates bookkeeping, but that is a cost of doing business in the four corners of the world."

"How much are guilders worth in pounds and shillings?" Gabriel asked.

The captain launched into a detailed explanation of currency exchange and the factors that could affect it. Then, perhaps noticing Gabriel's dazed look, he laughed and clapped his protégé on the back. "Do not think you must learn all the ins and outs of the shipping trade in a few weeks. I picked it up bit by bit over many years as —"

His voice trailed off.

"As what?"

"That can wait." Aaron Turner nodded toward a familiar-looking carriage that had driven into the yard between the warehouses and the counting house.

An even more familiar lady alighted from the carriage and peered around the bustling yard.

"Moira," Gabriel murmured to himself. "How did she know to look for me here?"

"Not from me." Captain Turner plucked the document out of Gabriel's hand. "Though I cannot answer for my wife. Since Miss Brennan has tracked you down, I suggest you find out what she wants."

Gabriel felt suddenly hollow inside. He could imagine a number of things Moira Brennan might want, beginning with an explanation for why he had left her in London without a word and never contacted her since then.

At the moment, he was not certain his reasons even made sense to him.

"I won't be long," he muttered in an apologetic tone.

"Nonsense!" Aaron Turner gave him a rough nudge in Moira's direction. "Take all the time you need. In fact, I order you to take the rest of the day off."

He had meant to pay a call on her at Ardmore when he felt ready, Gabriel reflected as he approached Moira. But she had caught him unawares, the way he had ambushed her at the Prince Regent's fête … and at Vauxhall … and at the Pulteney Hotel.

As she caught sight of him, Gabriel could not tell if she was any more pleased to see him now than she had been then. Should he have risked a conversation with her immediately after Stuart-Clark fled from the inn? Should he have driven back to Surrey with her and talked everything over during the journey? Could he expect Moira to understand why he hadn't, when he was not certain himself?

So much had happened between them in an impossibly brief time: a passionate tryst, a bitter quarrel, secrets revealed, disaster threatened. Where did one begin to talk about it all? Gabriel had hoped the passage of time would make it easier to broach the subject. Now he discovered otherwise.

"You found me." He winced at how obvious and foolish his words must sound.

Moira nodded. "It was not difficult. I asked your friends where you were. They believe it would be good for us to talk, even if you do not."

"I planned to come and see you," Gabriel insisted.

"Perhaps I *should* have waited for your visit," Moira replied, "but I could not. However, I can wait until you finish your day's business with Captain Turner."

For a moment Gabriel's spirits lightened. A smile tugged at one corner of his mouth. "I fear that would take much longer than you realize."

He told her about the opportunity Aaron Turner had offered him then added, "You may number him among the friends who believe we should talk."

"I thought I might." A faint twinkle flickered in Moira's blue-green eyes. Then she cast her gaze around the property. "Is there somewhere quiet where we could speak privately?"

Her question amused Gabriel in spite of his qualms. "Not here. But there is somewhere nearby that might suit our purposes."

He gave the coachman directions then helped Moira into the carriage.

"No chaperone?" he observed as he settled into the seat opposite her. "I hope Mrs. Trimble is not unwell?"

"I was not aware you were such an admirer of hers."

Was Moira teasing him? That might be a good sign.

"I was not," he admitted, "any more than she was of me. But we found common ground in our affection for … you."

As the carriage headed off through Southwark to Kennington, he told Moira how Mrs. Trimble had put him on the trail of her and her abductor.

His words erased any trace of levity from her features,

which Gabriel regretted.

"Then I owe her a debt of gratitude second only to the one I owe you," Moira murmured, "though I did little to deserve assistance from either of you."

"How can you say that?" he asked, though he had no doubt she meant it.

"Have you forgotten how I concealed our child from you?" Her rueful sigh assured Gabriel that he could not blame her for that any more harshly than she blamed herself. "I took such great pains never to tell you an outright falsehood, as if that could excuse the way I misled you."

"I knew you were not being altogether truthful with me." He recalled many times he had sensed something amiss. "Considering the way we parted after Lady Killoran's house party, I can see why you were reluctant to trust me."

"At first I was afraid if I told you about Nora you would insist on marrying me even if you did not love me."

He had tried so hard to keep her from making a loveless marriage, never guessing it was what she feared he meant to impose upon her. "I wish I'd never left you in any doubt of my feelings. But I could not acknowledge, even to myself, how deep those feelings ran. I invented any number of convenient excuses for opposing your engagement to Mr. Clarkson. The truth of the matter was that I could not abide the thought of you married to anyone but … me."

It was not easy, laying his heart bare for her to spurn as he had felt it spurned so many times in the past. But if she still cared for him at all, he could not bear for Moira to suspect that he only wanted her because he'd discovered she was the mother of his child.

Moira's gaze fall to her lap, where she toyed with her gloves in an anxious manner. Clearly his declaration did not meet with her approval.

She spoke her next words so softly that Gabriel struggled to catch them over the rattle of the carriage and the noises from the street. "If you felt that way, why did you say nothing after you and your friends rescued me from that horrible man? Why did you disappear and go off to work for Captain Turner?"

The carriage stopped then. Moira glanced out the window, perhaps surprised to recognize their destination.

"Shall we continue our conversation here?" Gabriel nodded toward Vauxhall Pleasure Gardens, where he had pursued her earlier that summer.

Moira replied with a subdued nod.

They found the gardens all but deserted. Perhaps Londoners were waiting to throng here in the evening for fireworks or some other spectacle. Gabriel was quite satisfied to have the place almost to themselves. The classical statuary put him in mind of the Muses of Farleigh and a day he would never forget as long as he lived.

As they had ambled down one of the wooded alleyways, he took up the tread of their conversation again. "I did not dare speak with you that morning at the inn. I was afraid of what I might say in the confusion of the moment and the intensity of my feelings. Like I did when Clarkson ... I mean Stuart-Clark overheard us talking on the footpath. If I had not stormed off then, you could have told me about our daughter, as you intended to. Then it would have not come as such a great shock and you would not have been subjected to that elopement ordeal."

"Perhaps I should not have tried to defend your mother's actions." Moira heaved a sigh. "But the way you condemned her struck so close to home. It was my own conduct I was trying to justify."

Recalling their bitter argument with the benefit of hindsight, Gabriel understood how his harsh indictment of his mother must have sounded like a direct reproach to Moira. "After my temper cooled, I thought a great deal about what you said. There was much more truth in it than I could grasp at first. Someday soon, I intend to have a long talk with my mother, hear her side of the story and tell her mine. Perhaps then we can lay the matter to rest. In the meantime, I choose to believe what you suggested — that she tried to do the best she could in an intolerable situation."

As he spoke, Moira nodded her approval. "I finally confided in Papa about the baby. He was far more sympathetic than I had any right to hope. He told me everyone makes mistakes in life. He said the important thing is to own up to our errors, learn from them and try to understand when others make mistakes that grieve us."

"A very wise man, your father." Not for the first time Gabriel wished for a closer connection with Mr. Brennan.

By now their wanderings had brought them to a private nook with a small wooden bench.

As they took a seat, Moira asked the question Gabriel had been dreading. "I understand why you chose not to speak with me before you went away, but why did you not go to see our daughter once you found out about her? You were prepared to do anything for Sarah even when you could not be certain she was your child. Does our daughter mean less to you?"

Moira's chin trembled and her eyes grew misty. A bitter note in her voice told Gabriel that her grief went back longer than the day he'd left her in London. All this time, had she begrudged his affection for a child who was not theirs?

He shook his head in a forceful denial. "When I left you that morning, I headed straight for Ardmore to see the baby. I was certain Mrs. Trimble would take me to her once I explained what had happened."

"I believe she would." Moira sounded relieved by his admission and relieved to hear that he had given some thought to their daughter. "What changed your mind?"

Gabriel fought to subdue his nerves. "I was afraid that if I saw her once, I would not be able to leave her again to do what I had to do."

Moira's delicate features furrowed into a look of bewilderment. "And what was that?"

Gabriel drew in a deep breath, like a drowning man who

had managed to breech the surface one last time.

"To make something of myself, the way Captain Turner did ... the way your father did. I never had any fortune but now you know I have no noble lineage either. If your father is prepared to give our daughter a home, then you do not need a husband in order to keep her with you. I wanted to have *something* to recommend me if I was to have any hope of persuading you to marry me. You and Nora deserve a husband and father you can be proud of!"

Suddenly the reasons that had seemed so important to him sounded hollow, foolish and cowardly.

Her full lower lip quivered, making him fear the worst. "I never cared about your fortune or your birth, Gabriel! Ever since our meeting at the Prince Regent's fête, you tried over and over to regain my trust and persuade me not to make a loveless marriage. How did I repay you? Not with the gratitude you deserved, but with the kind of deception and rejection you have experienced far too often in the past. I was afraid that this time you had given up on me at last."

He had left her dangling, with no indication of his true feelings, just as he had months ago. Even if he could succeed in making his fortune, she deserved far more from a husband than that. Gabriel choked back a lump in his throat that threatened to gag him.

Before he could *think* of any words, let alone speak them, Moira raised her gaze to meet his. Her chin tilted at an indomitable angle. "I decided the time had come for me to show that I will never give up on you or the happy future we deserved to have together."

"Now you know, I never gave up on you and never will." Gabriel took her left hand in both of his. "I look forward to the day when I can place a ring on your finger in token of all my worldly possessions, few though they are."

Lifting her hand to his lips, he bestowed a tender kiss on the base of her fourth finger. "But it will also be a symbol of all the love in my heart, which is boundless."

Moira broke into a smile that distilled the delight of a thousand dancing sunbeams. "That is all I ever wanted from you. I am willing to wait as long as you need to earn your success, but I believe with all my heart it will come."

"So do I." His words surprised Gabriel, yet his whole being resonated with the truth of them. "Almost as much as I believe in our love and the happiness our future holds."

Though he did not trust himself to speak further, nothing could prevent him from offering Moira the first of many blissful kisses, which she returned with boundless ardor. When she drew back at last, they were both flushed and breathless.

"Now," she whispered, "will you come back with me to Ardmore to meet your daughter?"

Though he shrank a little from facing her father, Gabriel took heart from what Mr. Brennan had said about forgiving mistakes. He answered Moira's invitation with an eager nod. "I must warn you that once I see her with my own eyes, I may lose all my scruples about making my fortune and insist we set the earliest possible wedding date."

Moira gave a sweet, mischievous chuckle. "That is precisely what I hope!"

Epilogue

October 1811

A MONTH AFTER Moira and Gabriel's hasty wedding, their daughter and little Sarah were both christened at Beckwith Abbey in the Killorans' family chapel.

When the ceremony had concluded, Moira's father carried his cherished granddaughter to meet a surprise guest, the Duchess of Cheviot. "Nora is named for my late wife, and though she is as pretty a child as I have ever seen, I cannot claim she bears any resemblance."

The duchess stroked the baby's plump cheek. "She is the image of her father at that age."

Nora greeted her grandmother with a bright smile which the old lady returned. "I see she has his winning ways too."

Hovering nearby, Gabriel overheard Lady Cheviot and exchanged a fond glance with his wife. True to his word, Gabriel had spoken at great length with his mother before the wedding about the circumstances of his birth. The account she gave was very much as Moira had suggested.

Though she'd cared a great deal for Gabriel's father, she knew that all her children would pay a high price if the duke divorced her. "I fear you paid the highest price of all for my indiscretion, dear boy. That has been the greatest regret of my life."

Happy as he was with Moira and their daughter, Gabriel had no room in his heart to nurse a grudge.

But when the duchess informed him that she had one

final secret to confess, he'd braced for the worst. "Is it about my father?"

His mother gave a wistful nod. "He knew you were his son and he wanted very much to acknowledge you. But he could not bear to ruin my reputation or cause you distress, so he kept silent."

"I understand," Gabriel murmured. "I would do the same for Moira and our daughter in that situation."

His natural father might have lacked fortune and rank, but Gabriel was proud to learn he had been a man of honorable character.

"He died several years ago." The duchess looked away, but not before her son glimpsed a single tear gliding down her cheek. "But he left me a large inheritance in trust for you."

"Why did you not tell me?" Even as Gabriel asked the question, he could guess the answer.

"I feared you might gamble the money away and I was ashamed to tell you the truth about what I had done. But now that you know and have reformed your ways, I shall be happy to carry out your father's wishes. Would you care to know how much you will inherit?"

"The amount hardly matters." Though it would give him a welcome measure of independence, Gabriel would have given that much and more to have known the father who'd cared so much for him, if only from a distance.

"Perhaps not," the duchess agreed.

But when she named the sum, Gabriel's eyes had widened. In the end, though, it only mattered to him for one reason. "Now Moira will never have reason to wonder if I married her for her fortune."

As Moira watched her father and Gabriel's mother dote over their precious little granddaughter, Annabelle Warwick sidled up to her. Jack's wife had an air of gentle radiance that made

Moira suspect little Sarah might soon have a tiny companion in the Warwick nursery.

"Jack tells me your husband has come into a tidy fortune," she confided in cheerful whisper. "I am so happy for you both. Now he will not need to worry about being accused of marrying for money. I know it troubled him a great deal at one time. Not that anyone seeing the two of you together could doubt for an instant that yours is a true love match."

Moira nodded. "We have been so happy these past weeks that I sometimes worry I shall wake up one morning and find it has all been a dream. Gabriel means to continue working with Captain Turner and invest some of his inheritance to form a partnership."

"An excellent plan," Annabelle replied. "Our husbands have certainly settled down from the wild bachelor existence they were living when Sarah first appeared on their doorstep. Do you suppose there is any hope for Rory?"

The two ladies chuckled at the notion of Rory Fitzwalter ever being domesticated.

"Who is that woman?" Annabelle nodded toward a well-dressed lady of about their age who had just entered the chapel. "Some relative of yours?"

"No." Moira peered closer, for the stranger did look somewhat familiar. "Good heavens! I believe it is Miss Delaney. She was a companion to Lady Killoran. I have not seen her since the countess's Christmas party. She certainly appears to have come up in the world since then."

Conversation among the other guests gradually fell silent as they also recognized the newcomer.

"Kitty!" Lady Killoran approached her long-absent friend. "How good it is to see you again and looking so well. We are celebrating a double christening — the young daughters of our friends Jack Warwick and Lord Gabriel Stanhope. What brings you back to Beckwith Abbey after all this time?"

"I heard about the christening. That is why I am here." Kitty Delaney's gaze searched the small sanctuary, finally fixing on little Sarah, nestled happily in Jack Warwick's arms. "I have come to reclaim my daughter!"

The End

Dear Reader,

If you have been waiting patiently (or impatiently) for Gabriel and Moira's sequel to *Scandal on His Doorstep*, I apologize for the looong delay. I can assure you I didn't forget about you and I appreciated folks who reached out to remind me there was an audience eager to read the next story. I didn't want to rush it, because nothing but my best work is good enough for my wonderful readers!

The upside of spending so much time with Lord Gabriel Stanford and Moira Brennan was that I got to know them really well and see why they were drawn to one another. I came to understand how their passionate romance, begun in *Scandal Takes a Holiday,* took a very wrong turn and how hard it was going to be for them to let their guards down again. In addition to protecting their wounded pride and broken hearts, both are protecting secrets. Their fear of the consequences if their secrets are exposed stands in the way of their rekindled attraction. Both have some difficult lessons to learn if they are to have a second chance at love.

That journey isn't all struggle and conflict. The beautiful Surrey countryside and the Muses of an abandoned estate help Gabriel and Moira fall in love all over again, deeper than ever. Writers often talk about our muses, so it was fascinating to learn about the original nine Greek Muses who inspired poetry, drama, history ... and two wary Regency lovebirds.

I hope you will find *Scandal in His Arms* worth the wait and I promise not to make you wait so long for the final book of the series, *Scandal Comes to Town.*

About the Author

Deborah's first novel won the Golden Heart award for Long Historical and was nominated for a RITA for Best First Book. Since then Deborah has written more than two dozen novels in the genres of historical romance, inspirational romance and otherworld fantasy. Her books have been translated into more than a dozen languages and sold millions of copies worldwide. Deborah invites you to visit her website for more information.

Website: www.deborahhale.com
Facebook: www.facebook.com/AuthorDeborahHale
Goodreads: http://www.goodreads.com/
author/show/133710.Deborah_Hale
Pinterest: http://pinterest.com/hrwdebhale/

"Hale's characters are so finely created they become real in her readers' minds and hearts."
— *syndicated romance reviewer, Sheryl Horst*

www.ingramcontent.com/pod-product-compliance
Lightning Source LLC
Chambersburg PA
CBHW050738180626
46814CB00002B/818